BOUND to ECSTASY

BOUND to ECSTASY

VONNA HARPER
P.F. KOZAK
LISA G. RILEY

APHRODISIA
KENSINGTON BOOKS
http://www.kensingtonbooks.com

APHRODISIA are published by

Kensington Publishing Corp.
850 Third Avenue
New York, NY 10022

All Kensington Titles, Imprints, and Distributed Lines are available at special quantity discounts for bulk purchses for sales promotions, premiums, fund-raising, and educational or institutional use.

Special book excerpts or customized printings can also be created to fit specific needs. For details, write or phone the office of the Kensington special sales manager: Kensington Publishing Corp., 850 Third Avenue, New York, NY 10022, attn: Special Sales Department, Phone: 1-800-221-2647.

ISBN-13: 978-0-7582-2222-0
ISBN-10: 0-7582-2222-X

First Kensington Trade Paperback Printing: November 2007

10 9 8 7 6 5 4 3 2 1

Printed in the United States of America

CONTENTS

RESTRAINT

VONNA HARPER

1

Heels tapping on the cement flooring, Evi Hult stepped into the middle of the set that had once been part of Dungeon Dames. Although she'd snorted with disbelief when she'd opened the door for the first time, standing and staring at the dimly lit set had produced an interesting change. No longer torn between laughter and disgust, she noted that her heartbeat was now nearly as loud as the sound her shoes made. And her skin felt as if it been sandpapered.

Dungeon Dames! Had the owners of the bankrupt adult film company her employers had just taken over honestly believed the name would entice buyers to purchase their videos? How about having a little class there, folks? What about dignity and self-respect?

Hell, what did it matter? Dungeon Dames was out of business and her task a simple one: inventory the several sets and prepare a list for a Wednesday meeting of the decision makers at Intellectual Properties, Inc., her employer.

Clutching her clipboard to her C-sized breasts, Evi approached the four-poster bed that dominated the set. Made of sturdy metal resembling cell bars, the head- and footboards were hardly what any sane and sensible human being would chose for bedroom decor. Bondage, it declared, bondage! Of course the leather restraints hanging from the metal did more than a little to help her come to that conclusion. Smiling, Evi made a mental note to include the leather straps in her list. For the moment, however, making peace with her too-sensitive skin came first.

A bed designed for sex, forced sex, albeit simulated forced sex, while cameras rolled.

Mouth dry, she placed her clipboard on the blood-red sheet stretched over the mattress and ran her fingers down what was designed to look like silk but, unless she was mistaken, was plain old cotton. The sheet looked and smelled clean, thank goodness. If it had been sex-spotted—

Not going to go there! Not with her fingers tingling and heat blooming between her legs. Damn, how long had it been since she'd been laid?

Months, came back the unwanted answer. Months because she'd been single-minded about her career.

Well, so be it. The window of opportunity to establish herself as a creative director in an ever-changing business might close or break if she so much as blinked.

No blinking today, no asking herself what kind of woman would allow herself to be spread-eagled naked on red *silk* with her limbs held captive so some porn industry stud could bury his well-used and impersonal cock in her. Just because the world included submissive women didn't mean she was going to waste her time questioning what made said females tick. She had better things to do, much better.

And yet against every- and anything sane, Evi sat on the side of the bed and reached for the closest strap. It came complete with an overly shiny adjustable buckle, obviously the better to quickly accomplish the job it had been designed for.

Not that she had any intention of locking it in place, of course. Only a fool would risk not being able to get out of the contraption.

Caught! Helpless against a man's will. Forced down into a dark place filled with secret needs and powerful fears.

Mouth still dry, she draped the leather over her wrist and leaned back so she could study the results. Interesting, from an artistic and only artistic point of view of course. Still, the contrast between brown leather and her *never have the time to get a tan* flesh would play well on a DVD. And her wrist was slender, fingers long and in serious need of a manicure.

Ah, nice. Softer than she'd expected, erotic even, the leather stroking her skin and adding to its sensitivity. As for what was chasing a heated path from the base of her throat to her pussy, well, a gal without a man in her life had to take her pleasures any way she could.

Eyes at half mast, she imagined that a macho member of the opposite sex out of central casting was responsible for what now roped her wrist. Another dark thought threatened to slam into her, but she forced it away. Damn it, in the real world she was alone at the warehouse-type building where Dungeon Dames had produced whatever they'd produced. Unfortunately, or fortunately, her mind had no trouble creating a hunk worthy of earning whatever the so-called masters or doms or whatever in the porn industry were paid.

Her hunk would be big and strong and supremely confident, of course. Hmm. How about wavy blond hair to contrast with her long, straight brown-on-brown hair? His skin would be naturally dusky so it'd play off her too-pale skin, and that way she'd be less likely to draw comparisons between him and the midnight images hovering at the edges of her mind.

Of course he'd speak with an accent that put her in mind of a Viking warrior, whatever they sounded like, but unlike some uncivilized ancient Viking, *her* hunk would have ready access to soap and running hot water. She didn't give a damn about his educational level, just the way he was hung.

He'd be naked of course because she couldn't imagine wanting to waste time stripping him down for action. First and foremost, he'd be steeped in knowledge about women's bodies and needs, their secret fantasies.

Ah, shit! Hadn't the heat been shut off in here?

Looking down with an effort, Evi took much-needed comfort in her dress-for-success knee-length black skirt, sheer panty hose, and two-inch heels. This was her, not the horny broad lurking at the back of her mind along with other images she had no business facing right now. Time to get back to what she'd come here for.

Only, oh shit, she hadn't really snapped that restraint in place, had she?

An experimental and nearly panicked tug only reinforced her fear that yes, that's what she'd indeed done. Even as her heart raced and she breathed in gasps, a part of her stood back like the stern and usually disapproving aunt who'd raised her, the older woman's pursed mouth saying that, once again, Evi had failed her because no self-respecting *good* girl would do something that irresponsible.

No, of course she hadn't, Evi tried to point out. It wasn't like this was a real leather cuff. It was part of a set and obviously designed to release. All she needed was to make the right move, trip the right clasp, something.

To hell with Aunt Margaret! And to hell with panicking because, after all, here she was in a place designed to enhance make-believe. Might as well go with the flow since that's what her subconscious wanted anyway.

Yes, yes, she was a prisoner in the Dungeon, a new captive anticipating her fate. With no choice but to wait for her *master* to walk into the room and have his way with her, whatever that entailed.

No reason to freak out or ask herself if, finally, her most unsettling images had moved from make-believe to reality. She didn't need a shrink, damn it, because there was no way she was going to tell some stodgy old man about her make-beliefs and have him label her sick and demented.

Feeling decidedly more relaxed than she had a moment ago, Evi scooted around so she was facing the door, a move which pulled her trapped arm back and to the side. A delicious tingle tiptoed up her inner arm. Imagining that the door was opening, she opened her legs as far as her straight skirt allowed. Head up and shoulders back, she waited—for what she didn't know.

Ah, there he was, the Viking warrior she'd ordered, naked with an erection that caused her mouth to gape and her cunt to flow. He had legs like tree trunks, washboard abs, shoulders out to there and beyond, no belly, and from what she could tell, the tightest ass allowed. His pale hair was long and raggedly cut but clean. He wore an earring in his right ear, his only adornment—except for the *I'm ready for you* cock. The deepest, bluest eyes she'd ever seen locked on her.

Melting inside, flowing into a hot puddle, lips tingling, legs shaking, fingers clenching, hard nipples jabbing at her bra, thigh muscles doing battle with her skirt—oh yes, that's what she'd become.

She felt no surprise when *her* Viking faded a bit; after all, who could concentrate on anything as mundane as mentally creating another human being when her cunt was on fire? Moaning, she stood as best she could and yanked up her skirt with her free hand. Then, giving in to the strain in her pulled-out-of-position arm, she sank back onto the mattress, but not before ramming her hand under her panties and panty hose. Grateful that she'd also positioned herself closer to the head of the bed so the strain on her left arm slackened, she concentrated on finding the source of her frustration and need. Only when she'd slipped her forefinger into her hole did she turn what was left of her attention back to her warrior. He had a grainy quality, as if he hadn't quite achieved three-dimensional status, but she was used to that, unfortunately. Too much fantasy time spent with fantasy fuck partners had that effect. One decidedly positive thing about having ordered today's hunk, she was in charge of his behavior, wasn't she?

"Come closer, please," she begged, head now tilting back and mouth agape so she could pull enough oxygen into her lungs. "I'm yours. Take me."

Cringing at the corny words briefly distracted her from what she needed her fingers to be doing, but a gal well-versed in self-pleasure knew the drill. Concentrating on her clit produced the desired results all right, but she'd never been a fan of wham-bam, especially at her own hands. A long, slow dip into her inner recesses reinforced what she already knew; she was wet down there, wet and hot enough for a fan to be a great benefit.

Visualization. Visualization had always been a vital part of getting the job of self-satisfaction done. Reminded of that fundamental fact, she tried to locate her warrior, but he wasn't where she'd left him. Damn, damn, damn. And what remained, a cheap setting consisting of the bed of course and three walls crudely painted to resemble a dungeon, wasn't helping.

There. All right. Get rid of the plywood walls and concrete floor. Keep the bed but make the sheet real satin and trade the single mattress for queen size. Throw in a little drum and guitar music, low and deep like rolling thunder. Nix the clothes. Have her surroundings be a real cave complete with thick granite walls, a barred entrance, burning candles in wall sconces the only light, shadows everywhere, the smell and taste and feel of sex.

And the Viking. Most of all the Viking.

Sweating, Evi leaned back as much as she dared and risked cutting off the circulation in her right hand by running it so far under her clothes and between her legs that she nearly reached her ass. A touch, a man's touch! Callused fingers instead of her soft ones, hot knowledge kissing her clit and taking her up, all the way to the top, holding her there, bringing her back down without allowing her to climax, and then starting up the mountain again while she mewed and begged.

"Be quiet," he'd order. Then he'd tell her that she was no longer in control of her body, he was.

She recognized her labored breathing and the fingers repeatedly collecting her wet excitement; even the fantasy was relatively safe and familiar, but she climbed on board anyway. There. In her mind's eye, she was on her back and both of her wrists had been secured to the headboard. Her legs were widely spread and kept that way via the ungiving leather lapped around her ankles. Of course she was naked and sweating even more than she had when her imagination started working because a man was sitting on the bed next to her, bent low so he could tongue and mouth-bathe her vulnerable pussy.

"No, no, no, please, mercy," she kept begging as she twisted this way and that trying to escape the unbelievable pleasure-pain. Climax after climax piled out of her. She couldn't stop them! Couldn't draw a calming breath! Another, oh shit, another! Being torn apart and knowing she'd die happy if everything ended today. "Please, please, please, master, please!"

"No begging!" the formless man commanded, coming up for air. "As long as it pleasures me to tease and torment you I will!"

"I understand, master. A moment of rest, that's all I ask, a moment."

"When and if I grant it," he growled as he went back to work. A single, hard contact with her shivering core ripped another explosion from her, causing her to strain against her bonds.

Unfortunately, the real-world increased burning in her left

shoulder did more than stop the blood-boiling fantasy. Straightening, she yanked her hand away from her core and clamped her sex-wet hot fingers over her cramping shoulder muscle. "Shit, shit. Oh, fucking shit!"

Hard kneading of her poor muscle wasn't getting rid of the knot so she turned toward the head of the bed, scooting close at the same time. The pain eased a bit, allowing her the thinking space necessary for releasing the buckle. There. Done. Not nearly as hard as she thought it would be, she acknowledged as she turned her attention to the pressure marks now around her wrist.

What the hell was the matter with her? She had a job to do and not much time to do it in! So get with the program already, starting with pushing her skirt back down where it belonged. Her own bed was the place for this kind of role playing, not here!

She'd stood up and was doing just what she'd ordered herself to do when something shifted. No, not a shifting, almost as if the whole set had started breathing. More intrigued than afraid, she swiped a hand over her eyes. Even before her vision cleared, she knew what she'd find.

A man.

2

"You've been searching for me for a long time, haven't you?" the tall, blond, proudly naked creature said. "Preparing yourself physically and emotionally even while your mind rejects the lengths and depths of your needs. I've decided to reward you. And challenge you."

Who are you? she should be asking. *What the hell are you talking about?* Instead, she nodded because every word he'd spoken had been the truth.

"Listen to me," he continued. "Because of where your mind and emotions are, I have become your only reality. The bridge has been crossed. Until and unless I say different, there's just you and me. Do you understand?"

On the verge of another nod, she ran her hands down her hips. The last time she'd felt this lightheaded, she'd just finished her third glass of wine, but she was stone sober. At least she thought she was. Lightheaded was good. Lightheaded kept her thoughts on the surface.

"I know about you, Evi Hult," the man with bottomless blue eyes and no clothing said.

"What? We've never met." *Except late at night when I bring you to life.*

"You believe you're responsible for my existence," he said as if reading her mind. "But I exist in ways you can't possibly comprehend."

"You—do?"

He didn't immediately answer, maybe because he was waiting for her to say more, but her mind had gone blank thanks to his formidable and bone-melting presence. "You're what the movie industry calls a creative director," he continued. "You work for a company that produces documentaries mostly for public TV. Your dream is to be put in charge of your own production company, where you'll be able to control content instead of responding to the demands of advertisers and money men. You were raised by an aunt because your parents were so focused on their international business."

"They shouldn't have had me. They didn't have time—"

"What is, is. Don't dwell on what can't be changed. Aunt Margaret was a lifelong virgin. Did you know that?"

"I, ah, I suspected."

"I'm sure you did. What did she teach you about sex?"

God but he was beautiful! Well over six feet tall with top-of-the-scale muscle development and a skeletal frame to carry it off. She couldn't judge his age and didn't much give a damn. Beyond a teenager and far from retirement age. His cock, although not completely erect, wasn't exactly hanging limp and disinterested. He'd been circumcised, something she didn't think happened to Vikings. He was blond just like in the majority of her fantasies, the hairs on his chest and elsewhere echoing what was on the top of his head. Yep, there was the earring. "Who are you?"

"Did I give you permission to ask questions?"

His tone was no-nonsense, a man who expected obedience. "No."

"No, what?"

Her skin again felt as if someone had exposed the nerve endings. She knew his voice, his presence, his promise and danger was responsible. As for his take-command air, that was the result of her imagination, of her needs, wasn't it? "No, sir."

"Sir, for now. Did Aunt Margaret teach you about sex?"

"No," she admitted although he must know the answer. Now she didn't know what to do with her hands so she kept moving them from her hips to around her waist, to folded in front of her belly. "No, sir."

"How did you learn?"

His voice was echoing a little and, without taking her gaze off him, she knew the plywood was gone and they were in a real cave. No, not a cave. A dungeon lit by candles. "Like most girls, I guess, sir. Experimentation."

"What kind of experimenting?"

"In the back seat of cars—although I lost my virginity at my boyfriend's parents' cabin."

"Why did you do it?"

Think, damn it, think! "Because I couldn't not, sir."

"And why was that?"

He'd run his gaze from her face to her crotch, just like that answering his own question but waiting for her to validate what he already knew. "Because I had itches. I was hot, hungry. When he touched me—"

"Did you climax the first time?"

What insanity was this? How could she possibly be standing fully clothed and free while a naked man grilled her about the most intimate aspects of her life? "No, sir."

"Why not?"

"It—it hurt a little. I didn't know what to expect. He came so fast." She might have said more if her throat hadn't threatened to close down.

"But you liked it well enough that you went back to him? Or maybe it was with another boy the next time."

Maybe he already knew the answer. Something about the heat in his gaze said he was ahead of her. He certainly held the upper hand when it came to self-control as witnessed by his still half-erection while it took every bit of willpower not to press her thighs together. "Not a boy the second time, sir. My boyfriend's older cousin. He—he was around thirty."

"And he knew what he was doing."

Oh shit had he! She'd lost his name to the years but not the power and impact of that first climax. She remembered screaming and crying, offering to suck his cock in gratitude afterward and being granted her request. She remembered agreeing to see him night after night for the better part of a month—once he'd made sure she was on the pill—and trying to tell herself that she wasn't falling in love with him; but if he continued fucking her out of her mind, she'd never want anyone her age.

Then his heretofore nonexistent wife had returned from wherever she'd been and that had been the end of that—except for feeling betrayed and being turned on to sex, that is.

Maybe she'd told the Viking that; maybe he'd read her mind. Whichever it was, she could only stand there with her secrets hanging from her and wait for what he wanted and said next.

"This is my place," he told her. "My present reality. I've let you into it because you're ready. From now on we do what I want, do you understand?"

Wasn't she already dancing to his tune? Maybe not completely but she sure as hell couldn't walk away since she didn't know where they were and the words *from now on* had turned her on even more. After years of directing the words and actions and emotions of men who existed in her mind, being confronted by one who'd never dance to any woman's tune was intriguing, and maybe dangerous. "I understand."

"I know you do." Stepping toward her, he laid his big, callused hand on her shoulder—the one that had cramped not long ago. "In time you'll understand why this is happening and your role in it, but I'm not ready for you to go there yet. First come the lessons."

"Lessons?"

"In understanding your body's needs."

Why are we doing this? she wanted to ask, but maybe she didn't. Maybe the journey was everything. Saying that her nerve endings were exposed didn't go nearly far enough in explaining what she was experiencing, especially now with his voice rolling through her, his bones and muscles and skin speaking to hers, his eyes working their way to her soul, and his cock promising everything.

The strength went out of her arms, causing them to flop by her sides. She had to lock her knees to keep from collapsing. And the drums—the drums had begun pounding. "You're what they call an independent woman, ambitious, dedicated to putting your career first."

"You make it sound like a negative," she managed.

"In your world, ambition is necessary, but you'll no longer need it."

A warning alarm went off. Still, unless she was terribly wrong, he was promising her something, not threatening. "What will I need?"

"Trust. Do you trust me, Evi Hult?"

"How can you ask that? I don't know anything about you." *And what if you were spawned in my mind's deepest recesses?*

"I'm Thorn, from a space and place where men understand what the word *trust* means and women listen to their bodies and don't fear them. Listen to yours now and tell me what it's telling you."

That I'm dreaming, drunk, delusional, maybe all three. "I don't know." Despite her denial, she sensed energy and anticipation. A naked man named Thorn sure as hell hadn't come to fix the plumbing.

"You don't know because you don't allow yourself to. You're afraid of your body."

"I'm what?" Much as she wanted to fold her arms over her breasts, she couldn't concentrate on the complex task. "You don't know what you're talking about. I exercise, take long walks, watch what I eat, and—"

"Quiet!"

Shocked by the harsh tone, she closed her mouth. As a young girl, she'd been the model student, the pleaser, sometimes the teacher's pet. She'd seldom gotten in trouble, only once had broken her curfew, hadn't received so much as a single traffic ticket. Still, there were times when she wanted to kick off the traces of that life, come to work without her bra, see if she could get away with shoplifting, say yes to a one-night stand.

"You walk a line that's not right for you," he said, sounding like a supervisor discussing her job performance. "You've been doing it for so many years that you're convinced this is what you want from life, but it isn't. The truth comes out when your defenses are down, at night, when you're alone."

"What do I want?"

"For the primitive bitch deep inside to break free."

Had he just called her the next thing to a whore? But instead of being indignant, she was intrigued. "What makes you think that's inside me?"

"I know. And I'm here to help the bitch emerge."

What was she supposed to do, thank him for the offer?

"You don't believe me, but there wouldn't be any reason for what we're going to do here if you did." The corner of his mouth twitching, he jerked his head indicating he wanted her to come closer.

She did, damn it, planted one numb foot after another like a cow plodding to slaughter. Only, she was approaching a prime example of the male animal, not a place of quick and bloody death.

"Turn around."

No, no! Not giving up control. "What are you going to do?"

"Turn around!"

His voice, like thunder and lightning. Not shaking, not even thinking, she did. Having her back to him changed little because she still felt him everywhere. Her spine was stiffening and losing strength at the same time, her heart thumping and wet heat blooming between her legs. What was this, the thrill of danger?

She couldn't say how long he made her stand there with her hands fisted and senses alert. When he pushed her shoulder-length hair aside and ran his teeth over the base of her neck, she nearly collapsed. Her quiet yet electric sigh went on and on.

"What are you thinking now?" he asked, his hand still in her hair and his breath warming the lightly abraded flesh.

Fuck. I'm thinking fuck.

"Answer me."

"That—damn, damn, that this is insane."

"It is." He nibbled again. "Now what are you feeling?"

"Alive!" she blurted. "Alive." Lifting her arms and running them behind her head, she tried to touch him. Her fingers brushed his cheek, but when she went in search of his mouth, he pushed against the back of her head and forced her to bend over.

"Listen to me. You have lessons to learn. I touch you when and where and how I want. You touch me only when I give you permission."

"Permission?"

Leaning down so far put her in danger of falling; she couldn't stop herself from clamping her hands around his wrist and trying to pry him off her. He responded by grabbing her hair again and yanking her first upright and then back until her shoulders pressed against his chest.

"Silence!"

She could hardly breathe. Her back ached. Her eyes were tearing. And her nipples had become so hard and tight that she longed to rip off her bra.

"Now, concentrate on my voice. And what I'm saying. You're going to do that, aren't you?"

She nearly said something before she remembered that he'd ordered her not to speak. Nodding as best she could, she counted the march of seconds in his grip. This was a powerful man, a confident male, unaccustomed to being disobeyed. And she'd always been obedient.

"I'm going to let you stand upright again but only because it pleases me to do so. Before we're done with each other, what pleases me will have the same effect on you, but you have a long way to go before you truly understand what that means. I expect you to fight me; your journey would be incomplete if you didn't. But no matter what happens, I want you to understand and believe one thing."

Finally, thank goodness, he helped her straighten. And when he released her hair and lightly closed his hands over her upper arms, she half believed he was comforting her and giving her courage. Instead of taking off at a dead run, she buried herself in his strong warmth.

"I won't hurt you. I'll never hurt you."

Just like that she believed him, believed with every fiber of her being.

"You're shaking. Are you afraid?"

The simple thing would be to tell him that yes, of course she was afraid, but she didn't want to lie to this man who called himself Thorn and was going to take her places she'd never been. "No. At least I don't think I am."

"Good. Evi, I'm not immune. I want you, in ways that we'll never forget. Do you want the same thing?"

I don't know what you're talking about. "Yes."

"Good. I'm going to let go of you now, but you're going to stay where you are, aren't you?"

"Yes."

He released her shoulders, and she sensed that he'd taken a backward step. Except for a slight shiver, she didn't move. The dungeon, if that was truly where they were, threatened claustrophobia. What had happened to Dungeon Dames and how had they gotten here? Even more important, when and how was she going to return to the world she knew and trusted?

When he wants, came the reply.

"Put your hands behind you."

Ah, something to do, a command to obey. But even as she complied, a part of her raged at the compliant pleaser who'd always done what people told her to. Another part warned of that damnable cave in her mind. If she'd been a rebel or stood up for—

What was that?

The answer came as a strip of leather closed around her right wrist. Squeaking under her breath, she tried to jerk free, only to have his hand tighten over her forearm. "Settle, settle, let it happen."

Although his grip lessened, she absolutely knew he wasn't going to release her. He'd told her to trust him and she'd believed him, back then. All she needed to do was return to that state. *No darkness. No thinking about absolute helplessness.*

Muttering something she didn't try to hold on to, he drew her arm back behind her, making it clear she was expected to keep it there. One-handed, he easily looped more leather around her free wrist, then pressed her palms together. Concentrating on the strain in her shoulders momentarily distracted her. A solid snap followed almost immediately by another told her what she didn't need words for. A short length of metal chain had been fastened to her leather *bracelets*. Tentative experimentation told her that the chain was no more than four inches long. Handcuffed; he'd handcuffed her. Those things happened in her mind's cave. Oh shit, was that where they were going?

"Step one."

How many steps were there and where would she be when they were over?

"Turn around, face me."

For the first time in her life, she was a prisoner in more than her imagination. The simple act of rendering her arms useless was having a powerful effect on her, not fear, thank God, but something so different she couldn't put a name to it. She was vulnerable and yet trusting, anticipating the unknown.

"I'm not going to tell you what I'm going to do; I'll simply do it. Your responsibility is to experience. That's all you have to do today, Evi, experience. And when I ask, you're to tell me what you're feeling. You understand, don't you?"

"Yes, sir."

A sardonic smile lightened his sober expression. Still smiling faintly, he tugged her three-month-old pale green blouse out of her waistband. Standing as he wanted her forced her to widen her stance slightly, and she deliberately avoided looking down at what he was doing. Once he'd freed her blouse, he tended to the buttons. As each button surrendered its assigned task, her sense of vulnerability grew. More than that, she could barely wait for him to be done. Already he'd taught her that she could be hot and cold at the same time, shaking and eager.

The last to go was the button between her breasts. She expected him to pull her blouse back, revealing her practical pink bra, but he left her with her modesty—not her freedom but a shadow of the modesty that was an ingrained part of her.

Or was it? Maybe not, because she was already anticipating what would happen once they were equally naked.

Stepping back, he cocked his head to the side and studied his prisoner, his captive, his what?

"What—what are you thinking?"

"That you're a beautiful woman. With long arms and legs, lean hips but with breasts better suited for a larger woman."

"They're—I can't do anything about that."

"Would you if you could?"

Starting to develop sexually at ten had nearly been her undoing. What did she want with breasts when all she cared about was playing basketball? And periods—whose idea of a joke was that! But she'd eventually resigned herself to the inevitable, to say nothing of attention from adolescent boys and envy on the part of her girlfriends. Now, although she kept that piece of information to herself, she was more than a little proud of the way she'd turned out. Yes, her size Cs were better suited for a larger frame, but they got her noticed. And on those nights when need outstripped opportunity, a little pinching and massaging of her mammary glands was sure to hurry her journey to a climax. Telling him that no, she wouldn't have designed herself for a B cup, she waited his response.

He didn't say anything, damn it. Instead, he reached out and, with a single, expert motion, undid her skirt's snap. Another practiced move dispensed with the zipper.

As eager and afraid as she'd been the night she surrendered her virginity, she balanced herself on shaking legs while he tugged the tailored black garment over her hips, down her thighs, past her knees and calves. He left it mounded around her ankles. A jerk of his head told her what to do but stepping out of it taxed her ability to remain upright.

Again looking amused, he turned his attention to her panty hose. Normally she wore slacks to work, but there'd been a meeting this morning and, thinking it might involve planning future projects, she'd wanted to present herself as a professional. Instead, she'd been told about the acquisition of the defunct porn studio and given her assignment.

Thorn didn't care about that. Thorn cared only about stripping off the damnable hose. Deliberately looking past his shoulder, she struggled to divorce herself from her body, struggled and failed. Layers were being stripped away, privacy surrendered.

She wanted it, and she didn't. She was scared shitless and so alive she wondered if she might take flight because bit by bit she was turning her separate self over to this stranger.

3

Slow, a delicious slowness that piled up around her until she was silently screaming. The nylon became silk and burlap on her thighs. Inch by inch, cool air stroked her skin, and always his fingers were there, touching, teasing, testing, leaving and returning. When he slid the heels of his hands over the outsides of her thighs, pressure resonated throughout her and settled deep in her groin. Knowing, absolutely knowing that before he was done with her, his hands would be all over her, sex flung her mind off into a dark space.

He met her in it, sheltering and challenging with nothing more than his fingers and deep eyes, and his cock of course. "What are you feeling?" he asked when at long last, her hose roped her ankles.

"I don't—I can't explain—I've never—"

"Do you love or hate your body?"

"It's never felt like this."

"Hmm. You can't walk, can you? If you tried to, you'd fall."

He was right; her panty hose made effective ankle restraints. Concentrating on not losing her balance distracted her from her humming and heated body and yet everything was flowing together, part of a threaded whole. How easily he'd restrained her. Despite her continued concern over not toppling over, just knowing he'd planned this held her interest. She who seldom kissed and had never fucked on the first date and had never allowed herself to be picked up had turned into what? Surely no one she'd ever met before.

Leaving her hobbled and with her heels on, he stepped behind her so he could unfasten her bra. "Watch," he ordered when he again stood in front of her. Several long blinks later, he'd come back into focus again. Watching her intently, he ran her blouse off her shoulders and down her arms until her cuffs stopped him. Sliding his hands under her bra, he cupped her breasts, captured them really. "Full. And warm, so warm."

Yours, you've made them yours.

"It's time for me to learn what I need to about them. I need you to be honest, you can do that, can't you, be honest."

"Why?" she whimpered. "Why are we doing this?"

"We? So you're acknowledging that you're as much a part of this as I am, a full participant, that's what you're saying?"

Of course she was; she didn't, after all, have any choice. But that was a lie, because she'd invited the man into her room and taken off her clothes. Back when Thorn had stepped into the room, she could have run away, refused to leave her world, insisted he not touch her.

Couldn't she?

But he was offering her something she'd long craved even as she'd denied bondage was anything more than a familiar daydream.

"Answer me!" Grabbing her nipples between thumbs and forefingers, he pulled her toward him. "You want this, need this."

Need pain? Need tears in her eyes and her nipples being smashed? "Please, please, don't hurt—"

"I'll do what I want, what you need." A tug reinforced the sharp words. "Go into yourself, Evi, deep inside."

Despite the danger and fear, she did, diving down through the layers to where that mental cave waited. And although the pain held and her breathing hissed, she found a molten pool in her cunt. Heated waves rolled one after another, and she sank into them. This was what the best of sex was about, the self-absorption, the joy in her body's capabilities, the never-ending exploration.

And when he released her nubs so he could bathe them with his tongue, she leaned over and kissed the top of his head.

"Do you understand?" he asked when he was done and the air was drying and dimpling her nipples. "Pleasure and pain can exist at the same time."

"I don't want, don't want."

"Yes, you do. You're just not ready to admit it."

"Why? Why?"

No answer, nothing except a hand pressing into the small of her back. "Next step, taking you down even more and awakening the animal."

How, she needed to ask but didn't because she now hated the sound of her voice. Coming so close that she wondered if he intended to bite the side of her neck or ear, he all but covered her body with his naked heat. He continued to help her stay in place via the hand on her back, and when, maybe, she'd become accustomed to his ever-increasing power, he ran his right hand between her legs.

"God, oh God."

"Not God, me."

Like that, just like that, he rendered her speechless. It took so little, a single finger on her labia and his palm pressing against her mons, but suddenly she wanted nothing more from life. Mouth open and head back, she dangled between his hands. The hose around her ankles prevented her from spreading her legs, but although he had to work at finding room for his large hand, she began to melt, to slide down and deep and true. She'd caught fire. Was bathing his fingers in her honest and raw heat. Her loose and swollen labia wept for him.

"Sing, Evi, sing."

"Ah, ah."

"A simple song, simple and honest."

"Do me, please, I need . . ."

"What do you need?"

Finger fucking her now, his rough-skinned forefinger everywhere and yet not deep enough, flames slapping the sides of her neck before burning a trench from between her breasts all the way to her ass. There wasn't enough air in the room and no way of going from need to explosion, just his fingers raking and fueling, making her sing, showing her how to dance.

"What do you need?"

"I don't know, don't know." Mindless to her balance, she thrust her pelvis at him.

"Yes, you do."

"A climax! All right, I need to come."

His hot breath exploded against her throat. "And after you have, what then?"

"What? I don't know. Please, I don't know."

"That's because you can't think beyond primitive pleasure, but it's not yet time for you to have what you crave."

"Why not? Are you deliberately teasing me?" The image of kicking him where it counted filled her.

"I'm not going to try to control your thoughts, Evi. If that's what you believe, so be it. Just remember what I said: sexual need is primitive and basic."

It didn't matter, damn it. Not a damn thing did in this world beyond sweet hot release, something he undoubtedly already knew about her. Grateful because for now at least he wasn't throwing his hard questions at her, she slipped back into her skin where delicious agony waited. On a level she couldn't begin to comprehend, she knew she'd allowed herself to become his slut. Eventually she'd have to face the ramifications, but right now only the present existed.

Again and yet again, he stroked her clit. Each time was new and clean, every touch locking her deeper into herself. He'd found her trigger and was expertly playing it, promising and yet not delivering. Much as she relished the pure primal experience, being kept on the edge was exhausting, as witnessed by her sweat and labored breathing and constantly having to remind herself to lock her legs in place. If she'd thought it would do any good, she'd beg for a moment in which to recover and prepare, but what if her plea angered him? What if he walked away from her? And so she gave him her body and its juices.

Finally, mercifully, he withdrew his hand from between her legs. The steadying pressure remained on her back. "Do you know what I've done?"

Talk. Say something, anything. "Played with me. Turned me into your whore."

To her surprise, he chuckled, the long, low sound seeping into her bone marrow. "Yes, that. But do you understand why?"

The question was important, maybe the most vital she'd ever been asked, but how could she concentrate on an answer with a volcano just beyond her grasp? "What do you want me to say, that I'm easy and cheap, that I have no self-respect?"

Feeling as if she'd just slapped herself, she concentrated on bringing his features into focus. When she'd first seen him, she'd looked into the eyes of generic man, masterful man, but now she noted the faint lines at the corners of his eyes and edges of his mouth, proof, maybe, that there was more to him than a lonely woman's stud.

What would she do with a fully realized human being?

"This has nothing to do with self-respect or the lack of it," he replied. "Honesty, it's all about you being honest with yourself and your needs."

"Why do you care?"

When he closed his eyes, they remained like that for long seconds. "Because that's a large part of the reason I was created."

Created, not born? "What? I don't—"

"I know you don't, but it doesn't matter because this is about you, not me."

All she knew was that for a moment there'd been a shift in their relationship and that he'd been on the verge of opening up to her about something, but he ended that by stepping back, folding his arms across his chest, and staring down at her.

How could she do anything except imagine what he was seeing, an effectively restrained and all but nude woman with the smell of her sex in the air and her cunt red and swollen? Was that it, he'd accomplished what he'd been *created* for by making sure she was hot and bothered to the max? Now he could ride off into the sunset leaving her with her arms behind her and her hose around her ankles and hunger clawing?

"We're going to fuck," he said abruptly. "but you aren't yet ready."

You want to take a bet on that? "What are you talking about?"

"I know who you are, Evi, what you do and what you think you want to accomplish in life. And what waits in the dark."

"Oh?"

"You're doubting me?"

"I'm—I'm not going to believe simply because you tell me something."

"Good. You shouldn't. All right, an example of what I know about you. You majored in the cinema in college because you wanted to use the camera to shed light on some of what happens in this world. That's why you went after the job you did; so far it's working out. For the past few months you've been gathering the material you believe you need to convince your employers they should do a documentary on the economics of higher education. You're disillusioned with aspects of your own education, specifically subject requirements you'll never use in the real world. You also want to expose higher education for what it is, a business complete with profit motive."

"How do you know? I haven't told anyone—"

"Because I selected you, Evi."

Don't go there.

"I'm not a stalker, at least not the kind you think of when you hear the word and should worry about. You intrigue me; that's why I brought you here today. My agenda, let's say that it will become clear to you in due time. For now all you need to understand is that my assignment is to open your mind and turn darkness into the freedom of light."

"What?" She was incredulous. "That's what this is about, to convince me not to expose the truth about colleges' determination to milk students for every bit of money they can, regardless of whether those students learn anything useful?"

"No, Evi, no." Smiling like an indulgent parent, he stroked a shoulder. "You have every right to be passionate about your project. But that isn't the one we'd like you to do."

"We?"

"People like me."

"Like you? There are others—"

A quick shake of his head plainly said he had no intention of answering. "Tell me, what's more important to you right now, convincing me you need to make your documentary or getting off?"

"Does what I want matter?" She indicated her forced-together legs.

"Not really." With that, he scooped her up in his arms and

carried her over to the bed. Leaving her standing, he sat. "I've been looking forward to this for a long time. Taking you on your journey is going to be as pleasurable for me as I intend to make it for you. Let's call it the perks of the job."

She might have asked what the hell he was talking about if he hadn't taken that moment to grab her hair and bend her over until her breasts and belly rested on his lap with her knees nearly on the floor. His cock was so close! What if she managed to get her mouth around it?

What was she thinking? She'd just *met* this man and would be the biggest fool on the planet to trust him. Still . . .

"It's time for you to go back into yourself," he muttered with his fingers trailing down her spine. "Learning the truth about oneself is a multilayered task. As an example, I've long known I had dominating tendencies. Perfecting that skill has been extremely rewarding. I love to be in control, especially when it comes to women."

A note of alarm sounded, causing her to try to look up at him, but he prevented her from doing so by grabbing her cuffs and pulling her arms up behind her. *Helpless. Malleable. Waiting and, hard as it was to admit, willing.* "Didn't you hear me?" He slapped her buttocks. "You must go back inside yourself where the truth lives."

Despite the strain in her shoulder blades she found herself not relaxing but focusing on the tactile aspects of what was happening to her. Her bare breasts pressed against his naked skin, and his knee was one with her groin. With her head hanging down, blood quickly pooled in her temples. He continued to force her arms up and out, the easier to slap first one ass cheek and then the other.

This was no parental spanking, no standard discipline, certainly not an erotic tease. Instead, the sharp but not painful blows resonated through her pelvic area. The rhythm was drumlike, a powerful man's wordless message of control and understanding. *I know what you're feeling,* they said. *The energy and excitement, the anticipation, even whispers of terror.*

She felt all that and more, damn it! In her mind she was standing off to the side watching as her buttocks shuddered and rolled in response to the relentless blows. Her flesh was soft and thus jiggly there, but she didn't care. Fire had already settled into her thighs, and her ass had to be reddening.

Not just her thighs, she acknowledged as he lowered her arms and started massaging her shoulder blades even as he continued the sensual spanking. Her pussy absorbed the drumming, lapped at the heat, wept and waited, silently begged to be touched.

"You like this. Like the fact that you can't do anything about what's happening to you." His words flowed like a warm rain over her. "You know you're on the road to giving up ownership of your body and going where I'm determined to take you, but it didn't matter. There's only me and admitting you're turning yourself over to me."

How seductive his words were! How hot and yet gentle his touch. How knowledgeable about her. Because she was off floating somewhere, she paid scant attention when he stopped striking her. Only when he ran his fingers into her crack did she roll as best she could toward him.

"Stay with me, Evi. Lose yourself in sensation. But don't for a moment forget that I'm responsible."

"I—I want," she said and tightened her buttocks in an attempt to keep his hand on her. He responded by probing deeper. Oh shit, a finger against her asshole!

He calmed her with nothing more than a thumb, running it over the base of her neck, around to the side, and then along the back of her ear. The finger against her butt remained in place, not forcing entrance but letting her know how easily he could plunder her there.

An ass virgin! Damn it, she'd never taken a man that way

because the thought overwhelmed her. How, exactly, was it done; could she get hurt; would her aunt spin in her grave? But as the seconds ticked by, she imagined what ass fucking would feel like. His cock was so damn big that she couldn't imagine being able to take him that way, but other women could and did and if Thorn insisted—could she do that, force herself to relax and accommodate him if that's what he wanted? Could she tolerate the act? Hell, what if she enjoyed it?

"You're shaking."

"I can't help it." Her voice was muffled and talking face down made her drool a little. "I keep thinking about what you might do."

"Nothing you don't want."

Nothing you don't want? Did that mean she was stretched out over his legs because she carried some secret, to her, fantasy about being a man's plaything? About to deny that the concept was even remotely possible, she held back. And as she waited for the truth to come to her, Thorn stroked her puckered ass, relaxing and softening her. Maybe starting with his pinky? Yes, if he showed her the way and let her control the pacing, she allowed as how her back hole could accommodate his smallest finger. But that was all.

Oh, what was that?

As when he'd placed her over his legs, he'd already changed position before she realized what he was going to do. He'd begun by hauling her back onto her feet and standing at the same time. He forced her to shuffle forward so her thighs pressed against the bed. Then he grabbed her wrist restraints and leveraged her forward and down so her breasts rested on the mattress. She managed to turn her head to the side but with his grip still holding her arms up, that was all.

There, the sense of standing off to the side again. This time she shook her head in amazement and amusement because Evi Hult's buttocks were now sticking up in the air. What do you know? Not the world's most dignified stance but ripe with possibilities.

Then she took note of the alignment between cock and cunt and contemplated possibilities. Her cheeks burned, and her breathing quickened.

Maybe he'd seen how red her buttocks were and had decided to take pity on her, which was why he was gently rubbing the still-sensitive flesh, but maybe he was only reminding her of what he'd done to them. Hell, it didn't matter, just being stroked and watched did.

"A man's hands wherever he wants on your body," he said in a sing-song tone. "How does it feel, Evi? Now are you afraid?"

Afraid? What was that? She knew surrender and contentment down to her core, everything revolving around her and growing energy in her pussy.

"Are you?" he asked again.

"No."

"And you don't want me to stop, do you?"

"No." The single word echoed against the stone walls.

"What about being fucked?"

"I want!"

"And after?"

There was no after, just his cock so damn close to her opening and her labial lips wet and hanging and her thigh muscles burning. "I don't know what you want me to say."

"You will by the time I'm done with you."

Don't be done! I don't think I could survive that.

The first time, his cock barely touched her labia. Suddenly quivering, she unsuccessfully tried to look back at him.

"Sensation, not sight," he warned. "Don't forget that."

"I don't know if—"

"Sensation! Experience. Surely you understand that."

"Yes, yes."

He waited until she'd calmed a little before again pressing

against her, firmer now, his organ telling her to prepare for something she'd never done. Despite her continued trepidation, if she had a knife, she'd slash her ankle restraints so she could fully open herself to him. A third touch, the strongest so far but still not enough to penetrate her firm walls. What incredible self-control he had, she thought, and for the first time wondered what this sexual journey must be like for him. Someday, somehow, maybe, she'd get him to explain it to her and then pay him back.

"Do you like doggy style?" he asked with his hands separating her buttocks and his cock nestled in her crack.

"I, ah, haven't had much experience. Never, oh shit, never like this."

"Restrained, you mean?"

That was only part of it. Always before she'd left the man in question understanding absolutely and with no doubt that she had the final say in the how and where and even the why of sex. Surrendering control or rather having control ripped from her was a new experience—except when it took place in her imagination. Now that what she'd told herself was a nightmare had become reality, did she have the courage to stop denying certain things about herself and milk these moments for everything she could? Belatedly remembering that he'd asked a question, she struggled to recall what it was, but what did talking matter when he'd opened her so he could study her holes and his fingers were gliding over her skin?

Exposed. Unbelievably exposed.

"Not used to this?" He brought home his comment by sliding both thumbs into her pussy.

"No, no!" Her spine was arched, her mouth open, muscles seizing and melting at the same time.

"Because you're a modest woman, a good girl."

A man's fingers housed strong and unyielding! Not pain but

not pleasure yet, new, so new! Oh shit, was there anything sacred about any part of her? And did she want or need back any of the modesty he'd stropped from her?

"Again no answer? Is it because you're trying to decide how to respond or because you can't think?"

"Can't think, damn it! Shit, shit."

Withdrawing his thumbs, he stroked her opening as if reassuring her that he was going to grant her at least a modicum of the modesty he'd spoken about, but that wasn't what they were about, what they needed.

"I want you to think, need you to concentrate on what I'm saying." His voice low but strong, he ran his cock from her tailbone down the length of her crack. "There are places and people who practice BDSM. You know what that is, don't you?"

"I—I have some idea."

"Yes, you do." His voice was seductive. "Subs and doms, Evi, lifestyles devoted to a master/slave relationship, where pain enhances pleasure. Your safe world stripped away to be replaced by what you're both afraid of and long to embrace."

Her mind boiled with familiar images, but his thumb, his solitary and talented thumb, was rocking over her butthole and each small stroke took him marginally deeper.

"I'm going to say certain things, not because you don't know what I'm talking about but because it's the only way you'll acknowledge the truth. Pain is just a part of the experience and as individual as the participants. Some subs get off on being beaten and can't climax without pain's stimulation while others crave being treated like an object." In. Oh—his thumb to the first knuckle now resided inside her! "Is that what you want deep down where you hope no one can see, to be handled as if you're a piece of meat, bought and sold and passed around, forced to service whomever your master orders you to? That turns you on?"

"No, no, no." And yet, yet, to be valued for her cunt and breasts and capacity for abuse, to fully dive into her mind-cave . . .

"Too much to think about?"

"Why? Why is this happening?"

"Evi, the questions I'm asking and the things I'm doing and the images I'm painting already exist in you. No, don't keep denying it! All I'm doing is helping you face your truth. Together we can bring it out into the open and celebrate your freedom."

Even as she silently begged him to take her there, that still didn't answer the question of why he'd taken on this task, let alone why he believed she needed to wallow around in her subconscious.

"That isn't enough, is it?" he asked as his thumb continued its slow and steady assault. She'd absolutely loathed her one rectal exam but his caresses were taking her deep into herself where, maybe, her hidden side indeed resided. "You still don't understand the why."

Did it matter?

"Answering that leads to freedom; don't ever forget that."

"Freedom?"

"Don't, damn it! You're trying to say that's at odds with the true meaning of BDSM, right? Still lying to yourself about your true nature. Listen," he muttered. "Concentrate. If you'd surrendered yourself to your slavehood, your master might fit you with butt plugs designed to open you here." He demonstrated with a quick shove into her ass. "You'd be expected to wear one for hours and to thank your master when the size keeps increasing." Up to the base of his thumb now, the intimate invasion complete, skewered on his digit. Accepting, accommodating. "You're an anal virgin, aren't you?"

"Yes," she whimpered with her eyes closed and her mind's eye full. If she'd been the one looking at the naked and restrained woman struggling to remain in place while a man reamed her asshole, she'd be filled with disbelief that any woman would willingly degrade herself this way.

Or would she?

"And yet this isn't new to you."

The hot humming running throughout made concentrating on anything nearly impossible, but he'd hit on something important. She could either lie and save what pitiful dignity she had left or tell him the truth.

"I've had fantasies—"

"That you believed no one would ever know."

"How did you—" she started but stopped because he was slowly slipping out of her. Too soon she'd be empty, lonely, waiting.

"How do I know what you think about in the middle of the night? I do, Evi, that's all you need to know, I do."

That made no sense but then nothing did.

4

Thorn had pulled her to her feet and turned her so her back was to the bed. He'd also produced scissors from a nearby nightstand and made short work of her bra and blouse, but she didn't care. He'd also helped her out of her shoes and cut off her panty hose and panties. She was still trying to decide what to do now that she could walk when he knelt and wound rope around her ankles, leaving no more than a couple of inches of play between them.

"You're beautiful in captivity," he told her, his ready cock cradled in his palm. "Sexual captivity brings out a woman's purest nature."

"It does?" Much as she loved hearing that and feeling his heated gaze over her body, all she really wanted was to be fucked. Had she been wrong to assume that was what he wanted as well? If he truly was into BDSM and here so he could force it on her—

"You're glowing, raw and wild. Think about that, Evi. Under the conservative clothes you wear and beneath the driven professional lives an animal screaming to be let loose. You can't deny that animal exists, can you?"

No. "Would it matter if I did?"

"It's still hard for you to admit, isn't it? Damn, but you're deep in denial."

"Why do you care?"

"Someone other than yourself has to. Otherwise, you're going to spend your life trying to live with your dual natures and that would be a pity."

"What do you want me to say, that BDSM intrigues me? If I do, will you leave me alone?"

He chuckled. "It doesn't work that way. Do you have the courage to admit the truth to more than yourself?"

"What does it matter?" If only she dared try to walk! How she'd love to launch herself at him and drive him to the ground, before wrapping her legs around him and demanding her reward, that is. "There's just you and me—whoever you are. The world doesn't know."

"But it could."

Alarmed by the possibility of what he might have in mind, she worked at getting moisture back into her throat.

"Let me put it to you another way. What if a camera was trained on us and a microphone picked up everything you say?"

"No!" Even more alarmed than she'd been a second ago, she studied what she could see of the candlelit cave. From what she could tell, there wasn't a camera lens anywhere. "Why would you do that?"

"Not me, you."

Not in this lifetime. "I'm not an exhibitionist."

"But you want to produce honest work and what's more honest than the range of the human imagination?"

"I'm one person. I can't cover all that."

"You can do a hell of a lot and you know it. The only thing standing in the way is your damnable insistence on shrouding your fantasies in darkness."

"Mine? Why should they be the only ones on display? What about you? Surely you have secret dreams and desires."

She read his answer in his darkened gaze and the way he stroked his erection. "Easy. Don't try thinking right now," he soothed. "It's time for you to go deeper inside yourself than you ever have. Peel away even more layers."

Yes, no!

Not taking his eyes off her, he again reached into the nightstand and produced a long black strip of fabric. Even before he placed it over her eyes, she knew what he was going to do, and although she could and should have fought him, she simply stood and trembled as he secured the blindfold in place. Locked in the darkness of her mind, she listened to the faint sound his feet made against the stone floor. That and her nerve endings let her know he was walking around her, his movements slow and thoughtful. A specimen. Yes, that's what she'd become.

"Exquisite in your helplessness. Like clay waiting to be molded."

If he hadn't already given her vivid and unforgettable examples of what he was capable of, she would have been terrified. Instead, she ordered herself to be patient, and as she waited, she imagined that they were at an important meeting in an opulent room decorated with leather and hardwood furniture. Thorn was magnificent in his designer suit, and all eyes were on him as he listened to and commented on input from the successful men and women under him and then issued his well-targeted orders.

But if those men and women looked under the table they were sitting around, they'd see her kneeling at his feet. Naked except for the weighted nipple clamps dragging her breasts down, she had her hands between her legs and her fingers pressed against her cunt in an attempt to feed her desperate hunger. Thorn's slacks were unzipped, his full cock exposed, or it would have been if it wasn't in her mouth.

She was his sex slave, his whore, his chattel. And her world was complete.

A harsh tug on her hair pulled her head back and killed the image. "Stay with me, Evi. You can return to your mind when I'm done with you." He punctuated his command by slapping her right breast.

She sighed but didn't cry out, and when he did the same to her left breast, she arched upward and offered herself in sacrifice. He turned her full mounds into his personal drums much as he'd done earlier with her buttocks, lightly striking her over and over again until the vibrations rolled throughout her.

"Your breasts are mine."

"Yes, yes."

"Are you deep inside yourself?" he asked as he released her hair. "Nowhere else you want to be?"

"I can't—can't go anywhere. There's just here."

No more slapping, no more energy running between them. Lost, she strained to see through the black curtain. She was still fighting the impossible fight when he claimed her nipples. "Your nipples are mine."

"I—know."

"Do you? Do you truly comprehend what it means?"

She thought she did. Turning her body over to him meant living in a place filled with sensation and anticipation. No longer made up of different practical body parts, she'd become a giant cunt, the primitive creature he'd called her. And when he rolled her nubs between thumbs and forefingers, instead of pain, she rode on the great heat centered in her pussy. It was all sex, everything.

"Dream for me, Evi. What do you want me to become?"

Wondering if he'd tapped into her fantasy about giving him

head in the middle of a high-level meeting, she went looking for a path through the darkness to where need lived.

"My master. Watching me being auctioned off and trying to decide whether to bid on me. Ordering me to bend over and spread my cunt lips so you can examine me."

"Are you worth much?"

About to reply, she realized he no longer had hold of her breasts, but even as the pain subsided, she remained solidly in her fantasy. "A great deal. Other men want me in their harem, their stable, their rooms, but you won't be denied. Once you've paid for me, you snap your leash onto my collar and haul me away."

"Where do I take you?" he asked from behind her.

Commanding herself to remain still, she told him that he lived in a moated castle complete with a secret dungeon. Supremely sure of himself, he barely looked at her while leading her down the steep stone steps. Because he'd bound her elbows behind her, she was afraid she'd fall, which distracted her from what she'd see at the bottom until they were there.

"A cage. You're putting me in a cage," she said as he lifted her arms as he'd done before, forcing her to lean over.

"Do you want to be there?"

"I—I'm not sure."

"Do you want to be here?"

In this windowless space she'd never known existed in a place and maybe a time she couldn't comprehend? Naked and helpless and bleeding with need? "Yes."

A nearly inaudible sigh told her he needed to hear that response. "Good," he muttered. He was still keeping her off balance; if he let go, she'd fall. "Tell me about the cage."

Cage. A place of not just confinement but quiet contemplation and escape from all responsibilities, all rights. "It's small, barely long enough to allow me to stretch out on the thin mattress. I can't stand. Rings have been bolted into the floor, and I know they'll be used to restrain me. I smell my fear."

Planting his foot in front of hers to keep her from stumbling forward, he reached between her legs from behind, swiped them over her lips, and then placed his hand under her nose. "Does your fear smell like this?"

"Yes," she admitted, the scent of sex assaulting her.

"Then it isn't fear, is it?"

She dangled in his grip, limp and ready to be used. Again her mind's eye provided the image the blindfold robbed her of. He was leaning back a bit to counterbalance her weight, the muscles of his forearm bulging. Staring at her back, he admired the way her shoulders were being pulled together, his free hand hovering over her ass. As for his thoughts, perhaps he was counting the minutes until he could bury his cock in the opening of his choosing.

"No," she said on a sigh. "I'm not afraid. Maybe of myself a little, but I trust you."

"Why?"

I don't know! I don't know. "I've—back when I was captured and trained as a sex slave, I kept hearing about you. They said you could be a harsh master, that you demanded absolute subservience. But you believed in giving pleasure as well as receiving it because pleasure breeds loyalty. As long as your slaves put you and your needs and commands above everything else, they were treated well. They wore your chains and brands with pride and worship your cock."

"What brands? Where were the chains placed?"

Head hanging and the world behind her unseeing eyes blood red, she dove even deeper into the world she was creating. She didn't know where the images and scenario came from or that she'd had the capacity for such a fully realized creation in her, but that was all right because she'd never felt more alive.

More restrained.

"I wore your collar. Made of leather with a locking device only you had the key to, you put it on me the night we reached your castle. You commanded me to kneel naked before you with my head uplifted while you locked it in place. You—then you clipped your chain to the ring in the collar and forced me to lean over so my head was nearly on the ground and fastened the other end of the chain to a ring driven into the ground. Not saying a word beyond ordering me to call you master, you left me like that for hours. All I could think about was what would happen when you returned, and by the time you did, I was drenched in hunger. Although I could see my cage, I knew I wouldn't be allowed to crawl into it until you were done with me."

"What did I do to you?" Pulling her upright again, he drew her against his chest with his legs straddling hers, his cock grinding against her backside, and his arms hard over her breasts and against her groin.

Not sure of the line between the dream she'd been trying to spin for both of them and being in his powerful embrace, she went in search of what she, and maybe he, needed.

"I think I'd fallen asleep, but you woke me by placing a vibrating egg in my pussy and turning it on. Because you'd used straps to hold the large egg in place and had fastened my hands to my collar, I couldn't pull it out. Although I tried to tell myself that I didn't want to be so helpless, I loved its feel in me and the constant reminder of what it stood for."

"Which was?"

"My place as your possession."

His hold increased until her breasts were flat against her rib cage. Despite the barrier caused by her pelvic bone, she had no problem imagining his finger penetrating all the way to her womb. When he repeatedly pulled her against his cock, in her mind, his finger became his hard and hot length. "Did you come?"

"You—you wouldn't let me," she stammered and forced herself back into the fantasy she was spinning for both of them. "Every time I came close, you used the remote control to quiet the egg. You were sitting in a chair, a drink in one hand, the control in the other and held high so I saw what you were doing. It didn't matter that there was more slack in the chain fixed to my collar because I couldn't remember how to stand. Instead, I writhed at your feet, begging."

"Was I pleased?"

How to concentrate? How to think of anything except his strength blanketing her and hot pressure powering through her? "I couldn't tell. I—I wanted to study your expression, but you wouldn't let me."

"How did I stop you?"

Stay there. Build images we can both feed off. "By ensuring that nothing except my cunt mattered. Your knowledge of my limits told me I'd never be as I was before. When I begged you to end the agony you'd brought me to, you laughed and said you knew what I really wanted."

"Was I right?"

Before she could begin to formulate an answer, he forced her onto her knees. Now untouched and alone, she strained to determine where he was. She sensed that he was nearby; he wouldn't have left her. But that was the only thing she knew, that and her starving, weeping, exposed body.

"Was I right?"

"Yes! I wanted to be your slave."

"And my slut?"

How far had she traveled since this morning? Miles and miles, and yet she couldn't begin to answer until she'd taken the rest of the journey. "I'm not sure I knew it then; it didn't matter. Finally when I was so weak that I could no longer lift my head and my throat was raw from begging, you removed the egg. At your order, I licked your feet in gratitude. After letting me go to the bathroom, you ordered me into the cage. How wise you were because you'd left my hands tied so I couldn't satisfy myself. Although I was exhausted, I don't think I slept. My need was too great for that."

"You don't think? This is a fantasy, Evi, not reality. You can control what happens in it."

Telling herself he was right, she worked to conjure up an image of her locked within bars, and discovered that it wasn't much different from what she was experiencing now. "Everything is swimming inside my mind. I know; you just said it shouldn't have been like that, but I can't help—maybe I deliberately made things vague."

"Why would you do that?" Going by where his voice was coming from, he was behind her but how close she couldn't be sure. Perhaps he was looking down at her, maybe studying her back but maybe positioned so he could see her breasts with their pale fullness and dark centers. Opening her knees as much as her restraints allowed, she once again went down.

"You're right. It was a fantasy, a way of stimulating myself so I could bring myself to climax. I'd—I've never told anyone this, but I've visited some pretty graphic Web sites and even bought some bondage videos to give me something visual to build on."

"How do you feel about that? Are you embarrassed?"

"At first," she allowed, no longer able to stop herself from trying to look behind her. "But the more videos I watched, the more comfortable I became."

"Then why didn't you tell anyone?"

"Why?" she repeated, unable to keep disbelief out of her voice. "That's hardly the kind of thing I'd share."

"You just told me."

"I know," she admitted on a sigh. Responding to his questions had distanced her a little from the fire in her core, but she'd be a fool if she told herself it wouldn't again flame.

"Go back to your fantasy," he said and brushed her hair off her shoulders. "Share."

Whimpering and leaning toward his touch, she nevertheless told herself that she couldn't possibly have become dependent on him so soon. Surrender didn't happen to modern, independent women.

Then what was she doing naked, tied, and on her knees?

"The next night you had guests, other wealthy and powerful men like yourself. They'd brought their slaves with them and passed them among themselves as they'd done many times before, but you said I wasn't ready to join them. Instead, you placed me in an arm binder that arched my back in such a way that my breasts were prominently displayed." Being caught within her dark world made it all too easy to form a mental image of herself as she trailed obediently behind Thorn—or whoever had been the man in her fantasy—watching the other slaves service their masters. Because the man in her images had also gagged her, she'd been a silent observer, and nearly as hungry as she'd become with the egg locked inside her.

"After they left, you removed my gag and changed my ties so my hands were in front, attached to a rope that went around my waist and between my legs. It was tight, but I didn't mind because the pressure on my cunt kept me horny and I wanted that. You fed me tiny pieces of food, the first food I'd had to eat since you'd bought me."

"Were you grateful?" He continued stroking her hair, and although she loved the touch, it wasn't enough.

"I begged you to let me give you head, but you said I had to wait a little longer."

"You pretty much made me a bastard in your mind, didn't you?"

Startled because his voice was so close, she tried to lean in that direction but nearly lost her balance. Grabbing her shoulders, he drew her toward him until the back of her head rested against him. She was still getting used to his touch after being alone for so long when he reached around so he could cup her breasts. "Why did you make me a cruel master?"

"Not cruel!"

"Then what?"

"You—you knew what I needed, to be taken down inside myself. I had lessons to learn about always putting you first and understanding that you were in control of everything I experienced."

"Even in control of what and when and how you ate?"

"Yes," she admitted. A wave of embarrassment slid over her at the reminder of what a perfect little bondage slut her imagination had made her. Then the image faded under the pressure on her breasts and the sudden and unshakable knowledge that he needed this as much as she did.

"A little while ago you mentioned brands. Did I brand you?"

As she spun off into the past that existed only in her mind, she described the day he'd decided the time had come for her to wear permanent proof of his ownership. By then he'd educated her in the art of sucking cock and when she pleased him, he allowed her to sleep at the foot of his bed. He still hadn't fucked her but had allowed her to satisfy herself while he watched.

On this day, he'd immobilized her with leather straps after giving her a pill designed to relax her. Although she hadn't been clearheaded, she'd taken pride in not so much as flinching as he pressed a hot, small S-shaped brand against the meatiest part of her right breast. The moment the S burned into her flesh, before she could scream, he slapped an ice pack on the spot and held it until the pain died.

"That night you ordered me to climb on top of you, straddle

your cock, and lower myself onto it," she finished. "Finally screaming the scream I'd been carrying inside all day, I came in seconds. When I'd recovered, I put all my energy into fucking you, and when you climaxed, so did I. We slept in each other's arms."

"Is that what you want? To spend the night in your master's arms?"

She was searching for an answer when he lowered himself to his knees behind her. One hand went around her throat while the other gripped her left hip. Bit by bit he increased the pressure on her windpipe until she again rested her weight against him. A thread of fear ran through her, but even as she worked at getting enough air into her lungs, she reveled in this latest proof of how much of her he controlled.

This was good, more than good, something she'd been searching for for a long time without knowing it.

"This is part of what BDSM is about," he muttered with his mouth near her ear. "What I want you to acknowledge and accept as you haven't so far is that in its pure form, the sub willingly gives up ownership because she trusts the dom. Do you trust me?"

The first time she'd allowed her darkest fantasy to slip past her barriers, she'd mentally imagined being in a harem, not a place of luxury and wealth, but a secret place in some unknown mountains where a powerful and savage warlord kept females he'd captured from his enemies in the valley below. Because he'd surrounded himself with handpicked henchmen whose loyalty had been bought with freely given cunts, the warlord was supremely confident. He devoted his days to plunder and killing, his nights to satisfying himself on helpless flesh. She'd been one of those women, of course. At first he'd beaten and humiliated her, sexually teased her and taught her that he and he alone fed, watered, and kept her warm. At length he'd broken her down, not with whips but crotch ropes. Bound and helpless, often with plugs in both her openings, she'd been forced to watch while he had sex with his more fortunate captives. After endless nights of hearing their delighted cries of gratitude, she'd begged to be allowed to receive his cock. And when he'd granted her wish, she'd groveled at his feet and then crawled after him as he walked away.

How could she possibly tell anyone, especially him, about that?

"Do you trust me?"

Unable to speak, she settled for nodding, but even as she did she wondered at the insanity or lust or hunger that had brought her to this point.

"You believe you do," he continued, his hand making inroads between her legs. "But what you have yet to learn is that this kind of trust is a never-ending journey. We both have to earn it."

Was he saying they were going to be together for a long time? Impossible because she had a job to do, bills to pay, responsibilities.

He must have known what she was thinking because suddenly he forced her head down to the floor. Although he immediately released her, she remained in place, in part because her leverage was restricted without the use of her arms, in part because knowing her ass was again offered to him was a turn-on. Calling up images of how she'd shown her gratitude to her warlord, she wiggled her rear end at Thorn.

Knowing hands pulled her buttocks apart. Expecting to feel his fingers in her intimate holes, she shuddered and moaned as his cock head slipped into her pussy. "What are you saying, that you want this?" he asked.

"Yes, please!"

"Please what?"

"Fuck me."

"No!" He punctuated the word with a familiar slap to her left buttock. "Not that."

What did he want? But even with the undeniable distraction of what she'd long been waiting to feel, she knew. "I offer myself to you, master. Please pleasure yourself with my gift."

"I love hearing that even if it's part of the role you're playing."

Was she assuming a role? Maybe and yet on another level she'd never meant anything more. Hoping to get him to focus on the physical, she rocked back toward him. Unfortunately, that caused her forehead to rub against the hard floor. "Master?"

"What, my pet?"

"I—can't we use the bed?"

5

That earned her another laugh but just as she was trying to lift her head, he pulled free, stood, and helped her to her feet. An instant later she could see; at least his shadow appeared. As she waited for her vision to clear, she concentrated on balancing her weight. She hadn't forgotten what he looked like, far from that, but being robbed of sight for a while had made it possible for her to concentrate on the stories and scenarios she'd long spun in her mind but had just shared with another human being for the first time. Concentrating on the man himself again served to bring back reality. She had been rendered helpless by a stranger. More than that she'd called him master and offered her body to him, more than offered, begged him to use her. And despite his greater height and nearly a hundred more pounds, she had absolutely no fear of him, at least not in ways she'd share with outsiders. How could she when he was giving her what she'd craved for longer than she dared admit?

"No more thinking," he said as he picked her up and threw her over his shoulder. Several long, easy strides brought them to the edge of the bed, and when he sat her down on the side of it, she knew it was far different from the cheap piece of furniture that had once belonged to Bondage Babes.

He sat beside her, his body angled toward hers, so she did the same. Even with urgency running through her, she saw the humor in what they were doing. Here they were, two brand-new acquaintances interested in getting to know each other, but instead of conversations about careers, pets, favorite vacation spots, and political affiliations, they were both naked, and she was tied up.

And they were going to have sex.

Eventually.

Hopefully.

"Have you thought about what catering to your needs so far has been like for me?" he asked after a long silence.

"You, ah, you have incredible self-control."

"Yeah, I do." After looking down at his hard-as-hell erection for a moment, he cradled it between his hands as if it was an old friend, a tired old friend. "I've learned how to distance myself from my cock, but it's never easy."

There must be something she could say, questions about why he was in this line of work, for lack of a better term, and where he'd come from and how he'd known what he did about her, but she didn't want to talk, didn't want anything more to get in the way of her goal. "I don't have that skill," she told him. "Not now after what you've been doing to me."

"In other words, you want to get to the main event."

Hadn't she already made that clear? She was pressing her lips against his chest even before she knew that's what she was going to do. Using her tongue to bring his taste into her mouth, she again slipped off into the hot sensual world she'd created for herself. To her wonder and gratitude, he wrapped an arm around her shoulder and held her there. And when he kissed the top of her head and lightly gnawed on her hair, she slid deeper into the heated fog of her mind.

Master or boyfriend, owner or husband, it didn't matter. She was a woman with needs and he a man who understood the depth of those needs even better than she did. "You're beautiful," she managed. "The most beautiful man I've even known."

"What makes me that way?"

"Your knowledge, your skill."

"In sexually restraining and teasing you?"

She'd gone as far as she could in her ability to think. Now his body was the only thing left, that and her body's need for it. "Master, please."

Cursing under his breath, he held her at arm's length. Anger blazed over his features but died a sudden death, making her wonder if she had more impact on him than she'd realized before and that he resented her power. "Damn you."

"For what?"

"For making me want you."

"Isn't this what your controlling me is about, so you can get off?"

"It isn't that simple, and you know it."

Nothing about today was, not that she needed to tell him that. Loving and hating both of them, she struggled to ignore the heat that threatened to take away her ability to breathe. When he released her, for a moment she simply sat. Then, acting on a force she didn't want to put a label on, she started to slide onto the floor, but although he must have known she wanted to take his cock into her mouth, he seized her arms and pushed her onto her back on the bed. She watched his every move as he lifted her legs on the bed as well.

His expression was impassive as he lightly stroked her thighs. Even when she gasped and tried to roll toward him, he held her in place while giving no hint of what he was thinking. Still, there was no denying the sweat along his breastbone or the way his cock danced.

Losing herself in sensation was easy and right. No matter

what the rest of the day brought, she'd live in these seconds while he painted her skin with his rough, knowing, and somehow gentle fingers. Beyond all reason, he was fueling flames that had come to life in her mind years ago.

And she took his gift.

"What are you feeling right now?"

Be honest. It's important. "I love having everything center around me. In my—always when I imagine things like this happening, I have to concentrate on the whole picture. It's my responsibility to make my imaginary man do what I need him to, and that's distracting. The way I am now, I can't do anything except experience it. You're giving me a gift, an incredible gift."

"Some gifts come with a price."

"What kind of price?"

"Maybe I should call it accountability. I hand you something, but I expect you to do the same in return."

If he'd wanted her to give her full attention to what he'd just said he wouldn't still be trailing his hands over her so-accessible and willing body, would he? *I'll think about that soon*, she longed to tell him. *Just grant me release first, please!*

"I know what you're thinking." Leaning down, he pressed his lips against her navel. "Do you have any idea how transparent you are right now?"

Oh shit, his breath running over her belly! Twitching, she couldn't guess that he was going to bury his tongue in her belly button until it was too late. "Arr!"

"No, no." His hands now pressing on her shoulders kept her from escaping. "I'm not cutting you any slack. Your job is to learn and acknowledge everything your captive body is capable of experiencing. Mine is to keep those experiences coming."

How right he was! How determined. Tongue and teeth and lips worked her from her neck all the way to her thighs. Maybe she'd learned her lesson; maybe she'd forgotten how to move.

Whatever the reasons, except for the uncontrollable twitches, gasps, and shudders, she held herself in place. It was a matter of pride—that and milking the erotic teasing massage for everything she could. If she dared, she'd tell herself that he worshipped her and that's why he'd slid his tongue through her fine pubic hair, guided her in bending her knees, and closed his mouth over her labia.

But that was a naive fantasy, a melting-to-the-core woman's disconnect with reality. Unlike her, Thorn didn't lose control. He had a reason for everything he did and lessons to impart to her.

Bottom line, her body belonged to him. She was his to mold.

Fine, wonderful, mold me.

Shit, the damnable ankle restraints were limiting his access to her sex. Struck by sudden inspiration, she planted her feet on the mattress and pushed off, briefly bringing her feet up over her head. Then gravity took over, causing her legs to slide back down.

"What are you trying to do?" That damnably intriguing amusement was back in his voice.

"Give you—give myself to you."

"You already belong to me." He demonstrated by repeatedly rolling her onto her right side and then her left. "Putty in my hands. Go on, tell me that's not what's happening."

"I'm putty all right! Stop, I'm getting dizzy."

"That's not dizzy." The moment she was on her back again, he slid his hands under her buttocks and lifted her lower body toward him, letting her know that she was to bend her knees as she did. "That's sensory overload."

No argument there. And no point in lying and telling him that she didn't belong to him. One thing about his little demonstration, he'd distracted her from trying to do anything on her own. Limp and receptive again, she lay there wondering if it was possible to melt into the mattress while his tongue repeatedly slid over her slit. Maybe not her entire body but her cunt, her *here's my gift to you* cunt. Not a muscle remained. She could be in the middle of a full body cramp and she wouldn't know it. There was him, him—first, last, and only him.

"Master, master," escaped her numb and yet sensitized lips.

"I'm not your master, Evi." He kept his mouth and thus his breath near her core. "Your body is."

"No! You . . ."

"I know. You still believe I'm responsible for everything you've been experiencing, but you're wrong." He slipped both thumbs into her and then separated them, effectively stretching her. "That's today's lesson. When you surrender yourself to someone who understands everything surrender entails, you become free to experience as you never have."

What was he talking about? "Master, oh, please."

"No reservations, Evi?" Although he relaxed the pressure on her pussy walls, his thumbs remained in place. "No modesty left?"

"Can't, can't."

"Can't or don't want to?"

Ah, that's what he wanted from her! "I trust you," she admitted around the tears clogging her throat and the fired energy centered in her clit. "With all of me!"

He didn't insist she repeat herself, and although she still would have insisted that everything in and about her belonged to him, she was thankful for the small gift of self-respect.

But was that what he had in mind, she wondered as he pulled out so he could stroke her wet and hot labia. Maybe, was it possible, maybe she had given him a gift with her words.

Wondering if that was true, she turned her head so she could study his features. What she found brought fresh tears to her eyes. Yes, he was still in control; nothing about him so much as hinted otherwise. But he wasn't a manikin or robot, and he was certainly much more than a figment of her imagination. Concentrating on her needs and lessons had taken their toil on him. Strain was etched on his face and in his eyes, and he'd again closed his free hand around his organ. His breaths were deep, yet rapid, and it wasn't warm enough in here for that to be responsible for the sweat glistening on his chest.

Despite the distraction of his so-knowing fingers on her clit, something shifted in her. Up until now, everything had been about her journey, but no longer. One thing, maybe the only thing she could give him, was the relief and release he deserved. And in offering a home for his cock, she'd receive her own reward.

"Thorn?" Swallowing against the lump in her throat, she tried again. "It doesn't have to go on like this. You've been incredible to me, incredible. I want to give you—please, think of yourself now." She demonstrated by trying but failing to fully open herself to him. "Release my legs, please, and let me wrap them around you. My gift—my cunt is my gift to you."

Although he could have rightly pointed out that she was in no position to be offering him anything, he didn't. Responding to a new light in his eyes, she rolled toward him, which unfortunately separated his finger from her clit. "Not my hands. You don't have to do that, but please, can't we have sex?"

"I could bring you to climax without that happening."

Of course he could. Just thinking about the ways and possibilities made her flush with anticipation. "But it's not what you want. Damn it, Thorn, think about yourself."

His grip on his cock tightened.

"You're on the edge. What are you going to do, force climaxes out of me until I can't come anymore and then walk away so you can jack off? You don't want that; I don't want it for you."

"Doms make those decisions, not the subs."

"I'm not your sub!" *Am I?* "And I haven't given you the right to be my dom. I'm learning, that's all it is, learning. Lesson over." She made her point by running her gaze from his *must be hurting* cock to her core. "Recess time."

"Recess?" He drew out the word.

"Play, party time, whatever you want to call it." Was there something else she could or should say? Maybe, but hadn't she already said enough and did either of their bodies need words?

One instant he was sitting beside her with his weight pulling her toward him. The next he'd stood and was stalking away from her. *Come back!* she longed to cry out but didn't. This was his journey, his decision.

Slowing, stopping, both hands at his groin, and his shoulders and back tense. Had she ever read anyone as clearly as she was now reading him? In countless ways they remained strangers, but she knew, absolutely knew, that his body was being truthful.

When he slowly turned and took the first step back toward her and the bed he'd placed her on, she smiled up at him.

"You have incredible eyes," he said. "There are flecks of gold in them."

"Are there?" *I saw silver in yours.*

"And they're so expressive."

"So are yours."

Although he was now close enough that she again felt his body heat, she knew he wasn't going to touch her until he'd had time to digest what she'd just told him. Of course he needed that. After all, his role as a dom was to present an aloof and mysterious image, right? A man in absolute and unwavering control. But underneath that image beat a man's heart. "Did I dream you up?" she asked. "I wanted a Viking and that's what you look like."

"I'm not a product of your imagination, Evi. I exist."

Thank God! "But where? Not in the world I understand and know." A wave of something beyond sexual need slammed into her. "You were going to walk away a minute ago, weren't you? Instead you came back to me."

"Yeah."

"Because we both want the same thing."

By way of response, he grasped her ankle restraints and lifted until she could see little except her shins and knees inches from her face. Her buttocks were off the bed, and her hands pressed against the small of her back. Even with anticipation running through her, she couldn't ignore what she looked like, an offered cunt.

Sighing, he positioned himself so one leg was bent and on the bed, the other still on the floor. What truly mattered was that he'd aligned his cock so it rested between her labial lips.

A single long, strong thrust buried him in her.

Filled! Full!

The press of his silken balls against her skin momentarily distracted her from the hunger crawling through her. This was a tough man, a powerful man, but not everywhere. His cock might be the obvious gift, but it wasn't the only one. This sac wasn't simply part of the package; in it waited his immortality, his unborn children.

Blindsided by fresh tears, she dove into herself. Not long after Thorn had entered her world, she'd taken a mental count of the days and came away knowing she wasn't fertile. But if she'd been, would she have stopped him?

Too deep. Thoughts were for later. This moment and the ones to come were all about sensation. Rewarding and being rewarded. Embracing a closeness time and distance could never alter.

He wasn't angry; she sensed nothing of rage about him. Instead, his need ruled him as he threw his strength at her. Sensing his frayed self-control, she wondered if she could reduce him to primal craving as he'd done to her, but for that to happen, she'd have to dismiss her own body. Acknowledging that she was too far gone for anything except this moment, this journey, she realized she was sliding along the sheet. When he tightened his grip on her ankle restraints, her legs started to come down, threatening to separate them.

"Wait!" she cried.

The instant he stopped, his muscles tight and jumping, she grabbed the sheet and used it to anchor herself. Supremely proud of her contribution, she smiled up at him. Maybe her legs made it impossible for him to see her expression, but maybe he could sense her mood as he resumed. In her mind, he powered toward her over and over again. His thighs became like hardwood. Sweat built upon the sweat already coating his chest; his mouth was open, and intensity contorted his features.

As hers must be.

Yes, slipping out of the self she'd long taken for granted to where hot sensation became everything. Yes, floating in heat. Yes, becoming both more and less than she'd ever been, loose and lost and—

Lost? Was that what it had come to, her will was gone, mind splintered, body ripped?

Assaulted by sudden and irrational anger, she whipped her head from side to side. He'd kept her on the edge for so long that falling into the deep hole of no return was only heartbeats away when she gathered the strength to fight what she desperately needed.

Not yet, not yet.

Sucking in air through both mouth and nose helped keep release at bay but only barely. Her inner muscles closed down around his gift, forcing him to work even harder. The nuance of each push and pull further tested her self-control. In yet another effort to delay the inevitable, she started rocking, but that only increased her awareness of the hot hard length grinding against her inner walls.

"Come, come, come!" she sobbed.

"I am. Shit, ah, ah!"

There was *her* Viking. Beneath knowledge and mastery lived

a savage and primitive creature who now ground out sounds without meaning. She loved the rough rage of noise coming up from his core, worshipped the wet flesh slide being played out in her pussy. Lifting her head allowed her to see his strained expression, but an instant later she fell back because every bit of strength she possessed was centered in one place.

Falling, the monster force pulling her out and up.

Had the same force gripped him? Would they climax together?

Too late! No thinking, no stopping.

"Oh, oh, oh my God!" she sobbed.

He bellowed, pushed, hammered, held strong and relentless against her. Then he flooded her.

And she took his gift, clung to it and him as her own climax exploded over and over again.

6

Steam fogged Evi's bathroom, saving her from having to look at herself as she stepped out of the shower, but because she'd already seen her naked body, she didn't need another reminder. Besides, her sensitive skin had demanded she apply soap as gently as possible. After blotting herself as dry as she gave a damn about, she wrapped the towel around her wet hair and rested her buttocks against the sink.

Spreading her legs, she made a careful assessment of what she could see of her pussy. Oh, no doubt about it, she'd been well and completely used, her labia and inner tissues demanding recuperative time. She was still warm down there and had no doubt that her inner sex was red and swollen. One saving grace: she was hardly in the mood for a repeat performance.

Neither did she want to be alone, but here she was, back in her apartment with only the vaguest recollection of how that had happened. Thorn was gone and that was all that really mattered. He'd been there to untie her and she'd fallen asleep nestled against his warmth, but not even his imprint had been on the sheet when she'd awakened. Not that she'd needed a dent in the mattress since his cum had still been both in her and drying on her thighs. Washing off the most vivid reminder of what had taken place between them had been hard, but she'd done the right thing. He was part of something unreal that was triggering her mind's dark potential when she needed back her world. Her sanity.

Bottom line, no way could or would or should she even try to plan her life around more of what she'd just experienced. Whether he was a figment of her imagination or a flesh and blood man, she'd be a fool if she told herself he'd be around for the long run.

Which was just as well since neither her body or mind and certainly not her heart could survive.

Sighing for what might have been the hundredth time, she put her mind on the complex task of applying lotion and putting on her underwear. She was settling her breasts in her bra cups when she noticed how abraded her wrists looked. Fortunately she didn't have to see anyone until morning and maybe makeup or long sleeves would hide the proof of what had happened.

But what had happened?

Thorn had given her entrance to a place where strong men proved their power over willing women and it had been incredible, nerve shaking but incredible. The real thing, she'd learned, had blown gaping holes through what her imagination had been able to provide. Then when he was done with her, he'd slipped out of her life as mysteriously as he'd entered it and deposited her back in what remained of Dungeon Dames. Not only that, he'd somehow supplied her with the materials inventory that had begun the whole adventure.

Adventure? No, that didn't come close.

Selecting a cream designed for scratches and scrapes, she applied some to both wrists and then to her ankles. She contemplated doing the same to her nipples but wasn't sure that was the right thing to do. Still, her breasts were much too sensitive for wearing a bra.

So take off the damn thing.

Wearing only underpants, she walked out of the bathroom, but by the time she'd reached her bed, where she'd left the rest of what she'd chosen to wear this evening, she'd determined that her labia was just as sensitive if not more so than her breasts. Tugging off the offending panties, she sat on the edge of the bed.

How long ago had she been on a bed, Thorn's bed? Other questions crowded into her mind, causing her to shake her head. Denying anything would be a lie and looking for answers would only make her risk what passed for her sanity. Fortified with that scant piece of information, she leaned over and spread her legs so she could study what he'd claimed in detail. There was where his balls had slapped and pressed and kissed. There, exposed by her less-than-steady fingers, was her opening, which yes, was indeed swollen and hot looking. Craving a return to the incredible moments when they'd been one, she slid her finger into her, but it wasn't the same thing. Another time masturbation might create its necessary magic; tonight only he would do. Maybe no sex until she'd healed but what about cuddling and getting to know each other, having him answer questions about his origins and a million other things, asking him why their connection had revolved around the BDSM lifestyle.

Like you don't know, damn it! Stop pretending you haven't long wanted to explore that road and might have actually done so if you'd had the courage.

What about tomorrow?

Falling back, she stared at the ceiling. Any other time and place and man and she'd be able to pick up a phone and make the vital connection, but Thorn existed in his own world or something. He'd come when he wanted—if he wanted.

And if he was done with her?

What did she mean, *if*? This was hardly a relationship designed for the long run. No way was she going to step into her golden years with Thorn at her side. He belonged to her imagination, her fantasies, end of discussion.

Determined not to cry, she stood on unsteady feet so she could traverse the vast distance to her dresser, where she pulled out a nightgown and pulled it over her head. As dressed as she could stand to be for the night, she stepped out of her bedroom. Although she needed to get something to drink followed by a search for anything digestible to eat, she wound up in front of her computer. After logging on to the Internet, she clicked on a heading in her Favorites and logged into a familiar site.

Yes, it was all there, pictures and videos of bondage-loving women and even a few men. Not sure what, if anything, she was looking for, she started scrolling. One update after another slid over her screen until she'd immersed herself in what had helped spawn her mind's secret cave. As graphic as they were, the images, like the places her imagination took her, were safe. Secret and safe.

Arms lashed behind her, her elbows forced close together while more rope tethered her wrists. Yet another rope led up from her wrists to an overhead pulley which effectively kept her arms high and her body arched forward. She was on her knees and kept that way via the rope tethering her thighs and ankles together, her knees bent. Even more rope ran both under and over her breasts, and thick strands circled the base of her breasts, forcing them away from her body. Large, silver nipple clamps gripped her nipples, and two weights hung from the chain that connected the clamps.

Hot discomfort ran through her helpless body as she stared at her unnatural-looking breasts. Someone—her master or cap-

tor—had placed padding under her knees, and she'd have to thank him for the small kindness. She wore the briefest of panties but they'd been pulled away from her crotch.

"Spread your legs."

By concentrating on the small, awkward moves, she managed to obey the voice. Then she looked up.

A cock, long and strong and aimed at her mouth.

"Master," she whimpered. "What do you want?"

"For you to satisfy me."

Desperate to obey, she leaned toward the cock, but her master was too far away. "Please let me—"

A disembodied hand gripped her hair and forced her head back. Blinking at tears, she waited, waited as she'd been taught to do.

"You please me, slave. Do you like the way I've rewarded you?" He demonstrated by tugging on the weighted chain.

"Yes!" Afraid her pained whimper might anger him, she took a steadying breath. "I love the feel."

"You'd say that no matter how much they hurt, wouldn't you?" He added another weight.

Breathing through the newest pain took all her concentration, but even as she did, the energy between her legs grew. Pain and pleasure. Subservience and power. "I will say whatever pleases you, master."

"And do what brings me pleasure?"

"Yes." When he released her hair, she again leaned toward the offered cock. This time her hungry lips made brief contact. "Master, let me please you with my mouth. I beg—"

"I know what you're going to say; I know everything about you, don't I, slave?"

"Yes."

"And why is that?"

"Because you demand absolute honesty." She struggled to lift her bound breasts toward him.

"And it brings you pleasure to do whatever I demand, does it not?"

"Yes." Pain had slid to the far reaches of her awareness, leaving her able to think about the gift of her body and what the man who owned it intended to do with it.

"Obeying me absolutely fulfills you."

"Yes, yes."

"Suffering because I desire it turns moments like this into your joy."

His cock was so close now, the heated smell seeping throughout her and igniting her pussy. "I am content when you beat me."

"But not as content as when I fuck you."

That was what it all came down to. When the lessons and forced obedience were over, he always brought her to climax. The explosions had become what she lived for. And were why she strained against the overhead rope until she closed her mouth around his cock.

Grunting, her master pulled off the nipple clamps and massaged away the hot sting. Then, as she drew him deep into her throat, he wiped sweat off her forehead.

The night after the most vivid and unsettling erotic dream of her life, Evi puttered around in her apartment until after midnight, but with her kitchen now disgustingly clean, everything ironed, and her personal files so organized it was scary, she crawled into bed. Focusing at work today had taken great self-control because every time her concentration slipped, she remembered what it had felt like to have her arms anchored behind her and her legs forced into a bent position while a faceless man, or rather his potent cock, approached. Every time that had happened, she'd managed to force the image from her mind but not the question of who the man was or why the experience had felt so real.

"If you're controlling my mind," she muttered to Thorn, "I

want you to knock it off. I'm not your puppet, got it? I'll think what I want, when I want, and the number one rule is that erotica and work don't mix. Rule number two, it's my fantasy, not yours."

Telling herself, perhaps not entirely successfully, that she'd gotten her point across, she finally gave herself up to her weary body's demands. For a few minutes work issues, specifically whether she would go out on a shaky limb and propose a project spawned from what had happened between her and Thorn, kept her mind functioning, but that didn't last long. Her last conscious thought was that she needed to do considerable research before taking the next step.

On her side on the floor, her arms behind her and anchored to the small of her back via rope around her waist. The secure tie kept her elbows bent and her shoulders back. Her ankles had also been roped together, and her knees were deeply bent. When she tried to straighten her legs, she discovered that a rope running from her wrists to her ankles were responsible. She was hogtied.

Lifting her head off the floor, she tried to look around, but the room or wherever she was was unlit. She was naked, but at least it was warm. A now-familiar fear mixed in with anticipation ran through her. Thorn had to be responsible. Who else—

Approaching footsteps stole her thoughts and, shivering uncontrollably, she waited. Sensing that whoever it was had positioned himself behind her, she tried to roll onto her back, only to be stopped by her bonds. A faint sigh served to let her know that the stranger had lowered himself to his knees. As for why she knew it was a man, no way could her body lie about that.

He was going to speak, he had to! His voice would identify him as Thorn and then she'd stop shaking, maybe.

A sudden snap followed by a sharp stinging sensation just below her breasts lifted her head. A moment later something struck her above her breasts. Furious and frightened, she tried to scoot away only to find herself anchored in place via a firm grip on her shoulder.

"I'm going to whip you. As for the reason, it's because I want to and can. Doing so brings me pleasure, and by the time I'm done, you'll feel the same way."

Was that Thorn's voice? Unfortunately, dealing with the stings now raining between her breasts and her thighs distracted her. He'd released her shoulder, and although she didn't want to and knew it wouldn't do any good, she writhed about. No matter how she turned or wiggled, what she'd determined to be a multistrand whip found flesh to attack. She couldn't say it hurt; it was more like never-ending assaults on her nerve endings. What soon had her moaning was knowing she couldn't do anything to stop him. She kept twisting, sweating, burning, experiencing.

When the whipping ended, she managed to turn her upper body so she was looking at the man the darkness hid from her, only maybe he'd disappeared because she no longer sensed his presence. Every inch of skin the whip had touched put her in mind of a fresh sunburn, tender and sensitive. Maybe she should be surprised by the amount of heat between her legs, but hadn't sex been why she'd developed and refined her fantasies?

What was that? By the time she realized the man had undone the rope between her wrists and ankles, he had her fully on her back with her body arched over her trapped arms. She put up no resistance when he pulled her knees apart so her cunt was exposed. Neither did she cry out when he whipped her mons. Instead, starving, she struggled to lift her buttocks off the floor and open herself even more.

Yes, her reward! Fire blooming over and over again along her labia. Flames building and threatening to burst.

And when he ran his fingers into her, she sobbed and came.

* * *

A week later, Evi stood so she could meet the gaze of everyone seated around the meeting table at Intellectual Properties. Her heart was going double time and her palms were sweating, but her condition had nothing to do with being stared at by the company's decision makers. Since coming onboard the better part of a year ago, she'd presented her plans for three video projects and had had two of them approved. The first, which had sprung from her frightening confrontation with an at-large dog and the owner's legal responsibilities, was already being shown on the local educational channel while the second, about the decision making necessary before new city streets could be built, was going through final editing. Via overheard conversations and a couple of out-and-out compliments, she'd gathered that she was now seen as an important member of the team, but what would they think of what she was about to say?

Wondering against everything that was sane if Thorn might be listening, she took a deep breath. Getting a decent night's sleep would have helped, but she hadn't had anything approaching one since he'd turned her into his personal bondage slut. Hell, just doing the necessary research for today's presentation had sent her running for her sex toys more times than she dared admit.

And that wasn't all. How many times had she spun fictional scenarios starring her and Thorn and featuring caves, dungeons, collars, ropes, nipple clamps, gags, blindfolds, and her mouth or cunt filled with his cock?

"Before I get into things," she began, her voice sounding labored, "I want to make it clear that it's all of your faults that I came up with this concept." Her attempt at humor apparently hit the right note as witnessed by the curious looks she was getting. "Remember when I was asked to inventory the contents of Dungeon Dames?"

"Yeah." Stan Harper who fancied himself a rebel against the

establishment of the day said, "What I couldn't figure out was why you got that assignment instead of me."

Deliberately not allowing herself to get sucked into that argument, she indicated her copy of the handout she'd passed around. "You'll see that I began with some statistics and trust they give you a hint of where I'm going to be going with this."

"Hard not to get it." This too came from Stan. "Psychologists are pretty much full of shit, but are they right, only five percent of people don't have sexual fantasies?"

"That's the conclusion several psychologists drew following extensive studies. As a result, most professionals now believe it's pathological not to have such fantasies. Contrast that with what Freud said in 1908."

Stan cleared his throat and read from his handout. "'A happy person never fantasizes, only a dissatisfied one.' I don't know about anyone else in here, but all I have to do is look at a number of movie stars to start thinking about them and me—"

"No one's interested in that," fifty-six-year-old Roberta Waylan interjected.

Evi shot Roberta a grateful look. "If anyone's interested, I have information about the methodology the researchers used to gather their material, but I'd prefer to have you ponder this." She took a moment to calm herself, and if she wasn't entirely successful, at least knowing what she was about to say distracted her a little from what was going on in her pussy. Damn it, did she think about anything except sex these days, specifically forced sex?

"According to another study conducted at a major university, some 51 percent of women's fantasies revolve around being forced to have sex and another third get off on pretending to be a slave who must obey a man's every wish." She'd planned a deliberate pause here; what she couldn't control were her flushed cheeks. Was this really her saying the things she was?

"That's unbelievable," Roberta said into the silence. "You can't mean women truly want to be raped."

"No, absolutely not. Remember, this is fantasy. When interviewing the female respondents who admitted that dreaming about ropes and chains turned them on, most made it clear that they have no wish for any of those things to happen in the real world and none wanted to be raped. In today's world, women have to carry their own weight and fight their own battles, but they can and do turn that on end in their fantasies. Not only are they able to explore the thrill of being the object of a powerful and undoubtedly handsome man's obsession, they're also saying they're granting said man, who exists only in their minds, full and uncensored control over their bodies. In exchange for that surrender, they get the sexual experience to top all sexual experiences."

"This is the project you want done here?" Roberta's husband, Andrew, who was one of the company's founders, looked as if he wanted nothing more than to find the exit. "We don't do porn at Intellectual."

"It isn't porn." Having anticipated Andrew's reaction, she was ready with her argument. "I'm proposing that we be the first to acknowledge what over 50 percent of women are already imagining and hopefully help them realize there's nothing dirty or sick about what they get off on. *Lifting the Veil on Sexual Fantasy* will be honest and direct. It'll go a long way toward explaining why such sites as Dungeon Dames flourish, at least the ones that are well managed. If the world can openly discuss such crimes as priests forcing themselves on children, why not this?"

7

Having expected her proposal to be brought up at a later meeting once everyone had had the opportunity to study her supporting material, Evi had left the meeting feeling she'd accomplished everything she'd hoped to. She wished she could sense that her idea had been received in a positive light, but at least she hadn't been laughed out of the room. The Waylans were a conservative couple and, although there were others with voting rights and responsibilities, the Waylans' standards heavily influenced the others in large part because their money had helped found the company.

Would she have to take her concept somewhere else? Maybe, but at the moment she couldn't think where that might be and she'd risk being fired by jumping ship. Why couldn't she just let it go and let the chips fall as they may?

Two reasons: one, she deeply believed female submissive sexual fantasies needed to be lifted out of dark rooms so women like herself could stop questioning their sanity and morals. Two, without Thorn shaking up her body and world, she had to get her itches scratched any way she could.

She was still deep in mental ramblings by the time she reached her desk. Determined to accomplish what else needed to be accomplished today, she picked up her messages to determine if she needed to make some calls. Why was she looking for his name in the stack and why in the double hell couldn't she get her mind away from between her legs? One *simple* session with the most mind-blowing man she'd ever met shouldn't have this much of an impact on her. Maybe she should cave and agree to go out with Stan.

Not in this lifetime!

"Evi?"

Startled, she swiveled to find Roberta Waylan standing behind her. "Sorry. I didn't hear you coming."

"Maybe you were distracted."

Don't tell me you can read my mind. "Just trying to organize my thinking."

"Do you have a minute?"

Roberta was the consummate professional. Collected and intelligent, she guided by example. Evi envied many of Roberta's qualities, maybe none more than her ability to look at every situation objectively. Yes, she had her strongly held opinions but never tried to push them down anyone's throat. She paid close attention to Intellectual Properties' bottom line and had become an expert at garnering grants for various projects. What intrigued Evi most was the sense that there were more layers to Roberta than came across during the business day. She dressed conservatively and conducted herself as a refined woman, yet loved off-color jokes. Victoria's Secret catalogs came to her at work.

"Of course," Evi belatedly said. "There's no place for you to sit in here. Do you want to go into the break room?"

"Why don't we go for a walk?"

Wondering if she'd crossed a line and was about to receive a dressing down or worse, Evi nodded and stood up. Saying nothing, Roberta led the way outside. Evi wasn't surprised when Roberta headed for the street corner because there was a small park less than a block from the building in that direction. Their heels made firm clicking sounds as Roberta stepped onto the cement path that zigzagged through the park.

"It's going to happen," Roberta said without preliminary as they walked side by side. "You'll get your video produced."

"The decision's already been made? How—"

"No, there's been no vote yet, but I'm going to make sure it happens."

Not sure what if anything she should say in response, Evi contented herself with matching Roberta's pace. Moving her muscles in the out-of-doors was helping to pull tension out of her. Maybe that's what she should do tonight. Instead of changing the batteries in her vibrator, she'd go for a long run.

Roberta changed directions, heading for a small picnic table under a large tree. When she sat on a bench, Evi chose the bench on the opposite side of the table.

"I'm afraid I gave you the wrong impression earlier," Roberta said. "I'm sure you thought I was shocked by your proposal and might be wondering if I think less of you because of where your mind went."

That had occurred to her. "The project is a total departure from what we've done so far. I can understand—"

"No, you can't." Smiling her perfect tooth smile, Roberta cupped her hands under her chin. "Evi, I'm one of that fifty-one percent."

"Fifty-one percent?"

"Of women who fantasize about turning control of their bodies over to a man."

Although she couldn't say what she did next, Evi wouldn't have been surprised if her mouth had gaped open.

"Two of my friends know that. Thanks to one of them I know where to go for the kind of reading material I crave. But you're only the third person I've ever told about what goes on in my mind."

"I, ah, I would have never guessed."

"I'm not surprised." Roberta smiled. "We all play roles after all; the one you see is the buttoned-down one. You, on the other hand, I've wondered about."

Surprised that Roberta had ever given a thought about the hidden corners of her mind, she could only nod.

"Oh, don't worry. It's not like I've been following you around checking on what you do after hours. You conduct yourself like a professional on the job, just like I do. But there's something about you that tells me you aren't quite sure what to do with the messages that healthy young body of yours is giving you. You haven't jumped on the marriage bandwagon, and I compliment you on that. Also, I'm told you don't do much dating. It's because you're searching, isn't it?"

No more. I've found what I need. I just don't know how to find him again. "Until recently I didn't know what I was looking for."

"Interesting. I think I've known since I was a teenager. It just took a long time to admit it to myself. Once I did, I became much more comfortable in my own skin."

That was how Evi had felt since being with Thorn, as if certain pieces of her were coming together. "You weren't embarrassed?"

"Of course. And to be honest, that was and still is part of the appeal." Roberta winked. "Kind of like slipping out after curfew and getting away with it. My husband isn't aware of this side of me; I trust you won't say anything."

"Of course not."

Nodding, Roberta stared at her perfect nails. "Evi, what you presented is a dry and technical approach where there could be passion."

Fighting to keep her mouth closed, Evi waited.

"I understand why you took the approach you did. You didn't want to shock anyone or harm the company's reputation, right?"

"That's the last thing I'd want."

"Which is politically and maybe ethically correct, but you're going to miss the audience you most need to reach that way."

Evi was still trying to decide what to say when Roberta started laying out what she had in mind. Instead of relying almost solely on study results and statistics, she wanted to begin with an example of a bondage fantasy, tastefully done, of course, which could be accomplished via shadows and carefully controlled camera angles. She foresaw no problem hiring people who were either into the scene or portrayed that lifestyle on camera, possibly even former Dungeon Dames employees. Relying on narrative from the woman's point of view would lift any veil of secrecy about what the female submissive was thinking and experiencing.

"Direct," Roberta finished. "That's what keeps running through my mind. Keep things direct and factual and real." She winked conspiratorially. "Damn but I'd love to have one of my favorite kinks front and center."

Damn? Had she ever heard that word from the older woman? "What do you mean?" was the best she could come up with.

Roberta leaned forward, and her eyes clouded over as if she was going deep into herself. "I'm on a pirate ship, not one of those leaky, stinky things that kept real pirates from drowning, at least most of the time, but one with hot running water and expensive, clean sheets. I'm a native woman who was living on a lush island when I was kidnapped. The lead or head pirate took one look at my naked and tethered and of course ripe body and knew he had to have me for himself."

Roberta paused, but instead of simply waiting for her to continue, Evi mentally created the pirate ship and peopled it with strong, virile sea outlaws, although to be honest, she didn't bother providing details beyond the captain or whoever now stood over her own tightly restrained body. He was blond, tall, strong, knowing.

"There are ropes running both over and under my breasts, which of course haven't been touched by gravity," Roberta said, winking. "I'm wearing a red ball gag and have on a crotch rope. My pirate grabs the rope, then starts pulling, which presses the strands against my labia."

Lulled by the vivid image, Evi didn't bother trying to meet Roberta's gaze. Hell, for all she knew, Roberta's eyes were closed.

"I moan and struggle. That makes him angry and excited so he slaps my breasts to get me quiet. But I can't because of the pressure on my slit. He hauls me to my feet and leans me against a pole."

"He has to tie you to the pole because your feet are bound together," Evi added, her voice breathless and her panties soaking.

"Yes! When he has me where he wants me, he shows me these exquisite gold nipple clamps and orders me to watch while he puts them on me."

"And—and he tells you that they'll stay on until he decides differently. He says, he says you're beautiful in bondage."

"Yes!" Roberta too was breathless. "Then he grabs my chin and lifts my head and tells me that he's taking me to his island, where I'll learn to suck his cock and kneel at his feet."

"You'll wear his brand."

"His brand? Oh, yes. Yes. On the fleshy part of my right breast."

"Skull and crossbones."

"Holy shit." Roberta sighed. "We work well together, maybe too well."

"We think the same way." Trying for a casualness she didn't feel, Evi fanned herself with her hand.

"And we're hardly the only ones. That's what this project

will make clear. It'll let women know that no matter how vivid or graphic their sexual dreams are, it's all right."

Maybe the sun had gone behind a cloud, although maybe she'd only imagined it. Whatever the reason, Evi no longer saw the park. Instead she was back in an unlit room and helpless on the floor while a man, Thorn, fingered her to climax. "Roberta?" She swallowed. "Do you ever feel as if you've lost control, that your fantasies have taken on a life of their own?"

"That's what's happening to you?"

"Sometimes." That was the best she could give the other woman. "Sometimes."

Oh shit, she really was insane!

Although she and Roberta had spun out their sex-flavored tale before noon and it was now night, Evi's body continued to hum. When they'd run out of words, they'd walked back to Intellectual Properties without speaking or looking at each other. As for whether they would push for the pirate role playing, well, she supposed they'd talk about that once they'd had time to consider all the aspects, and calm down.

So when was the calm down going to come?

When she'd gotten Thorn out of her system?

At the moment she was standing in her shower with her wet hair obscuring her vision. She hadn't intended to shampoo tonight, but after mentally spending that much time on a pirate ship, running hot water had seemed more a necessity than a luxury. Besides, this way she had ready access to her naked body.

Sighing, she leaned against the side of the shower and widened her stance so the sharp spray reached her mons. Stinging water wasn't the same as Thorn's hands but brought back memories she'd almost managed to bury this afternoon. Now there was no longer any need to keep a lid on her libido, and with no one looking or caring, she could do what she wanted to herself.

After adjusting the showerhead a few inches lower, she arched so the heat now pelted the front of her labia. No matter how much she wanted to remain still so she could fully experience, energy turned her from side to side. Mouth open and panting, she spread her cunt lips and leaned her head against the wall.

She was no longer in a shower. Instead, she was outside—at an isolated ranch—yes, a ranch. Thorn had secured her to a horse hitching pole in such a way that the horizontal pole pressed against her shoulder blades. Her arms were outstretched and tied to the pole at the wrists, forearms, and upper arms. Rope had been knotted into her long hair and secured to a tree behind her, forcing her head back. As for her legs, oh yes, her legs—Thorn had positioned them so far apart that her pussy was easily accessible, and with her ankles tied to metal rings in the ground, she couldn't move.

Thorn stood in front of her. Although she couldn't see him with her head so far back, she felt his gaze as it raked over her vulnerable flesh. He focused on the long, taut line of her neck, traveled down to her breasts so he could study the way they looked flattened against her ribs. Next came her concave belly—one good thing about the position. He didn't linger there because he had plans for her pussy, plans that revolved around the nozzle gripped in his right hand and attached to a water hose.

Waiting, helpless and eager, she listened to the sound of her heart slamming against her ears while hot anticipation oozed down her inner thighs. No matter how she tried, she couldn't relax her stomach muscles, and she couldn't stop thinking about the way her puckered nipples surely stood up from her pale, full breasts. He had to approve of what he was seeing; he had to.

"The water's cold," he announced. Almost before he'd stopped speaking, a harsh blast slapped her labia and clit.

Gasping, she fought her restraints, but no matter how much she strained and pulled, the ropes held fast, and the message received clear and clean. She belonged to him, every bit of her mind and body.

On and on the icy spray attacked her sex. Unable to do

more than rock a few inches in one direction or the other, she had no choice but to take her punishment, to shiver and whimper and beg. But even as her thighs threatened to cramp and the strain to her neck brought tears to her eyes, this was her gift to him, her master. He wanted her to dance and cry for him and to have her sex fully exposed. He wasn't washing her because she wasn't dirty. Neither was his intention to punish because despite her noisy cries, she wasn't in pain.

Dancing on the edge of release, that's what it was, everything in her system zeroed in on a single part of her body. Her clit, her living, breathing, feeling clit existed for this, for him. She might be the one sobbing and shaking, but her clit was hard and overloaded because he wanted that for her.

Slow awareness of her surroundings, along with the strain in her shoulders, pulled Evi back into the world defined by a real shower in a real bathroom. Wishing it was otherwise, she said a reluctant but necessary good-bye to what had existed only in her mind.

With her fingers still cradling her barely touchable clit, she turned off the water. So weak she could hardly summon the strength to step out of the shower, she gave a towel only a fleeting thought.

Dripping, she pushed her hair out of her eyes. Her thoughts, if they could be called anything that organized, revolved around how much easier facing the rest of the evening would be if Thorn was there to direct it—and her. However, the only times he'd shown up since their one session together had taken place in her imagination. A long distance relationship, even one this intense, couldn't continue. Somehow, damn it, she'd find the remote and turn off the TV of her mind.

"You're getting your carpet wet."

Before alarm had time to pull her into a fight-or-flight response, recognition seeped through her. Feeling intensely alive, she swiped the water from her lids.

Yes! There he was, this man who'd stormed into her life and then slipped out of it, who'd shaken her to her core before deciding he didn't want anything more to do with her—until tonight. Only, instead of being naked, he wore a conservative shirt and slacks, and his black business shoes had recently been polished. Awareness of her nudity begged the question of whether he'd dressed this way in deliberate contrast to her condition. "Where have you been?" Her tone was more whimper than question.

"Watching you."

Was that possible? Hell, hadn't she already learned that nothing was out of the realm of possibility when it came to him? "I didn't know. I had no idea—"

"Because that's the way I wanted it. How do you feel about seeing me? Are you going to welcome me, or maybe tell me to get the hell out of your life?"

How seductive and dangerous his challenge was! Arms at her sides, she searched her heart and mind for the answer. During her time away from him, she'd regained a measure of her independence and freedom. True, things were different during her *dreams,* but the submissive creature who'd embraced everything he'd done to her had faded to be replaced by an employed and bill-paying woman. That was the familiar Evi and the only one she'd believed existed under her skin until Thorn had walked into her world.

But did she want to hold on to that creature?

What did she mean, did she want?

"I'm waiting."

"I'm certain you are," she shot back. "Been enjoying yourself, have you? What does it take to program my mind with those bondage images? Maybe there's some kind of BDSM chip you planted in my brain."

"You believe I'm responsible for your dreams?"

Hadn't he just answered his question by bringing them up?

Either that or this impossible man could tap into her subconscious. "I never used to have anything like that."

"Didn't you?"

She almost laughed at herself because she, naked and dripping, was going toe-to-toe with a man who looked as if he'd just gotten home from the office. "I don't need to answer that," she countered. "I might, eventually, but only once you tell me where you've been and why you're dressed the way you are."

"Are you saying you'd rather have me the way I was before?"

"I don't know," she admitted. "The whole Viking thing was pretty intense, magnificent but intense."

"Which is why I'm offering you this contrast. First time I was responding to what you wanted, now you're getting something more familiar."

On the verge of thanking him, she repeated her question about where he'd been. She was starting to chill but other than hugging herself, she couldn't think how she might change the condition. Strange how being barefoot made her feel small, small and yet sensual. But maybe it wasn't her since just being in his presence had kicked up her awareness of her body's potential.

"I told you," he said. "I've been watching you. Learning about you."

"Were you at work when I made my presentation?" What kind of insane question was that?

"Yes."

Struck by a sudden realization, she stalked closer. "Answer me one thing, just one thing! And if I believe you're telling me the truth, I'll let you do anything you want to me, even burn a brand into my breast." Her breath caught, but she shook free of the image.

"Ask."

Maybe he already knew what she was going to say. If that was true, then he'd had time to tailor his response so it became what he believed she needed to hear. "Everything that's happened between us, the whole dungeon thing followed by my vivid whatever-they-are followed by my decision to try to get approval for my project, was it all part of your plan?"

Not sure she'd said what she'd intended to, she stalled by squeezing water out of her hair. To her relief, he took off his shirt and draped it over her shoulders. A little warmer now, she pulled her thoughts back together. "Here's what's occurred to me. You, either alone or part of some worldwide BDSM organization, decided it was time to present your lifestyle to the *normal* world. And who better than a naive, horny woman to launch your damnable educational program? You started by messing with my mind and body, kept working on my imagination and libido, then decided to show up again to hammer home another lesson. But as soon as your work with me is done, you're out the door."

Exhausted, she pulled the shirt over her breasts.

Instead of answering, he walked past her into the bathroom, then emerged carrying a towel. Turning her from him, he began towel-drying her hair. Much as she tried to hold on to her angry suspicion—or was it insanity?—she couldn't help relaxing. Her arms dropped to her side, and she closed her eyes. How long had it been since she'd seen him, felt his warmth, heard his voice?

When he was done with her hair, he took back his shirt and slowly, carefully, maybe even lovingly dried her off. Damn but she did enjoy being treated like something precious! Eyes still nearly closed, she tracked his progress. Maybe he was looking at her breasts and the V between her legs, a possibility that effectively pulled her out of her lethargy. Sighing, she opened her stance so he could dry her pale pubic hair, then opened herself even more while he tended to her inner thighs. Small shivers tracked her spine when he massaged the small of her back. Finally he wrapped his arms around her and drew her close. With his heat bleeding into her, she stopped shivering.

"Do you still want an answer?" he asked.

A question, yes, she'd asked him something. Not wanting to, she nodded.

"I'm not part of some well-organized BDSM recruiting organization; in fact, I doubt one exists. For the most part, it's just individuals with common interests and needs seeking each other out. I lend my energy, for lack of a better word, to some of the bondage sites you frequent, which is how I became aware of you."

"Why didn't you get in touch with me before you did?"

"Because I wanted to study you, to learn if your curiosity about bondage went deeper than voyeurism. Although you were hesitant to admit it, I discovered it did. You simply needed the right introduction."

"That introduction consisted of you stripping off my clothes and tying me up. Not particularly subtle."

"There wasn't any need."

How right he was. If she wasn't a closet submissive wannabe, she would have run screaming from Bondage Babes the moment a naked man walked on to the set. "I was really that transparent?"

"Only because I have the same itches."

"Thorn, I'm not the first, am I?"

"No." He met her gaze. "But you're the only one now."

"You mean that?"

"I'll never lie to you, Evi. I promise you that."

"I want to believe you."

"Then do. I don't control. I simply facilitate what already exists."

"Already exists?" she asked, not yet fully ready to take that huge step.

"Men like me don't change any woman's nature. We're simply there to help let it happen."

Guiding, not controlling, freeing, not forcing. Weakness nearly knocked her feet out from under her. Fighting tears, she took in his strong features. This was no figment of her imagination, no actor from central sex casting. He was real, maybe not real in any way she'd experienced before, but a vital part of her world.

"How long are you going to be here?" she whispered around the lump in her throat.

"How long do you want me?"

Why was she so lightheaded? "Maybe—maybe forever."

"Then you have your answer."

Letting instinct rule her, she wrapped her arms around his neck, stood on her toes, and kissed him. As the soft and sensual contact spun out, she acknowledged that although he'd already claimed every part of her, this was the first time they'd kissed.

Needing to be the architect of their relationship, she parted her lips and pressed her tongue against his. The moment she did, he opened his mouth and welcomed her in.

Short minutes later, they were on her bed with Thorn's discarded clothes littering the carpet. Instead of casting them in darkness, he'd turned on a lamp so gentle light played over his prone body. At the moment, he was stretched out on his stomach while she knelt beside him so she could massage his back. He hadn't said anything about wanting her to assume a submissive position. Instead, she'd sensed he was letting her control and guide what was happening, at least for now.

Fine, good, she knew what she wanted and prayed her desires would trigger the same response in him. Her fingers burned with anticipation and awe as she worked his powerful muscles from shoulder to thighs. Even now he was her master in ways that went far beyond having his ropes on her. And obeying his every command said only a little about her commitment to him.

"Where do you live?" she asked with her hands resting on his buttocks.

"I'll show you. Evi, I don't exist in a vacuum. Much of my time is spent in the company of others like myself."

Good. She didn't want him to be a loner. "And their slaves? Are they there, too?"

"Yes," he muttered. "But until your training is complete, it's going to be just the two of us. I want you to fully understand what you're getting into."

"Thank you."

'Thank you what?"

"Master." The word was accompanied by a contented smile. Then she bent over and kissed the base of his spine. "I love taking care of you. Whatever you want, please let me know."

"Oh, I will," he said and rolled over. Grabbing her wrists, he pulled her down so her upper body rested on his chest. "By the time we've completed our journey, you'll know what I want without my having to say a word." Taking hold of her hair, he lifted her head so their eyes met. "In very separate ways, we'll cater to each other. I need to be in control while you need to be controlled. It's a dance."

A lifelong dance? Reminding herself not to take anything beyond this moment, she nodded. "I want to wear your collar."

"You will. Even when you're at work, you'll always have on some reminder of our relationship."

A memory of her fantasy when he'd ruled her responses via a vibrating bullet caused her cheeks to flush, and when he released her hair, she feathered kisses over his forehead, nose, and chin before closing in on his mouth.

"You're trembling," he muttered.

"With excitement."

"No reservations?"

"No," she said without hesitation.

"Demonstrate."

Propelled by the single word, she straddled him with her weight on her knees. She didn't take her eyes off him as she reached for his cock and positioned it between her legs so his tip just touched her entrance. "Take my gift, master. House yourself in this cunt that exists for you and, if it pleases you, gift me with your cum."

His expression shrouded beneath his half-closed lids, he slapped first one breast and then the other. "Do it. Now."

Do it, she silently repeated as she lowered herself onto him and his cock slipped into her. *Exist for his pleasure and through it, find your own.*

Thinking of his pleasure and his alone, she didn't wait for him to start thrusting but called on her thigh muscles to do the job for both of them. Even as her legs burned and her back ached, she smiled down at the man who'd come to rule her world and she'd do anything for.

Holding him tight and secure within her melting pussy walls while allowing his cock to repeatedly dive deep and then retreat became her only existence. Heat flooded her muscles, her veins, her bones even. Quick! So quick! Despite her impending climax, she managed to tune in to what his body was telling hers. He too was close, closer, nearly there, tension and promise roping him. Vulnerable but only for these few seconds.

Me too! I'm so exposed!

As it should be.

Yes, Master.

There! Yes, there!

His cries of release filled the room. Then she added her own explosion, gasping like a wild animal, like a woman fulfilled.

And filled.

MIRRORS WITHIN MIRRORS

P.F. KOZAK

1

The taxi stopped in front of what appeared to be an abandoned warehouse, a drab brick shoebox several stories high. Patricia checked the address again. "Excuse me driver, are you sure this is 200 East Third Street?"

"This is it, at the corner of Avenue B, just like you said."

Patricia was already annoyed that she had to travel to the Lower East Side for these appointments; this decrepit building further irritated her. She didn't want to go near the place, let alone have sessions here several evenings a week. As she paid the driver, she wondered what she had been thinking when she agreed to this insanity.

Not feeling safe standing alone on this street, she hurried to the door, only to find it locked. A metal plate with rows of buttons attached seemed to be the only way in. She couldn't read the numbers. The address said 4D, so she counted four rows up and four buttons in. She pressed the buzzer, hoping she guessed correctly.

A male voice answered. "Hello?"

"Marc? It's Patricia."

"Well, this is a step in the right direction. You showed up! Take the elevator. It's down the hall, to the left." The speaker clicked off and the door buzzed.

Taking a deep breath, she went in. Half expecting garbage on the floor and rats scurrying past, she was surprised to see newly painted pale gray walls, with triangular sconce art deco lamps lighting the hallway.

Her heels clicked on the granite floor tiles and echoed in the empty hallway. She found the elevator, pushed the button, and waited. Nothing happened. Then she realized it didn't open automatically. She pulled the heavy door open and pushed the iron gate to the side, reversing the process after she stepped in.

When she got out on the fourth floor, the lingering smell of paint again filled her nostrils. The gated elevator, gray walls, and art deco lamps made her feel like she had teleported back in time to the 1930s. Smiling, she realized this place wasn't the dump she first thought it to be.

After knocking on the door of 4D, she remembered she had promised to turn off her BlackBerry. She had just pulled it out of her bag when the door opened.

"Hello, Patricia." Marc crossed his arms over his chest. "I'll wait until you check your e-mail one last time before inviting you in."

"I'm turning it off, like I said I would."

"Good. I would rather you turn it off yourself than my having to confiscate it."

Patricia forced herself to turn off the unit without checking her incoming messages, and then put it back in her bag. "There, it's off. May I come in now?"

"Certainly." He escorted her into the newly renovated loft. "Have a seat. Let's talk first and make sure we're on the same page about this."

She sat on the leather sofa. "Isn't the Lower East Side slumming for you? Why aren't we meeting in your Park Avenue office?"

"This is the East Village, and this loft is a good investment in a gentrifying neighborhood. It's also a good space for our sessions. There are no distractions here, for either of us. That is, if you keep that damned BlackBerry turned off."

Patricia glanced at her purse, remembering her unread messages. "That damned BlackBerry, as you call it, keeps me in touch with my office." She picked up her bag and stood, meaning to leave. "I'm sorry. I don't think I'm ready for this."

"I think you are, and so does Dr. Richards."

"Lately, Dr. Dick hasn't known his ass from his elbow when it comes to what's going on with me. I told him to stick his Freudian analysis up his bony ass!"

"He noted that conversation in your records."

"You have my records?"

"Of course I do. You're the one that requested an alternative to traditional therapy, and you agreed you were comfortable having me handle it. Perhaps you should have read the fine print on the release form before you signed it."

"My dear Dr. Forrest, I signed a consent form allowing Dr. Richards to consult with you, if necessary. I didn't realize he would open the confessional door."

"I've known Philip Richards for many years. He trusts me. If we are to make any progress with this, you have to let go and trust me, too. Isn't that why you're here?"

"And if I decide I can't do this?"

"There's the door. I'm sure you can find your way out."

Patricia squeezed her purse, the BlackBerry hard in her hand. The compulsion to check her messages nearly overwhelmed her. She dropped her purse onto the sofa and sat back down. "You know, the urge to always be on top of things is like craving heroin."

"And it can be just as destructive, if you allow it to control your life."

"Dr. Dick says that's what I'm doing."

"His name is Dr. Richards, and that's why he recommended this form of alternative therapy. He knows you have to regain the balance in your life. Based on what you've told him about your dreams and fantasies, Phil thinks experiential role playing might give you the breakthrough you need."

"Oh, then you prefer I call him Dr. Phil?" Patricia laid her head on the back of the sofa and closed her eyes. "Well, then, how many of my dreams and fantasies did Dr. Phil put in my file?"

"There are notes on every session. Whatever you've told him is in there."

"Jesus Christ, then you know it all?"

"I know what your subconscious is telling you."

Patricia sat up and slid forward, her legs sticking to the leather. "Why the hell did you get a leather sofa?"

"I like leather, so I bought leather furniture. There's more coming later this week. I thought leather furniture would work well in this space, especially considering the role playing we will be doing."

"This role-playing thing. I don't understand how it will work."

"I talked this over with Phil. We both think that your dreams are the best place to start. We'll take a scenario from one of your dreams and act it out together. From there, we'll see where it goes."

"If you've read his notes, then you know they've been over the top lately."

"I know they're edgier than I expected. Why didn't you tell me something had changed?"

"Yeah, right!" Patricia stood and paced around the sofa. "And tell you what? That I'm a pathological submissive and I want to be slapped around?"

"Tricia, that's not what this is about."

"Don't call me Tricia. You know I don't like it. My name is Patricia."

"That's what this is about."

"Excuse me? That one flew over my head."

"I think it's about damn time someone called a spade a spade with you! You're beyond the pale with your obsessive need to be in control. You compulsively dictate what people can or can't do, and your micromanagement of every detail is isolating you. You're like this tyrannical despot no one can get close to. Your subconscious is finally saying enough!" Marc stood and held her stare. "I prefer calling you Tricia, and that is what I will call you!"

"You're an arrogant son of a bitch! You know I have to be on top of my game in order to stay there. If I didn't pay attention to detail and work at being a good manager, I wouldn't be where I am today! I'm still the only female partner at Swenson Securities, and my investment portfolio is the best they've got!"

"You're not dreaming and fantasizing about your investment portfolio, now are you?" Marc walked over and took her hand. "And you're so damn angry and frightened about losing control over yourself you can't see straight."

"You need to read some more of Dr. Dick's notes. And I prefer calling him Dr. Dick. Dr. Phil is so over."

"Come here and sit down. I want to ask you some questions." He led her back to the sofa. Before he sat down, he picked up her purse and tossed it onto the leather chair where he had been sitting. "Best that thing is out of reach."

Patricia crossed her arms and glared at Marc. "What could you possibly want to know beyond what you've read?"

"I want to know the last time you had an orgasm, and how it happened."

"Why?"

"Because it will help me to understand what you need. Since you've been having difficulty feeling sexual, I want to know what excites you."

"All right, you asked for it! I had another dream last night, and I got off in the shower this morning thinking about it."

"Tell me about the dream."

"Now you really sound like Dr. Dick."

"Tricia, the whole point of this is to help you, before your life spirals out of control. If things don't change, and change soon, all you'll have is your precious career and nothing else. Is that what you want?"

"No. That's why I agreed to this bizarre experiment in self-abasement."

"Then tell me about the dream."

"I can't just sit here and tell you. I'm too damn stressed."

"Then get up and walk while you talk. Just tell me."

Patricia hugged herself as she walked, squeezing her upper arms hard enough to bruise them. "This dream starts the way they usually do. I'm in a large house. The house feels familiar, but I'm not sure what I'm doing there. I hear someone calling my name from one of the rooms. When I open the door, an older man is there wearing a robe. He yells at me, telling me I'm late.

"I remember I'm supposed to draw his bath. He follows me into the bathroom and takes off his robe as I run the water in the tub. I know he wants me to wash him, and I'm to wear nothing but my panties while I do. He gets in the tub, and then watches me take off my clothes.

"When I kneel over the tub, I see he has a hard-on, a big one. He feels up my tits while I wash him. When I touch his cock, he gets very angry. He accuses me of being a cockteaser and tells me I have to be punished.

"He gets out of the tub, dripping wet, and takes a razor strap off of a hook by the sink. Then he tells me to take off my panties and bend over. The anticipation of having that strap across my ass makes me crazy. When he swings it, and the leather bites into me, I am close to coming. He continues to strap me, the whole time telling me this is what happens to cockteasers. I want to come, but can't unless he fucks me. He never does."

Even with her hand trembling, Patricia needed to brush the beads of sweat off of her upper lip. "Can you open a window or turn up the air or something?"

Marc went across the room and adjusted the thermostat. "Then you didn't have an orgasm in the dream?"

"No. But damn, it turned me on! When I got in the shower, I finished it, imagining him fucking me from behind. In the dream, his cock was so hard, like concrete." Patricia leaned against the window sill. "I fucked myself with the handle of the bath brush, thinking about being bare-ass strapped and then fucked."

"Did you climax?"

"Hell, yes! That's the only way I've been able to have an orgasm in several months! Why do you think I'm still seeing Dr. Dick?"

"Do you know if you can feel sexual with a partner?"

"What's the female equivalent of not getting it up?"

"Frigid?"

"There you have it. That's what happens when I think about having sex with a partner. Except for my dreams, I would be a total ice queen."

"Phil thinks that if you can find orgasmic release alone, you can also do it with someone. I agree with him. But it has to be the right partner."

"Do you think you're man enough for the job?"

"I'm sure of it. But, as they say, it takes two to tango. I can't do this alone."

"The other day, I overheard a couple Generation X associates joking about how I wouldn't be such a bitch if I got laid. I could have had them fired on the spot. But I didn't. Do you know why?"

"Why?"

"Because I think they're right." Patricia chuckled bitterly. "They call me Ms. Piranha. Instead of sleeping my way to the top, they say I've eaten men alive to get there."

"Tricia, you excel at what you do. The investments you made for me paid off tenfold. Men can be crass when it comes to a woman holding her own in their world."

"Yes, but Marc, what price have I paid to get there? I'm so fucked up! I don't know how to be a woman anymore."

"You've recognized that, and now we're going to do something about it."

"You aren't afraid I will eat you alive?"

"My dear, that should be your concern, not mine."

"Confident, aren't you?"

"Yes."

"Dr. Dick thinks you are a natural alpha male, and that you can handle my proclivities. Is he right?"

"You wouldn't be here if you didn't think so."

"Why do you think I'm here?"

"To find out who you really are. Your career is not you. The real you is sending you messages in dreams and screaming at you to stop pushing what you really want into your shadow."

"Great! I get up from Freud's couch and lie down on Jung's. What is it with you guys? Everything I say or think is psychologically categorized and analytically pigeonholed!"

"Why does that make you angry, Tricia?"

"Because I am so fucking sick of it! I don't want to talk about it or think about it anymore. I just want to turn off my mind and feel!"

"Feel what?"

"Anything! Maybe that's why my dreams are becoming more intense. It's getting harder for me to feel anything. At least with a leather strap across my ass, I feel something!"

"And what if we make that more than a dream? What if we make it real?"

Patricia's stomach tightened. "I don't know if I can do that."

"All you have to do is to trust me and allow yourself to feel. I'll do the thinking."

"Now there's a scary thought!"

Marc chuckled. "What, you don't believe I'm capable of thinking?"

"You're a shrink. Who knows what you're capable of?"

"Shall we get started?"

"Now? Just like that?"

"I don't see why not."

Patricia glanced at her bag on the chair. "You're not going to let me check in while I'm here, are you?"

"Absolutely not! If need be, I will lock your BlackBerry in the closet, if you find it too much of a temptation."

"You don't need to lock it up. Just put it somewhere where I can't see it."

Marc took the purse and put it in the closet. When he opened the door, Patricia glimpsed what seemed to be a skirt, among other garments hanging on the rod. "What do you have in there?"

"Costumes."

"Costumes? Halloween isn't for several months."

"My dear, those aren't for Halloween. They are for our sessions."

"You can't be serious!"

"I am absolutely serious. In the notes Philip took, there are some colorful descriptions of the clothes you've mentioned. I thought it a good idea to invest in a few of the things that recur in your dreams and fantasies."

"That's a bit extreme, isn't it?" The reluctance Patricia felt did not quell her curiosity. She strained to see the closet contents behind Marc.

Marc closed the door. "What's in there will be seen and used when I decide it is appropriate, not before."

"Really!"

"Yes, really. We will start slowly, to make sure you can handle this scene."

"And what do you know about this particular scene?"

"Enough." As Marc stood looking down at her, Patricia noticed his expression changed. The lines in his face became more defined, and his ruggedness evident.

"Do you know you look like Sean Connery when you get serious?"

"You've mentioned that before. I don't see it."

"I do." He didn't look away and neither did she. The challenge in his eyes drew her in. She knew he meant to see this through. She waited for him to make the next move.

"I think we need to establish some ground rules, which in this space will be obeyed."

"All right, what are they?"

"First and foremost, I am in charge. You do not call the shots here. I do."

"And if I don't agree to that?"

"There's the door. Don't forget your BlackBerry on the way out."

Marc moved from in front of the closet door. Patricia could see he meant what he said and would not try to convince her to stay. She also saw an erection growing in his trousers, which he made no attempt to hide. Her clitoris pulsed with anticipation. "I'm not leaving. I accept your condition. What else?"

"You agree to play the role I select. Some will be familiar to you from your dreams, others may not be. There may also be times when we will be ourselves. Whatever it is, you agree to follow my lead and wear what I choose."

"I'm not much of an actress. But if that's what you want, why not?"

"I also reserve the right to discipline you if you overstep your boundaries or break the rules. That includes being a bitch and mouthing off inappropriately."

"I can't wait to hear you ask 'Who's your daddy?' while I'm over your knee."

"That is a distinct possibility, given your mouth."

"Do you know you have a hard-on?"

"Yes. I'm not ready to do anything about it yet."

"And when you are?"

"You'll be the first to know." Marc came closer, standing directly in front of her, his erection only inches from her face. "There are two more things we need to discuss."

"Which are?"

"Protection and a safe word."

"What? Do you mean birth control?"

"Yes, and being tested. I've been recently tested and am clean. Are you?"

"I had my insurance physical last month. My blood work came back normal. I'm also still on the pill, so that's covered." Patricia stood. Marc did not move. She could feel his cock against her leg. "What's a safe word?"

"It's a word you use to stop the action if it is too much. We agree on the word and that you will only use it if there is a serious problem. You will let me know if there is too much pain or discomfort, or if I inadvertently injure you."

"Christ, what are you thinking of doing, resurrecting the Marquis de Sade?"

"Have you dreamed about him yet?"

"No, thank God." Marc shifted slightly and pressed his erection deeper into her thigh. The tingling in Patricia's clitoris intensified. "What is the word?"

"There are three. Red is stop the scene. Yellow is stop doing that, but don't stop the scene. Green is I'm fine. If I ask you what your color is to check on you, you will respond with one of those three choices. Do you understand?"

"I have a master's in business management and finance. I think I can remember red, yellow, and green."

"When a scene is happening, your financial prowess will not help you. Red or yellow will."

"How do you know all of this? You're talking like a regular player at a BDSM club."

"I didn't agree to this until I had done the proper research. Phil suggested I do some exploring several weeks ago."

"This is news. He only mentioned it to me last week."

"He's a smart man." Marc abruptly turned, went back to his chair, and sat down. He calmly asked, "Shall we?"

Slightly disoriented by his unexpected movement, Patricia remained standing. "Shall we what?"

"Get started?"

"You're in charge, so I've been told."

"Then you won't mind taking off everything underneath your skirt."

Patricia thought he might be bullshitting her. But his demeanor said otherwise. He sat in the chair, his erect cock clearly outlined inside his trousers. He watched her closely, studying her reaction to his request. She understood that what she did now would mean her staying or leaving.

"If that's what you want, then that's what I do." She kicked off her shoes. "Where's the bathroom?"

"Do you have to go?"

"No. I want to do what you asked me to do, take off everything under my skirt."

"You'll do it here, in plain sight."

"What do you want, a striptease?"

"For now, just take off your underclothes."

Patricia pulled up her tight skirt. The business suit allowed her no modesty. She had to pull the skirt up around her waist to hook her fingers in the waistband of her panties and panty hose. Balancing herself against the sofa, she lowered them to mid thigh, stopping to pull her skirt back down before taking them off.

Marc reached behind the chair and picked up a bag. "Here. Put these on."

Patricia took the bag. Her curiosity definitely piqued, she opened the package. "These are lace thigh highs."

"That's what they are. When you come here, you are to wear this style of hose only, unless I tell you I would prefer a garter belt. Oh yes, and no panties."

"I suppose you want me to wear these to work?"

"That is optional, but if you would, it would please me."

Patricia sat down on the sofa to put on the stockings, only realizing after the fact how badly her sweaty skin would stick. When she pulled up the stocking, her thigh made an obnoxious sucking sound breaking free of the leather. She tried to hide her embarrassment. "Could you cover this sofa with something, so I don't stick?"

Marc simply said, "No."

She already knew not to argue. So, she stood, smoothed her

skirt down the backs of her legs, and sat back down. "Oh, I'm sorry. Do I have to say, 'Daddy, may I sit down?' "

"Not yet." His smirk made her squirm. "But I think you do have to take off that jacket and open a few more buttons on your blouse."

He had her off balance and obviously knew it. Feeling more flustered than she expected to be, she took off her suit jacket and unbuttoned two more buttons.

"Do another one. I want to see some cleavage."

She opened the next button, and saw Marc staring at her breasts. Patricia realized she was nearly as turned on as she had been that morning waking from her dream. "Should I open my bra?"

"Do you want me to see your breasts?"

Patricia flushed as she answered. "Yes."

"That pleases me, Tricia. Open your bra."

She unclasped her bra and tucked the cups inside her blouse. When she sat back, her breasts were almost completely exposed.

Marc came over to the sofa and sat next to her. "You are doing very well, Tricia. How do you feel?"

"Vulnerable, mostly, and nervous."

"That's good. Your defenses are coming down." Marc leaned over and kissed her neck. Patricia shivered. "What is your color?"

"Green."

"Good. Open your blouse the rest of the way and ask me nicely to squeeze your tits."

Patricia could hear Marc's breath change as she undid her blouse and pulled it wide open. "If it pleases you, I would like you to squeeze my tits."

"Very good! Your invitation is appreciated." He took his time squeezing and caressing each breast, all the while watching her reaction to his touch. When he unexpectedly pinched her nipples, she moaned. He did not lessen the pressure, and in fact, pinched harder. "Do you like that, Tricia?"

She squirmed under his hand. "God, yes! I like it."

"Then perhaps you will like these." Marc reached into his coat pocket and pulled out what looked to be a silver necklace. "These are nipple clamps on a chain. This part goes around your neck." He clasped the silver links around her neck. The clamps dangled down her chest, hanging on two long chains. Without asking her permission, he screwed the clamps onto her nipples, tightening them until she winced.

"Yellow!" She didn't want them any tighter. He immediately stopped.

"You're catching on, my dear. That also pleases me. Now, lean forward." When she did, Marc removed her blouse and her bra. She now wore only the thigh highs and her skirt, and the nipple clamps.

The sensation piercing her chest made her breath catch, but it didn't hurt. "Marc, help me to understand what is happening."

"We are playing, Tricia. Right now, you are on the brink of eroticizing pain. This is what they mean when they say, it hurts so good."

"Christ, it does."

"Are you ready for more?"

"Yes!"

"Then take off your skirt and bend over the back of that chair." Without hesitation, she unzipped her skirt and let it fall to the floor. With only the nipple clamps and thigh highs on, she felt sexier than she ever had before. Marc further instructed her. "Bend over and spread your legs wide apart."

She did as he told her and waited. The excruciating anticipation of what would happen now had her on fire. Marc stood in front of the chair, in full view. He opened his trousers and exposed his cock. She could see him leaking, the pre-cum shining on the head of his penis.

As she watched him, her knees turned to jelly. He pulled his belt out of his pants and doubled it over. "I thought you said we were starting slow."

"Gorgeous, this is slow compared to where we're going."

Patricia dug her fingers into the back of the chair, bracing herself for what she expected him to do. She yelped with surprise when the first stroke of the belt did not connect with her ass, but instead, landed between her legs. As the second stroke hit, again between her legs, she heard Marc say, "This lends new dimension to the term pussy-whipped, wouldn't you say? Having a man do it to you is long overdue!"

Spreading her legs wider, she tried to position herself so the belt would connect directly with her clitoris. Marc noticed. "So, you like how this feels. Turn around, so I can see those pretty tits bounce when you come for me."

She turned around and pressed her ass into the leather, so the chair would support her. Before she could brace herself, Marc again connected with her labia, the sting moving through her clitoris like an electric shock. Her knees started to buckle. "Tricia, stand up and spread your legs wide!" The command in Marc's voice made her jump to attention. "We aren't stopping until you come." He swung the belt again.

Patricia could hardly breathe, the intense sensation overwhelming her. She managed to rasp out, "Faster, I need it to be faster."

Like the piston of a revved-up engine, Marc swung the belt, the strokes coming one on top of the other. With explosive force, Patricia's orgasm hit, her entire body convulsing with the spasms. Marc did not slow down, not one bit. The belt bit into her labia, sending shock waves through her pelvis. For what seemed to be an eternity, her consciousness swam in sensation, until finally, the strokes slowed, and then stopped.

Before she had caught her breath, she felt Marc's hands on her shoulders, pushing her down to a kneeling position. "Now, Patricia, you may thank me with the best blow job you have ever given, and you will swallow every drop."

She willingly did as she was told.

2

Patricia checked her watch. If she left her office in the next five minutes, she would have just enough time to run to the ladies' room and change her hose before hailing a cab downtown. Looking at the stack of files on her desk, she hesitated. Before last night, she would have stayed as long as necessary to finish her work. But Marc made it clear that missing a session without twenty-four hours' notice would terminate the agreement. She knew he meant it.

After organizing the folders so she could go through them quickly in the morning, Patricia went to put on the thigh highs. It would be easier to wear them all day and not have to change, but she couldn't bring herself to do it, at least not yet. Marc had given her a pair of sheer black hose with lace tops to wear. She didn't realize until she took them out of the package that they had seams up the back. With these stockings, no panties, a black suit and black pumps, she felt like Bettie Page.

The elevator bell dinged as she came out of the ladies' room. She ran to catch it and bumped into another senior partner when she jumped inside.

"Oh, Earl, I'm sorry!"

"That's all right, Patricia. You're in a hurry!"

"I have an appointment. I don't want to be late."

"Must be important."

"It is."

"New client?"

"No, this is personal."

"So, that's why you put those black stockings on. I wondered about that."

Surprised he even noticed, Patricia suddenly remembered she didn't have any panties on. Trying to retain her professional composure in spite of feeling flustered, she changed the subject. "When do you need those quarterly reports?"

"By the end of the week." The elevator reached the lobby and the doors opened.

"I'll have them ready." Grateful for the opportunity to escape her partner's scrutiny, she added, "Have a good evening."

He smiled and winked. "You, too." Earl held the elevator door for her, and then followed her into the lobby. As she hurried toward the door, she wondered if he noticed the seams on her stockings.

The cab dropped her at Third Street and Avenue B. She knew the building now and hurried toward the door. Remembering her BlackBerry, she checked her messages and then turned if off before she rang the bell.

"Marc? I'm here."

He didn't say anything, just buzzed her in.

Relieved that she had arrived several minutes before the designated time, she knocked on the door. When he opened the door, she almost laughed. "What the fuck do you have on?"

"Come in, Patricia." He led her into the room. "Welcome to biker night."

She turned around and looked at him again. As if the black

leather pants and boots weren't enough, he had on an open leather vest and nothing else. "Where did you park your Harley?"

With crassness she had never seen in him, he grabbed his crotch. "Right here, baby. And if you're lucky, you may get to ride it later."

What she saw on the sofa squelched her urge to laugh. A pair of low cut leather shorts with lace up sides lay beside a black vinyl silver studded crop top that had barely enough material to cover her breasts.

"I see you wore the stockings. Take off the skirt. I want to make sure there are no panties."

"Have you lost your mind?"

"No, sweetheart. My mind is right where it needs to be. Now, take off the skirt."

Patricia tossed her purse on the chair, not even giving her BlackBerry a second thought. Marc picked it up and stashed it in the closet. When he came back, he dropped a set of leather lace-up cuffs onto the sofa with the other clothes. "I almost forgot these. Accessories are important."

Framed in the leather vest, his chest caught her attention. She followed the hairline from his sternum to his navel, stopping when she saw his erection encased in his leather pants. "Not wasting any time, are you?" She continued to stare at his pants as she unzipped her skirt.

"Not with this boner waiting! C'mon baby, show me some pussy."

Hearing Marc use such language while blatantly leering at her made her uncomfortable, but it also did something else. It made her feel deliciously sleazy. Her skirt fell to the floor and she kicked it to the side. "You see, no panties. I did as you asked."

"Very good! Is your pussy wet yet?" Patricia didn't answer, embarrassed that she did indeed itch as her juice ran. "What's the matter, baby, cat got your tongue?" Marc grabbed a handful of her hair and pulled her head back. He forcefully kissed her, pushing his tongue into her mouth while simultaneously squeezing her pussy. Patricia instinctively tried to break free, but her hair pulled in his fist and she stopped.

He continued to kiss her as he violated her cunt with his fingers, ramming them into her vagina. He pulled them out and rammed her again, fucking her with his hand. Without releasing her hair, he lifted his head, his hot breath blowing in her face as he spoke. "I'll ask you again, is your pussy wet yet?"

"You motherfucker, yes my pussy is wet. It has been all goddamn day!"

"See how easy it is to take on a character. You are now a biker babe." In one continuous motion he released her hair and her pussy, and shoved her backward onto the sofa. The leather surface stung her bare ass. "Now, put on the fucking clothes."

Patricia glared at him as she took off the rest of her suit. "This isn't one of my dreams!"

"No, but it's one of mine. At least it used to be. I resurrected it just for you."

"How magnanimous and thoughtful!" She picked up the shorts, trying to calm herself down enough to figure out how they worked. She glanced up at Marc, who still stood directly in front of her. He stood there, rubbing his cock while watching her. "You fucking pervert, you're masturbating in front of me!"

Marc's laughter rang though the loft. "Christ, that's rich! You're calling me a pervert? I remind you, you are stark naked, except for a pair of black stockings. What man wouldn't jerk off watching you right now?"

Now royally pissed off, Patricia struggled with the laces on the sides of the shorts. They finally loosened enough for her to pull them on. Then she had to redo them. Marc interrupted. "Make sure you tie them in pretty little bows, so when the time comes, I can untie them without having to rip them off of you."

Not caring that she stood there topless, Patricia laced up the shorts, being careful not to knot them. Then she put on the top, which only had one hook to hold it shut. Both the shorts and the top fit her like a second skin, the black vinyl top barely covering her tits. She put on the wrist cuffs, which she noticed had small metal rings attached. "I can't lace these up myself. It is impossible to do it one-handed."

Marc took her arm and managed the laces for her. "What's your color, Tricia?"

She knew he had just given her the opportunity to walk away. But she didn't want to leave. She honestly answered, "Green."

"Good. Then we will continue." He went to the closet and took out a pair of ankle-high black boots with stiletto heels. "See if these fit. They told me these run small, so I got an eight wide."

Patricia sat down and put them on. When she stood, she wobbled a bit, not being used to the ultra-high heels, but the boots didn't pinch. "They seem fine. Now what?"

"Now we go out to a leather bar down the street."

"Now wait a damn minute! I never agreed to go out like this!"

"Are you calling yellow?"

Patricia looked down at her boots. She had seen women wearing these on the street, but never thought she could pull it off. "May I look at myself in a mirror before I decide?"

"There's a mirror on the inside of the bathroom door."

Patricia went into the bathroom and closed the door. When she looked at herself, she nearly fainted. The image staring back couldn't possibly be hers. Marc had tousled her hair when he grabbed her, giving it a just-got-out-of-bed look. The sexy leather costume made her look like she had stepped out of a porn magazine for bikers. She had on just enough clothing to avoid being arrested for indecency.

She noticed the shorts outlined her labia, leaving nothing to the imagination, and that her breasts never looked as full as they did in the tight top. Feeling this sexy had never been her experience. It surprised her to realize she liked it.

When she came back into the room with Marc, she simply said, "Green."

"Tricia, are you sure?"

"I'm sure. If it gets to be too much, I'll call yellow or red. You'll honor that, right?"

"I will. I know your envelope is being pushed with this. I'll tell you this much. I've checked this place out and have an arrangement with the owner. As long as you're with me, you'll be safe."

"So, I won't be gangbanged bent over a pool table?"

"Not unless you want to be." Marc took out his cell phone and dialed. "Hello, Lenny? Yeah, it's Marc. We're on our way."

"You're on a first-name basis with the owner? What the hell? Have you been leading a double life?"

"Not until now." He gave her a once-over. "You're one hot slut tonight. Now, give me some biker babe attitude and strut your stuff."

He took her arm and led her to the door. Patricia watched him closely as they rode down in the elevator. His demeanor had changed. Somehow he seemed more masculine, more rugged. She had to admit, he looked hot as hell in leather. Going to the gym had obviously paid off. For the first time, she noticed that under the body hair, he had definition. Why the hell had she never noticed his abs before? She muttered, "Too damn preoccupied!"

"What did you say?" Marc pushed the elevator gate to the side and waited for her answer.

"Just muttering to myself."

"That's not like you. What did you say?"

"Christ, Marc! All I said was 'Too damn preoccupied.' "

"About what?"

Marc stood in front of the heavy elevator door, obviously not intending to open it until she answered him. Again, his chest and abs caught her eye. Framed in that leather vest, she had a nearly uncontrollable urge to grope his pecs.

"All right, you want to know? I'll tell you. I wondered why I've never noticed how ripped you are. You are fucking hot! All I can figure is that I've been too distracted."

"Well now, this is a quantum leap forward!" He ran his index finger down the crack of her cleavage. "I'm also noticing what a hot bitch you are."

"You like that, don't you?"

"Hell, yes! It's what I've wanted for years."

"Why didn't you tell me?"

"Would you have listened?"

"Probably not."

"Well, you seem to be listening now. Listen to this." Marc slipped his hand between her legs and squeezed. "My cock will be in your pussy before the night is over, and you will beg me for it." A wave of heat moved through her that made her chest flush red.

Marc didn't wait for a response. He pushed the elevator door open with such force it banged against the wall.

"Jesus, Marc! Be careful! You'll chip the paint."

"Then I'll have it repainted! Are you coming?"

She had never seen Marc like this, so commanding, and actually crude. She could either play his game or not. In the few seconds it took to step out of the elevator and close the gate, Patricia made her decision. "Baby, if I don't come before the night is over, it's your fault, not mine." She slipped her arm though his and added, "Let's go."

The tight line of Marc's jaw softened as he smiled. "Then, it's still green?"

"Emerald City, lover." If he could do this biker thing, so could she.

Marc wrapped his arm around her waist and pulled her close.

"I'm proud of you, Tricia. This is a big step." His fingertips dug into her flesh.

"You know I'm scared shitless."

"But you're still doing it, and you're doing it with me."

"You're the only one I could do it with. I feel safe with you, I always have."

"What we are doing wouldn't work without trust. Phil knew that, which is why he contacted me." Marc put both hands on her ass and pulled her pelvis tightly against his. "Tell me what you want, bitch."

"I want you, Daddy." She rubbed her pelvis against his. "And this."

"Learn to say the words, Tricia. What do you want?"

Patricia took a deep breath and exhaled the words. "I want your cock in my pussy, I want you to make me beg for it."

"Oh, yes, better, much better."

Tricia wobbled as they walked down the hall. "You'll have to slow down. I'm not used to walking in these heels."

Marc steadied her. "Understood. Just remember, you have to reek with attitude."

"I do that every day. This just puts a new twist on it."

"You got that right."

By the time they were on the street, Patricia had found a comfortable stride. Marc matched her step and allowed her to set the pace. "How far is this place?"

"Not far. It's a few blocks uptown, just south of Tompkins Square Park."

Just then a bicycle messenger rode past and yelled, "Yo, Mama! Lookin' good!"

Patricia flipped him the bird. "Is that enough attitude for you?"

Marc laughed. "Damn good thing I took that karate course at the gym. I may need it before the night is over."

"I wasn't aware you'd finished it."

"I have my brown belt. I'm working on my black belt now."

"I didn't know that."

"You didn't ask."

"Is that why you're so cut? I mean, you are in better shape than I remember."

"Thank you for noticing. I had to do something to blow off steam. So, I stepped up my classes. I've been going three times a week. I'm back to once a week now, since we're doing what we're doing."

"What are we doing, Marc? Really, why is this necessary?"

"Tricia, walking uptown dressed like this is hardly the time to discuss why this is necessary."

"But I need to know. It will help me when I feel like it is too much for me to take."

Marc stopped. "I've already told you why it's necessary. Your controlling behavior has alienated everyone in your life, including me. Your subconscious is regurgitating in your dreams and making you miserable. If you don't do something drastic damn soon to turn it around, your whole life will spiral out of control, including your precious career."

"I've been round and round with Dr. Dick about this!"

"You're damn lucky Phil has hung in as long as he has, considering how often you kick him in the balls with your sarcastic remarks. He told me flat out it's only because we've been friends for so long."

Marc had raised his voice sufficiently to draw even more attention from passersby. "Keep it down, Marc, before we get arrested for disturbing the peace!"

Marc pressed his erection into her leg. "It's too damn late to keep it down, sweetheart. It's up and hard. I expect it to be that way for the shank of the evening."

Patricia glared at him, but at the same time, her heart thumped in her chest. "Then I guess we're both in this up to our ass cheeks."

"I guess so." He wrapped his arm protectively around her waist as a group of teenage boys walked by, obviously checking her out. "We'd better get going. The bar is up the street."

"Tell me about this place. How did you find it?"

"One of my former clients is a regular. He's a self-proclaimed hedonist, and frequents several of these clubs."

"I thought you said it was a bar."

"It is. Anyone can go in for a drink. It attracts mostly the tattooed leather crowd. Bikers love the place. But there is also a private club downstairs, which only members are permitted in."

"And you're a member?"

"As of last week. It's by referral only. I asked my client about it and he introduced me to Lenny, the owner. I can either go alone or bring a guest."

"This Lenny knows about me?"

"He only knows I'm bringing someone new to the scene. He recommended coming early the first time, before the regulars show up. Things really heat up after midnight."

"You've been there after midnight?"

"Yes."

"You're just full of surprises these days!"

"Baby, you don't know the half of it." Marc stopped. "This is it." The large neon sign in the window flashed JUGS AND PUDS BAR AND GRILL. Several smaller neon signs advertised a variety of beer brands.

Patricia looked past all the neon in the window to see inside. She saw a jukebox and a pool table, and several men standing at the bar. The waitresses wore leather bustiers and short leather skirts.

"Charming! I wonder how *Zagat* rates this place?"

"I don't think they've discovered it yet. But *New York After Dark* gives it nine out of ten."

"How reassuring!"

Marc escorted her inside and took her right to the bar. He spoke to the bartender. "Hey, Lenny, how the hell are you?"

A muscular man in jeans and a black sleeveless T-shirt came over and shook hands. "Good to see you again, Marc. This is your lady?"

"Tricia, this is Lenny, the owner of this fine establishment. Lenny, this is Tricia."

Not knowing what Marc expected of her, she tried to sound down with it. "Hello, Lenny. How's business?"

"Not too bad." He looked directly at her cleavage when he added, "With you here, it's bound to get better."

Marc put his hand on her ass. "I told you I had a lady ready for some action. Which room are we in?"

Lenny handed Marc a key. "Room Two, downstairs. You know the way."

"Did you leave us a bottle and some glasses?"

"There's Jose Cuervo Gold and shot glasses. Good?"

"Oh, man, very good! Thanks, buddy. How long do we have?"

"You've got the room all night, if you want it. Too damn bad you're hiding this one away." Lenny caressed her breast with the back of his hand. "Doll, let me know when you want more."

Patricia pushed his hand away. "Marc keeps me happy. I have no complaints."

"Well, if you ever do, you know where to find me."

"Lenny, you should know they call her Ms. Piranha. She eats men alive."

Patricia nuzzled Marc's neck. "He's the only one able to keep me in line."

Marc smiled and held up the key. "Shall we?" Ignoring both Lenny and the other men at the bar, Marc led her to a staircase in the back marked EMPLOYEES ONLY. When they got to Room Two, Marc opened the door and turned on the light.

"Oh my God!" It took Patricia several seconds to take it all in. The stone walls had a variety of chains and shackles. On the table with the tequila there lay paddles and whips of different sizes and shapes, as well as a selection of dildos, vibrators and butt plugs. There were other benches and tables in the room, some with leather straps attached. Dazed, she turned to Marc. "This is a frigging dungeon!"

"That's what it is, fully equipped and ready for action." Marc closed the door and locked it. "In this room, Tricia, you do as I tell you. Remember your colors. That's your only safety net here."

"What are you going to do, torture me?"

"There are degrees of torture, my dear." Marc approached her and held her wrist. "Sometimes the psychological torment is as delicious as the physical."

Patricia did not resist as he led her to the stone wall. He picked up a short length of chain attached to the wall. Taking her wrist, he clipped the chain to the hooks on her wrist cuff. Patricia's hand trembled as he did the same to the other wrist. "What's your color, Tricia?"

"Pale green, but still green."

"Then spread your legs." She did as he asked, opening her legs as much as she could while balancing on her heels. Marc wrapped leather straps around her calves and buckled them. When he finished, she stood spread-eagled against the wall, immobilized. "Would you like some tequila?"

"Do you have a straw?"

"No, but I would be happy to hold the glass for you. Do you want some?"

"Yes."

Marc poured them each a shot. He bolted his back before taking Patricia hers. "Did you see how I drank mine?"

"Yes."

"Open your mouth and knock it back when I tip the glass."

In one smooth motion, Patricia tilted her head and Marc

poured the shot of tequila into her mouth. She swallowed it the same way she had swallowed his cum the night before. The warmth spread through her and she began to relax. "May I have another?"

"Of course." Marc repeated the process. Once the second shot hit, her nervousness calmed.

"Do I get to make requests?"

"It depends. What do you want?"

"Open your pants so I can see your cock."

"Why?"

"When you did it last night, it really turned me on to see how hard you were."

Marc traced a line down her bare belly with his index finger. Patricia shivered. "It turned me on to see you with those stockings and nipple clamps and nothing else." He reached into his pocket and took out the clamps he had used the night before. "I'll open my pants when I'm ready. First, we undress you."

Marc unhooked her top. Patricia's tits tumbled out of the constricting material. Before he attached the nipple clamps, he untied the strings of her shorts and yanked them off. He stroked his cock as he looked at her. "Goddamn, Patricia! You are so fucking hot! Lenny should see you now!"

Patricia panicked. "If you bring him in this room, I call red!"

Patricia could see Marc's jaw line harden. "Calling red ends the scene. Do you want it to end?"

"I agreed to be here with you, no one else. If you bring anyone else into this room, it ends. With only you, it's still green."

Marc relaxed, his smile softening his jaw. "Understood." He tickled her pubic hair. Her pelvis tipped toward his hand. "You may change your mind once you adjust."

"Are you my pimp now?"

"I could get off watching someone else fuck you."

Patricia's anger fueled her arousal. "You are a freaking pervert, aren't you?"

Marc rubbed his cock against her leg as he attached the nipple clamps. Patricia winced, but did not call yellow. He gave the screw another half twist before he stopped. "You bring it out in me, Tricia. You always have." He reached down and rubbed her clit. She tried not to move, but the intense sensation made her hips undulate against his hand. "Oh yes, you are heating up. Let's get you hotter."

Marc stood directly in front of her, took off his vest, and tossed it to the side. Then he unzipped his pants and exposed his prick. "Do you like what you see?"

Patricia stared at his cock, and then followed the line of hair up his chest. She couldn't hide her reaction. Her entire body flushed. The utter helplessness of being so exposed simultaneously sexed her up and angered her. She spit her answer back at him. "Fuck, yes! Isn't that obvious?"

"That's good, Tricia, that's very good." Marc went to the table and picked up a large rubber dildo. "You should be wet enough to handle this. They call it a Jeff Stryker, modeled after the porn star. Ever use one of these, Patricia?"

"Hell, no!"

"Pity. I expect it would work much better than the handle of the bath brush you have been using."

"Christ Almighty, Marc! That thing is huge! Yours is the biggest prick I've ever had. *You're* not even that big!"

"It's a ten-incher, so they say. Let's see if you can handle it."

Patricia involuntarily pulled against the restraints when the tip touched her labia, but she didn't call yellow. Her pussy burned with the need to have a cock fill it. She knew Marc wouldn't fuck her so soon, and she wanted to be fucked.

He rolled the dildo against her clit, coating it with her cream. With excruciating slowness, he wedged the head inside her cunt. She squirmed, trying to force it in deeper. Marc pulled it out. "What the fuck are you doing, Marc? Put it in!"

Marc dragged the dildo up between her breasts. "My, my, Patricia! You are a slut tonight, aren't you?" Patricia glared at him and didn't answer. "Patricia, I asked you a question. Are you a slut tonight?"

With her cunt itching from her juice and also with wanting to be fucked, she hissed her answer. "Yes, you motherfucker, I'm a slut tonight! Fuck me with that goddamn thing!"

"Not yet." He touched her nose with the tip of the dildo and then pressed it against her lips. She could smell the acrid odor of rubber mixed with her genital perfume. "Have you ever tasted yourself, love?" Patricia turned her head away. "No, I didn't think so." Marc pinched her chin between his thumb and forefinger and turned her head toward him. Before Patricia had the chance to call yellow, the head of the phallus filled her mouth. "Suck it, Tricia. Suck it like you sucked me last night."

She tasted the dildo commingled with her own musk. Marc humped her leg as he pushed the dildo deeper into her mouth. She remembered her hunger when she blew Marc last night, and how much she wanted him to come in her mouth.

She wanted to blow him again, and circled the dildo with her tongue as if it were his cock. Spit ran down her chin onto Marc's hand as she voraciously tongued and sucked the dildo as if it were him.

"I always knew you had a whore buried in there. She's finally coming out of the closet." Marc yanked the dildo out of her mouth. Patricia gasped for air. "Now, sweetheart, you're going to be fucked." With no preamble, Marc shoved the rubber head between her legs, found her hole and pushed the entire length of the dildo into her pussy.

Patricia screamed, and her whole body shook. Her ankles turned in and she wobbled on the stiletto heels. Marc steadied her. "Patricia, I want you to listen very carefully. I'll take your boots off, but you have to grip the cock and hold it inside. If it falls out, the boots stay on. Do you understand?"

"Yes! Take the fucking things off before I break my ankle." Patricia remembered reading somewhere that clenching the PC muscle when you have to urinate also clenched the vaginal muscles. She squeezed as hard as she could, the same way she would if she really had to go. Marc released the dildo. It didn't slip out.

He lifted one foot and pulled off the boot. She gritted her teeth and grimaced with the effort to keep the phallus in. It slipped slightly and she pulled up harder. He lifted the other foot as sweat ran down her cheek. The second boot came off. She nearly cried with relief when she felt his hand push the rubber fully inside her again.

"Nicely done, Tricia. You've earned yourself a royal fucking." Now able to balance herself, Patricia opened her legs as wide as the leather straps would allow. Marc pulled the dildo out and rammed it back in. She pushed her pelvis toward him with each thrust, not caring how lewd it looked. She wanted to come.

Suddenly, he stopped and pulled the dildo completely out. Nearly whimpering, she pleaded for him to keep going. "Marc, please, I'm burning up! I need to come!"

"Oh, my dear Patricia, it's much too soon for that. You haven't been strapped yet."

"You're going to fucking kill me, aren't you?"

"No, darling. I'm going to make you feel more alive than you've ever been!" Marc unhooked the clips from her wristbands. Then he taunted her, promising complete freedom. "If you fondle my balls with loving sweetness, I'll release your legs."

Hoping he would unshackle her, Patricia put one hand on his chest and cupped his balls with the other. She gently caressed the soft sacks. Marc moaned softly each time she squeezed, the veins on his cock obviously pulsing. She ached with wanting him to fuck her!

Marc finally stopped her, taking her hand and kissing her fingers. Then he unbuckled the straps around her calves. "What's your color, Patricia?"

"It's still green! But I'm telling you right now, you had better have your cock in me soon, or it will be fire-truck red, and this whole dungeon scene will be over!"

"I have every intention of fucking you! My hard-on is purple, it needs it so bad. But I'm not frigging ready yet, Tricia. You will beg me for it, I swear to God, you will. Now, bend over the spanking bench and spread your legs wide." Marc pointed to a sloped bench with a kneeler. "If you can maintain the position, I won't strap you in. If you can't or won't, then the straps will be used."

"I'll hold it. You don't have to strap me into the damned thing!"

"We'll see."

Patricia knelt on the leather padding and had a flashback of kneeling in a confessional when she went to Catholic school. "This thing is over the top! How bloody Freudian can you get? Maybe you should put on a collar and robes."

Marc walked around to the front of the bench, where she could see him. He held a razor strap, almost identical to the one in her dream. "Recognize this?"

"Jesus Christ! Where did you get that?"

"Lenny found it for me. I described it to him and he found one."

Patricia began trembling uncontrollably. "Marc, I need another shot."

Without saying a word, Marc went to get the bottle and a shot glass. He handed her the glass and poured. She bolted it back and held it up for another. He poured again and then put the cap back on the bottle. "That's enough. You want to feel this, don't you?"

Patricia couldn't deny the truth of what Marc said. "Yes, I want to feel it." Before he had a chance to tell her to, she bent over the sloping part of the bench and spread her legs the width of the kneeler. Her dream filled her mind, and her pussy oozed with need.

The first stroke of the strap made her teeth grit. She grabbed the legs of the bench and held on. The second stroke would have brought her to her knees had she been standing. Marc did not hold back with the third and fourth swing. He strapped her with sadistic pleasure, grunting with his increasing arousal.

By the fifth stroke, she thought she might lose consciousness, but she did not cry yellow. Sensual delirium had replaced any concern for her well-being. She only wanted more sensation.

Somewhere in the fog of her arousal, she heard Marc's voice. "Patricia, answer me! What is your color?"

She heard a voice laughing and suddenly realized it came from her. "You mother-fucking bastard! It's fucking leprechaun green!"

Suddenly, heat surged deeply into her belly. Marc had mounted her from behind, shoving his cock so far in she thought surely it hit the back of her throat. "You're my bitch, Tricia. Say it! Tell me you're my bitch and beg me to fuck you!"

Marc didn't move. With his prick buried inside of her up to his balls, he didn't move. She screamed at him, "I'm your bitch, your slut, your whore! I'm whatever the hell you want me to be! Fuck me, you son of a bitch. Fuck my pussy and make me come!"

He pulled out and drove himself back in, putting his weight behind each thrust. With her ass up in the air on the slanted bench, his cock drilled her like a jackhammer. "Come for me, you bitch!" Marc reached under her and harshly rubbed her pussy lips with his hand. The unexpected pressure caught her unaware, and she pushed back against him. He pinched her clit and she squealed.

With strength she didn't know she had, Patricia nearly knocked Marc backward as her orgasm seized her. He forced her to bend forward as she convulsed, pounding her with brutal force. His climax followed hers. As he emptied his balls into her, he growled, "Fuck, yes! You cunting bitch, yes!"

Marc's thrusts finally slowed, and then stopped. Still holding her pussy in his hand, he rolled onto the floor and pulled her over with him. Unable to manage any sort of balance, Patricia fell on top of him. He held her tightly, and whispered into her ear, "Tricia, I'm glad you're finally realizing how hot you are. And I'm glad you're doing it with me."

3

Patricia had just finished the paperwork left over from the day before when her assistant, Betty, buzzed her. "Patricia, Marc is on line three."

Surprised that he would call her at the office, she picked up the phone. "Hello, Marc?"

"Good morning, Tricia."

"You don't usually call me here. Is everything okay?"

"Everything is fine. I wanted to make sure you are all right today."

Patricia lowered her voice, just to make sure no one walking by her office would hear. "My ass is sore, but other than that, I am quite well today."

"You know, if we ever have phone sex, you have to use that sultry voice. It's hot as hell."

Patricia smiled. Marc had never spoken to her like that before. "I'll be sure to keep that in mind. Why aren't you in session? You told me you were booked solid today."

"My ten o'clock cancelled at the last minute, so I have an hour free. I wanted to ask you a couple of things."

"What?"

"Did you have any dreams last night, like you have been having?"

Patricia hesitated and glanced at the open door to her office. "I really can't talk about that here, Marc."

"I understand. You don't have to go into detail. I only want to know if there is any change."

"There is."

"Can you give me an idea of what?"

Practically whispering into the phone, Patricia told him. "I dreamed about you. The orgasm I had in my sleep woke me up. That has never happened before."

"My dear, that tells me we are making progress, and that we are on the right track. Oh, and you just gave me a hard-on with that sexy voice."

Patricia burst out laughing. "You are a piece of work! Speaking of which, I have to get back to work."

"I'm sure you do. I know we aren't scheduled for tonight, but I thought I would check with you anyway. Any chance?"

"Marc, I would like to, but I can't. I have to get the quarterlies done by Friday."

"Yeah, you told me that. I thought I would take a shot. Then, how about this? Friday night, you come to the loft and plan on spending the night."

"Are you serious?"

"I wouldn't ask if I weren't."

"Will you tell me what you've got planned?"

"No."

"Well, in case you would like to know, I've reconsidered something."

"I'm listening."

"Lenny. I might call green if he comes to the loft, but it is still red otherwise. Understood?"

"Oh, yes, very much understood. Then, you'll come?"

"That's up to you, isn't it?"

Marc chuckled. "Let me rephrase that. Will you meet me at the loft on Friday?"

"I'll be there. Do I bring my toothbrush?"

"No need to bring anything. I'll supply everything you need. One thing you can do. Wear a garter belt this time with sheer black hose, and again, no panties."

"You like this, don't you?"

"Tricia, you're not the only one exploring your shadow. I've become a bona fide spelunker, complete with a caver's helmet and carbide lamp."

"I'll have to buy that piece of clothing."

"Get a black one. And while you're at it, a matching bra."

Patricia's assistant poked her head in the door and pointed to her watch. "Damn, Marc! I have to go. I'm late for a meeting."

"That's also progress. That means you lost track of time while talking to me. I'll see you on Friday." The phone clicked in Patricia's ear. For the first time in her professional career, she walked into a partners' meeting ten minutes late.

During the next two days, Patricia focused on her work, staying at her office for nearly fourteen hours both days. At ten o'clock Thursday night, she left her quarterly reports on the managing partner's desk. After sending a quick e-mail to her assistant saying that she would be in late on Friday, she took a cab home.

Even feeling exhausted, Patricia lay awake for some time thinking about Marc. For as long as she had known him, she had never realized he could be so forceful and dominant. She had been too busy trying to control everything in her life to notice. It never occurred to her that he needed her acquiescence to show this side of himself. How totally fucked up had she been not to see it?

When the alarm went off at seven o'clock, Patricia rolled

over and hugged her pillow. She didn't remember falling asleep. It couldn't possibly be morning already.

A dream about Marc floated in her head, a dream she wanted to continue. Then she remembered! Tonight she would be with Marc, and she would be spending the night with him. She threw the blankets off and jumped out of bed.

After taking a shower, she chose the sexiest, lowest-cut blouse she had, and matched it with a tailored black suit. Marc would no doubt have selected the costume of the day, but nonetheless, she wanted to look sexy for him. Before going to the office, she would shop for the garter belt, stockings, and bra, and put them on later. Maybe she could find a new pair of shoes to go with the lingerie.

By the time Patricia arrived at her office, it was well after eleven. She hadn't realized the stores didn't open until ten. Trying to put on her best pit-bull face, she got off the elevator.

Her attempt to walk in without being noticed or spoken to didn't work. Earl saw her with her shopping bags and asked if Christmas had come early this year. One of the Generation X associates she had considered firing stopped her and told her how lovely she looked today. Even Betty wanted to know whose birthday she had missed.

By the time she got to her office, she knew the whole floor would soon be buzzing about her coming in late with Victoria's Secret shopping bags and Charles David shoes. She didn't care.

She had a lunch appointment with a client, which she almost forgot about. Betty reminded her. Grateful for the distraction, she spent a couple of hours at a fancy restaurant talking business, before returning to the office.

Finally, the day started to wind down. She had an hour before meeting Marc. She gathered her shopping bags and went to the ladies' room to change before making the trip downtown.

She knew which button to press now; she didn't have to look for it. Marc buzzed her in without saying anything. When she knocked on the door to the loft, her heart thumped in her chest.

The oddest thing happened when he opened the door. Neither of them said anything. They just stood there looking at each other. Marc had on a black Armani suit, a white shirt, and gold cuff links. He had not buttoned the first two buttons of his shirt, revealing the top part of his chest. She had the urge to brush his exposed chest hair with her fingertips.

Patricia still had her shopping bags. It should be obvious to Marc she had done what he asked. When he looked down at her feet and saw her shoes, he smiled. "Very nice, Tricia. You look lovely this evening."

"Thank you. And you look like you stepped out of a James Bond movie." Patricia tried to see behind Marc. "Are we alone?"

"For now." Marc took her shopping bags and her purse. "Please, come in." Feeling like Alice stepping through the looking glass, Patricia followed Marc into the loft.

She looked around for some clue about what the evening would bring. The room appeared neat and devoid of any evidence. Marc put her bags and purse in the closet and closed the door.

"No costumes tonight?" It surprised her to feel mildly disappointed.

"I'm wearing mine. You're already wearing part of yours. The rest is hanging inside the bathroom door."

"What is it?" She couldn't imagine what he had dreamed up for tonight.

"You'll know soon enough." He squatted in front of her. "Let me see those shoes." She lifted her foot and he held it in the palm of his hand. Turning her foot from side to side, he closely examined the black stiletto pumps she had bought. "How high are the heels?"

"Four inches."

"Are they comfortable?"

"Actually, yes. The heel is a little wider than the boots you gave me. And the ankle strap holds them in place. I wore them here with no problem."

"Good. Then we'll use these instead of the ones I bought."

"You bought me more shoes?"

"I told you I would supply everything you needed. I meant it." Before he stood, Marc gripped the back of her leg and slid his hand up under her skirt. He didn't stop when he reached the garter belt, but continued up to her ass. He watched her reaction when he tickled her pubic hair before removing his hand and standing. "Kudos, Patricia. You gave me exactly what I asked for and then some."

"It's good to know you appreciate it."

"I do."

"Are you going to tell me what is on the boards for tonight?"

"Eventually. Right now, tell me how you're feeling."

"Nervous."

"Any more dreams?"

"Fragmented ones, nothing I remember very well."

"Do you recall anything?"

"Just that you have been in them, and I woke up feeling really turned on."

Marc unbuttoned her suit jacket and caressed her breast. "Do you like how that feels?"

"Yes."

"That's good, Tricia." Marc took off her suit jacket and tossed it onto the back of the chair.

"You got more stuff in here. That's new dining furniture. It's beautiful! And bookshelves, too!" She looked in the corner where there had only been a sink, a coffeepot, a microwave and some cupboards a few days earlier. "You also got a refrigerator and a stove! This looks like a real apartment now."

"Thank you. I cleared my afternoon to be here for the delivery yesterday. They put the bedroom furniture up there." He pointed to an overhead mezzanine. "I've decided not to sell this place. I'm going to keep it."

"You are?"

"There is a sense of freedom here, to do what we are doing. Don't you agree?"

"I hadn't thought about it, but I suppose you're right."

"It's our private safe space, where we have no distractions. Speaking of which, is your BlackBerry off?"

"I turned it off in the taxi."

"You have come a long way this week, Tricia. Tonight you will go farther."

"You're making me feel like a mouse, and you're the cat playing with me."

"Then let me tease you some more. Shall I tell you a bit of what's ahead?"

"If you don't mind."

"Philip noted a dream in your records about a French maid. Do you remember it?"

"Marc, you wouldn't!"

"Oh, yes, Patricia, I would. Lenny should be here shortly. I asked him to bring along some food, so you can serve us dinner before we get down to business."

"What is my costume?"

"Why, a French maid uniform, of course. Isn't that what you described in your dream?"

"Christ, I saw that damn yogurt commercial before I went to bed one night. My subconscious took it and ran."

Marc laughed. "Tricia, what you dreamed was no yogurt commercial."

"Does Lenny understand the situation?"

"He does and he's cool with it. He'll only go as far as you want to go. If you call red, it stops."

"Even if he's really into it?"

"He would stop. I would see to it."

"No shit! The man looks like a bodybuilder, his arms are huge! What would you do? Karate-chop him?"

"If I had to, yes, I would."

"When the hell did you get so macho? You're a bloody shrink, for God's sake!" Marc said nothing. But Patricia saw him grit his teeth and knew she had hit a nerve. Goading him even more, she added, "I suppose you drink raw eggs for breakfast now."

Ignoring her derision, Marc went to a cupboard in the kitchen area and took out a bottle of Jack Daniel's. He poured himself a drink. Turning back to her, he raised his glass toward the bathroom door. "I suggest you go and change clothes now, unless you are calling red." He sipped his whiskey and waited.

Patricia glared at him. But the glare became a stare when she really looked at him. Standing there in his Armani suit, holding a tumbler in his hand, she couldn't stop the heat that moved through her body. She remembered the first time she saw him. The same thing had happened. With no conscious intent, she smiled. She wasn't an ice queen anymore.

"I will change clothes, but don't I get a drink first?"

"So you're staying?"

"I never said I wouldn't."

"You know I'm going to push you tonight."

"I would be disappointed if you didn't. Do I get that drink?"

Marc poured whiskey into another tumbler and set it on the table. "If you want this, you have to work for it."

Patricia knew a challenge when she heard it. She wouldn't back down. "What do I have to do?"

"Strip to your sexy underwear. Then come over here and blow me."

"What if Lenny shows up?"

"Then I suppose you'll be blowing both of us, because

you're answering the door when he knocks. I don't give a shit what you have on, or don't have on, at the time."

"Who are you trying to prove something to, Marc, me or yourself?"

"Perhaps both, perhaps neither. It doesn't frigging matter does it, as long as we both get off on it?"

"Is getting off all this is about to you?"

"No, Patricia, it's not. I thought you knew that." Marc glanced at his watch. "Lenny will be here by seven o'clock. It's up to you how the evening starts."

Marc wasn't bluffing. Patricia knew that. If she wanted to stay, and she did, she had to play by his rules. She opened her blouse and took it off, then unzipped her skirt. As it fell to the floor, an unfamiliar sensibility overshadowed her spitefulness. Subjection replaced superiority, and emancipation trumped control.

"Do I keep the shoes on?"

"Oh, yes, Tricia, the shoes stay on."

Marc did not move from where he stood. Patricia picked up a pillow from the sofa and dropped it on the floor in front of him. The alchemy of self-consciousness and vulnerability acted as an aphrodisiac. She could smell her own musk as she knelt in front of him.

Patricia opened his belt. Before she could unzip his trousers, he stopped her. "Look at me, Tricia." She tilted her head and looked up, appearing to pray in pagan worship. "Tell me how much you want to suck my dick."

The abject humiliation of this moment inflamed her. She did want to blow him, and she wanted him to know it. "Marc Forrest, I want to lick your cock until you come."

"Will you swallow my cream, Tricia?"

"I will suck you and swallow your cum when you finish."

"You are not permitted to have an orgasm now. After you

blow me, you will immediately put on your uniform and get ready to greet Lenny at the door. Do you understand?"

"I understand."

"What's your color?"

"I am so green I could play Elphaba in *Wicked*."

Marc unzipped his trousers. It surprised her to see he wore no underwear. He always wore some sort of jockeys. Keeping her surprise to herself, she carefully exposed his cock. The smell of him made her heady, the odor of sex and arousal hitting her like a popper.

When her tongue touched his tip, he grunted. Setting his glass on the table, he braced himself by putting his hands on top of her head. She had wanted to kiss him and lick him before taking his prick into her mouth, but his weight forced her head deeper into his groin. She had no choice. She opened her mouth as his cock pressed against her lips. Marc pushed forward, nearly gagging her as his organ filled her mouth.

Quickly pulling her head back as far as she could, she managed to grab the base of his prick. By doing that, she regained her balance and could better manage his thrusting forward. The front of his coat fanned her as she sucked, his scent filling her like incense.

She could tell by his rhythm it would be soon, the force of his thrusts increasing with his need. Wrapping her arm around his ass, she pulled his pelvis against her, restricting his ability to move. With the sound of a wild animal being caged, Marc shot his load down her throat. As she struggled to swallow his cream, he shouted at her, "You fucking hot bitch, do me!" She took the compliment to heart.

Remembering that Lenny would arrive at any minute, Patricia stood and threw the pillow back on the sofa. She scooped up her clothes, intending to go straight to the bathroom.

"Patricia?"

She turned around just as Marc zipped his trousers. "What now?"

"Don't forget your drink. You've earned it. Oh, yes, and for tonight, your name is Cosette."

"How totally Victor Hugo of you! Don't tell me, you're Jean Valjean and Lenny is Javert."

"It's nice to see your mouth is hot, no matter what the situation. No, my dear Cosette, Lenny and Marc will do for tonight. Lenny is my guest, here to share the charms of my maid." Marc handed her the glass. "Now go and get ready for us. Put on what's in there, except for the shoes."

After closing the door, Patricia tossed her suit over the shower rod. Grateful for a few minutes to regroup, she looked in the mirror over the sink. "Shit!" Her lipstick had smeared on her face and she had left her makeup in her purse.

When she turned to go back out and ask Marc for her bag, she saw the maid's costume on the back of the door. She couldn't believe how closely it resembled the one in her dream. The black uniform trimmed with white lace and the attached frilly white apron barely had enough material to cover her tits and ass. Wondering how she would work up the nerve to put it on and walk out the door, she muttered, "Ooh la la. My name is Cosette. Please fuck me."

Marc was talking on his cell when she opened the door. "Hold on, Lenny, I'll be right with you." He put the phone down. "Yes, is there a problem?"

Paying no attention to his terse tone, she explained. "A minor problem. I need my makeup. Could you give me my purse?"

Marc retrieved her purse from the closet. Before handing it to her, he opened it and took out her BlackBerry. "Contraband is not permitted in the dressing room."

"Fuck you!" She took the bag and slammed the door shut.

Not believing she would stoop to spying, she paused by the

door and listened, hoping to hear some of Marc's conversation with Lenny.

"Make sure the ropes and blindfold are buried in a shopping bag. I don't want her to see them. By the time we get that far, she'll be ready for it." Patricia took the costume off the hanger and went to fix her makeup. She had heard enough.

Patricia took her time getting herself together. Marc didn't interrupt, which meant Lenny had not yet arrived. She had trouble fastening the white lace cuffs, but did manage it without asking for help. She noticed the cuffs had the same silver loops that the leather ones had earlier in the week. Now she knew how they were used.

The last accessory was a white lace collar to match the cuffs. It also had silver loops. In spite of the queasiness she felt putting it on, the implication of their use excited her.

When she finished, she took a deep breath and looked in the mirror. Her reflection shocked her. The garter belt, clearly visible under the short, pleated skirt, hid nothing. The bottom curve of her ass cheeks could be seen when she stood straight. Bending over would expose her ass and her pussy. The snug fit of the bodice pushed her breasts up into exaggerated cleavage, the black lace of the bra seeming to be part of the dress.

She knew both Marc and this other man, Lenny, would see her in this, and it would be lewd and sleazy. She also knew they would use her in ways she couldn't even imagine. The costume of the day would serve its purpose, and she knew that was exactly what she wanted.

Cracking the bathroom door open, she peeked out. Marc had his back to her, digging in the closet for something. Lenny had not yet arrived. She quietly came out, and waited for Marc to turn around. When he did, he had a leather paddle in his hand. She stared at the paddle while he stared at her.

"Well, now, don't you look like you just stepped out of a French porn movie! *Très passionnante*."

"And don't you look like a male dom poster boy!"

Marc held up the paddle, and then whacked his leg with it. "Isn't it a beauty? It's the best one I could get. I found it at Purple Passion on Twentieth Street. It's a great store. Ever been there?"

"No, Marc. I don't usually frequent such places."

"I expect that will soon change. Come here." Patricia came closer. "Now turn around and bend over. Let's see if it does the job."

Again Marc challenged her. She knew she could refuse. But remembering the sting on her ass from the strap, she knew she didn't want to say no. She liked the intense feeling of having her ass smacked, she liked the sting and she liked feeling it at Marc's hand.

Without complaint or objection, she turned around and bent over. She heard Marc's breath change, and knew the view he had must be worth the price of admission. Even in her submission, she felt a rush of power at evoking such a response from him. She knew that shortly, another man would be lusting after her in the same way. She didn't understand it, but she wanted it.

Before she could think it through, Marc swung the paddle. It connected solidly with her ass. The sting made her stumble forward. She caught herself on the arm of the chair. The paddle connected again, this time slightly lower. Her pussy tightened with the impact, the sensation flowing through her groin. Bracing herself for more, she spread her legs wider. But Marc stopped.

"That's enough for now, Tricia. My glass is on the table. Get me another drink."

Patricia slowly stood, disappointed that Marc had stopped. Reminding herself that she had agreed to play by his rules, she picked up his glass. He watched her walk across the room to the cupboard.

When she gave him the refilled glass, she noticed two things.

He had unbuttoned two more buttons on his shirt, exposing most of his chest, and he had an erection. Fighting the urge to make a wisecrack, Patricia attempted to be a proper servant.

"Your drink, sir."

"Thank you, Cosette."

Hearing him call her Cosette made it difficult to keep a straight face, but she managed. "When is your guest coming, sir?"

"He's waiting in the lobby. I told him I would call him when you are ready. I think you're ready." Taking his phone out of his jacket pocket, Marc dialed. "Hello, Lenny. C'mon up. We're in 4D." Marc sat down in the armchair. Patricia understood he expected her to answer the door not as Patricia but as Cosette.

Patricia jumped when Lenny knocked. It didn't help that Marc chuckled at her nervousness. Determined to play the role she had been handed for the evening, she opened the door. "Good evening, monsieur. Please come in."

"Well, hello again, doll." Lenny winked at her and then checked her out. "Ohh la la, you're a little piece of heaven tonight!"

"Cosette, please take Lenny's bags."

"Cosette? I thought her name was Tricia."

"For tonight, she is Cosette. She is here to serve us, however we choose."

"Hey, man, I'm in. I haven't done a scene like this in years." Patricia reached for the bags Lenny held. "Here, Cosette, take these three. This one is for Marc."

Lenny gave the bag to Marc. After glancing inside, Marc smiled. "I see you also brought dessert."

"I didn't have to. She's already here."

Patricia put the bags on the table. She bent over to look inside. When she turned around, both men were leering at her. Realizing they had seen her ass and her pussy, she flushed. Struggling to maintain her composure, she began unpacking the food.

Marc came over to examine their dinner, casually rubbing her bare ass as he looked. "What the hell did you bring, Lenny? There's enough food here to feed a frigging army!"

"You wanted French, so I did French. Since you're paying for it, I did it right. The appetizers are French onion soup, pâté, and escargot. I didn't know what the hell the entrée names were, so I asked for one of each. And for dessert, crème brulee and chocolate mousse, and of course, her!"

"Well, man, we sure as shit won't go hungry tonight."

"Damn straight we won't, not with her serving."

Marc sat down at the table. "Lenny, please take a seat. Cosette, we'll have dinner now."

Again, Tricia felt at sea in this situation. Not only did she wonder what they would eventually do with her, but now she had to actually be a maid! She had never backed down from a challenge, and she wouldn't now. "Sir, you will have to tell me where to find the dishes and silver. I am new to this."

"Why, of course, Cosette. The cupboard over the sink has dishes. The silver is in the drawer next to the refrigerator. And there is wine with the other liquor."

While Tricia put together the place settings, Marc quietly spoke to Lenny. She strained to hear what he said, but couldn't manage it. She did hear Lenny say, "Hell, yeah, I'll tickle her pussy when she comes back."

Tricia brought enough dishes to the table to set three places. "Excuse me, Cosette, there are only two for dinner."

Marc really threw her with that one. Staying in character, she kept her cool. "I'm sorry, sir. I thought I would also have some food."

"What do you think, Lenny? Should we give her a little something?"

"Between the two of us, Marc, she'll get more than a little before the night is over. As for food, we have plenty. But servants never sit at the table with their masters."

Turning to Patricia, Marc feigned surprise. "You hear that, Cosette? Servants never sit at the main table. Lenny, would it be acceptable for her to kneel between us? We could give her a bite or two, if she is a good girl."

"Come here, sweetheart." Lenny motioned for her to come closer.

Patricia hesitated.

"Cosette, my guest made a request. I expect you to be gracious and see to his needs."

Feeling both nervous and a bit frightened, Patricia went to Lenny. "Yes, sir?"

"If you want any food, you have to be a good girl." Lenny put his hand on her thigh and slowly slid it up her leg to her ass. "Are you a good girl?"

"I try to be, sir."

"Do you let men touch your pussy?"

"It depends, sir."

"Depends on what, Cosette?"

Patricia glared at Marc. "It depends on whether my master permits it."

"Marc, do you permit it?"

"Not usually, Lenny. But you are my special guest. Cosette's charms are yours tonight."

Without warning, Lenny's thick middle finger slipped between her pussy lips and found her clitoris. Tricia instinctively pulled back. Steadying herself on the table, she apologized. "I'm sorry, sir, you surprised me."

"That's all right, Cosette. Let's try this again." Lenny again reached under her skirt and found her clitoris. "Ahhh, Cosette, you must like our company. You're already slippery." Lenny rubbed harder.

Patricia tried to stay still, but Lenny's relentless rubbing made that impossible. She squirmed against his hand, already feeling the need to orgasm. Marc's voice cut through her increasing arousal. "That's enough, Cosette. Serve us dinner now."

Reluctantly, she stepped away, breaking the connection with Lenny's finger. Trying to focus on the food, she served the two men. She scooped food onto their plates until they were overflowing. Several unopened containers still sat on the table. Then she opened and poured the wine.

Taking the opportunity to calm herself, Patricia retrieved the same pillow she had used earlier with Marc. Tossing it on the floor between the two men, she sat down, curling her legs around the side of the pillow, and waited.

4

Marc brushed the hair off of Patricia's forehead. "You see, Lenny, what an obedient hired girl I have? Cosette is not only lovely, she is willing."

"Let's see how willing, and how hungry, she is. Come here, little girl." Lenny swiveled her around and pulled her up to a kneeling position between his legs. Spreading a thick layer of pâté on a piece of French bread, he brought it close to Patricia's mouth. When she leaned forward to take a bite, he pulled it away.

"Not so fast, pretty lady." He took her hand and put it on his erect cock. "You have to rub this while you eat. When you finish what I give you, you have to kiss it and say 'thank you, sir.'"

A wiseass remark tumbled out before Patricia could stop it. "How do you know I won't bite it instead of kissing it? Remember, when I'm not Cosette, I'm Ms. Piranha. And I'm hungry."

"Well, now, Cosette, let's see how hungry you are. All right with you, Marc?"

"If she's says green, it's fine with me. Cosette?"

Looking over her shoulder at Marc, she negotiated. "If I do what he wants, then I am allowed to sit at the table with you and have some dinner. Otherwise, I'm yellow."

Lenny laughed. "You've got yourself one sassy bitch here, Marc. I like her." Lenny put his hand flat on her cheek and turned her head back to face him. "If you sit at the table and eat, you'll be paying for it all night. There won't be any more yellows, only red to stop the scene. And I leave. That's it, sweetheart. Take it or leave it."

"If you aren't afraid I'll bite it off, then I'm not afraid of what you'll do, either. If it's too much for me, I'll call red and show you to the door."

Lenny roughly groped her tit. "Doll, where have you been all my life?"

"Nowhere you would have gone." For some reason that baffled her, Patricia enjoyed sparring with Lenny. "When do I get to eat?"

"Right now, sweetheart." Lenny unzipped his jeans and his cock bulged out the fly. He also wore no underwear.

Patricia wasted no time. She wanted to prove to this man that she could hold her own with him. The competitive behavior that had pushed her into a successful career surfaced, and she aggressively licked his cock. For a moment, she forgot that Marc sat behind her watching. Then she felt his hand under her skirt.

"Lenny, I think she's forgotten who is in charge here." Marc pushed two fingers into her pussy. "She has to understand that she does what we tell her to do, and nothing more."

"For Christ's sake, Marc, don't stop her! This is fucking good head I'm getting."

"I'm not going to stop her, but I am going to smack her ass." Marc picked up the leather paddle from the chair and then leaned close to Patricia's ear. She had Lenny's cock in her mouth when he whispered, "When the paddle connects, you keep sucking, Cosette. This is our guest. It would be damn rude to bite him."

Lenny grunted, and then muttered, "She'd better not fucking bite me, if she knows what's good for her."

"I would take to heart what the man says, Cosette. You don't want to make him angry. I've seen what he can do when he's angry, and it isn't pretty."

Patricia knew Marc would not let Lenny hurt her, but she also understood the not-so-veiled threat in what he said. She had set herself up for a rougher night than she had anticipated. The only way out now would be to call red and end it.

Lenny had a thick cock, thicker than Marc's. It filled her mouth like a fat sausage she had eaten at the San Gennaro festival in Little Italy. She wondered if she could be losing it, unable to control the images floating through her mind. The picture of sucking that Italian sausage out of the hero sandwich would not go away.

The flat leather surface of the paddle connected with her ass. Marc did not hold back. He really whacked her. Forcing herself to stay relaxed, she kept licking and sucking Lenny's prick. She thought to curl her lips over her teeth, to keep from scraping him. The paddle connected again. The intense sting caused her to lurch forward. She regained her balance by leaning on Lenny's lap.

He reached down and fondled her breast. Marc whacked her again just as Lenny pinched her nipple. She moaned, and spit leaked out the corners of her mouth. She could taste Lenny's pre-cum, and hoped this lumberjack of a man would finish soon. She didn't know how long she could hold out, and shuddered to think of the consequences if she didn't.

When Marc smacked her a fourth time, something changed. The endorphins must have kicked in, because she stopped thinking. The sensation traveled through her body and filled her mind. She moaned again. Lenny's cock slipped from her mouth. She rubbed it against her face and licked it, like a dog relishing a bone.

"Oh, yeah, mama, you like dick. Do me some more. I want to come in that pretty mouth." Lenny stuffed his prick back in her mouth, and she obediently sucked. Marc continued to paddle her, each smack of leather against flesh taking her higher. Suddenly Lenny grunted and raised his ass off the chair. "Fuck yes, swallow it, bitch, swallow all of it." With one last crack of the paddle to punctuate the moment, Patricia swallowed Lenny's cum.

Lenny pulled his cock out of her mouth. Feeling dazed, she laid her head on his lap.

"Here, Cosette, sip this." Marc handed her his tumbler of Jack Daniel's. She lifted her head and took the glass.

"Marc, hand me a napkin. I need to clean up." Marc gave Lenny a napkin. He wiped himself off, and then tucked his business back into his jeans and zipped up.

Patricia still leaned against Lenny's knees. The whiskey burned her throat, but it did revive her. When she looked up at Marc, she saw him studying her. "Why don't you go to the bathroom and fix your lipstick? It's smeared on your face again. When you come back, you can tell us if you're still green."

She wobbled a bit when she stood, and Marc caught her arm. "Take the drink with you. When you come back, we'll have some food."

Her legs felt numb from kneeling so long. Pins and needles jabbed her feet as the nerves woke up. With as much dignity as she could manage in her disheveled state, she went to the bathroom and closed the door.

Taking a few minutes to collect herself before looking in the mirror, Patricia considered the implications of continuing. If she stayed, it promised to be a challenging evening, and surely there would be rougher sex ahead. She knew Lenny had the ropes and blindfold in the bag he gave to Marc.

She took a washcloth and wet it with cold water. Her ass burned like hell. Putting a cold cloth on it helped. After using the toilet, she also washed herself, realizing her thighs were sticky with her juice. When she rubbed her clit with the washcloth, she had a nearly overwhelming urge to bring herself off. Marc hadn't said not to, so she would still be playing by the rules.

But she decided against it. If she had an orgasm, she wanted them to give it to her. She had been rubbing herself off for months. Tonight, she didn't have to manage it alone. In fact, she didn't have to manage anything. They would do it for her. In that moment, she decided she wanted to stay, and she wanted whatever they would do to her.

She washed her face with cold water and fixed her makeup. There were two glasses with whiskey sitting on the sink, the one she hadn't finished earlier and the one Marc just gave to her. Combining them, she swallowed what was left in one gulp, washing away the last traces of Lenny's semen in her mouth. She chuckled, hoping the alcohol would also kill any germs he left behind. Still smiling, she opened the bathroom door.

Walking past the men sitting at the table, she went to the cupboard and refilled Marc's glass. She brought it, along with the bottle and two more glasses, back to the table. After giving Marc his glass, she poured some for Lenny and for herself. When she gave Lenny his glass, their eyes met for a moment, and he winked at her. Without really understanding how, she seemed to have won his respect.

"Do I get some food now?"

Marc smiled. "Help yourself."

She loaded up a plate with even more food than she had given the men, and also helped herself to the container of French onion soup, which no one had touched. Before sitting down, she walked around the table and stood in front of Lenny. Pointing to the pâté Lenny had spread for her, she asked, "Do I get that now?"

"I expect you do."

Knowing full well Marc could see her ass and pussy and that Lenny could see her tits, she bent over and waited for Lenny to feed it to her.

Lenny held the bread up to her mouth and she took a bite. She chewed and swallowed without standing, and then opened her mouth for more. When Lenny held up the rest of the bread, Patricia closed her mouth around it, as well as the tips of his fingers, licking his hand as she took the pâté.

After finishing her prize, she went back to her chair and sat down, the cool wood soothing her still-warm ass. Marc had said nothing since she returned to the table. Patricia glanced at him, and saw him obviously grinding his teeth. Figuring he might be jealous of the attention she had given Lenny, she couldn't resist chiding him. "You asked me to let you know if I'm still green. I am. Are you?"

"My dear, I won't be the one to stop the scene. What about you, Lenny?"

"Hell, no! Not with this hot lady for dessert!" Pointing to her container of onion soup, he added, "Cosette, could I have some of that?"

"But of course, monsieur." She handed him the container and a spoon. If flirting with Lenny made Marc jealous, she might have found his Achilles' heel. Watching Lenny fuck her might just push Marc more than he expected.

Both Patricia and Lenny ate ravenously. With some food in her stomach, Patricia felt much steadier and able to cope with whatever they threw at her. She noticed Marc only picked at his food, but continued to drink the Jack Daniel's. Not wanting him to get falling-down drunk, she interceded.

"Monsieur, is the food not satisfactory?"

"It's fine."

"Ah, but it must be bad. You have not eaten enough to keep a bird alive." Remembering the yogurt commercial that had inspired this evening, she slid out of her chair and sat down on Marc's lap. "Let me taste." She took a fork full of food from Marc's plate and ate it. "It is delicious! Perhaps Cosette will help you eat?"

Patricia shoved a fork full of food into Marc's mouth. He had no choice but to chew. "Monsieur Lenny, will you spread some pâté on the bread for me?"

"You got it, doll." Lenny slathered pâté on a chunk of bread and handed it to her.

It didn't matter that Patricia had a terrible French accent; she enjoyed being Cosette, the saucy French maid. She held the bread up for Marc, and he bit into it. "You see, I knew you would eat for Cosette. Maybe you will reward me and tickle my pussy?"

Marc nearly choked on the bread, and quickly swallowed what he had left in his mouth. Lenny offered his two cents. "Hey, man, if she wants her pussy tickled, do it. And pull down the front of her dress so we can see her tits. It'll get us warmed up for dessert."

Patricia kept feeding Marc while he tugged her dress and bra down. The elastic snapped back under her breasts, supporting them and pushing them up. Being preoccupied with her tits, Marc hardly noticed she continued to stuff forksful of food into his mouth.

He ate what she fed him, the tumbler of Jack Daniel's forgotten on the table. By the time he reached under her skirt, he had eaten most of what he had on his plate. When his middle finger found her clit, she squirmed on his lap. "Monsieur has a big appetite tonight. What else can Cosette do to make him happy?"

"Lenny, what can she do to make us happy?"

"She can clear the table." Lenny got up and found the shopping bag he had given to Marc. He took out the ropes and blindfold, as well as a vibrating dildo and a butt plug she recognized from his club. "Sweetheart, like I said, you're dessert."

Remembering her dream, she knew what to expect. Unless Marc deviated from the notes in her file at the last minute, she understood why Lenny told her to clear the table. Patricia quietly said to Marc, "This is it, isn't it?"

"Yes, unless you want out."

"I don't."

"Then clear the table, Cosette."

After she closed all the containers, she packed everything into the refrigerator. Marc and Lenny methodically tied lengths of rope to the table legs. Once she had wiped the table clean, they were ready for her. All thoughts of making Marc jealous by flirting with Lenny disappeared when Marc picked up the pillow and put it on the table.

"Bend over the table. Use the pillow to cushion your stomach, so the wood doesn't cut you."

Lenny startled her when he reached around and cupped her breast in his hand. "Make sure you're comfortable, pretty lady. You won't be getting up for a while. Marc, you said you have nipple clamps?"

"They're in my pocket." He gave the clamps to Lenny and then took off his coat. "I think I'd better turn up the air. It's fucking hot in here."

"You can say that again. And she's doing it!" Lenny circled around and stood in front of Patricia. "Pull your dress down to your waist and take off the bra."

Lenny's demeanor had changed. He seemed more ominous, even dangerous. For the first time that night, Patricia felt scared. As she undressed, she glanced at Marc for reassurance. He offered none. It really hit home that Marc intended to turn her over to Lenny. She almost called red.

Her mind racing, she stood still while Lenny put the nipple clamps on. She had agreed to no yellow calls, which meant she had to endure what happened or stop. Lenny tightened the clamps until she winced. He gave each screw another turn before he stopped.

"Now, bend over the table." Patricia bent over, adjusting the pillow to protect her stomach. Then she waited.

She felt Marc's hand on her foot, pulling her leg to the side. He looped the rope around her ankle a couple of times and then tied the end to the table leg. He did the same thing to the other leg.

Lenny stretched her arms straight out in front of her, as far as they would reach on the table. He secured her wrists with pieces of rope attached to the table legs at the other end, making sure to allow enough slack to reach under and fondle her breasts. When they finished, she lay bent over the table, spread-eagled, tied hand and foot. Except for the addition of the pillow, it exactly matched the image in her dream.

The blindfold was superfluous. She couldn't see anything but the surface of the table. But Marc still put it on her. The cessation of light did make a difference. She was bound and blind and the sense of helplessness enveloped her. Rather than causing panic, somehow it calmed her. She had no control over what happened now, no decisions to make. She had to endure whatever happened; they had left her only one option.

She felt a hand sliding up her leg, an anonymous hand, as she had no way of knowing if it was Lenny or Marc. Unless one of them spoke, she wouldn't know which one did what.

Then Lenny did say something. "Marc, in the bottom of that bag there is some lube. Get it for me."

Patricia heard paper rustling. "What the hell is this?"

"It's a ball gag. I brought it just in case."

"I don't want to gag her."

"We won't have to if she is quiet. With her mouth, that one's up for grabs." The edge in Lenny's voice both frightened and excited her.

She heard a squirting noise. Marc must have given Lenny the lube. "Ever had a butt plug, sweetheart? This one's a beauty. Too damn bad you can't see it."

Patricia felt something hard at her anus. With no thought given to gentleness, Lenny shoved a cone-shaped object into her rectum. She squealed, more in surprise than in pain. "Ever had her up the ass, Marc?"

"Are you kidding? Until this week, I haven't fucked her in months! Before that, she spent more time at her office than she did with me."

"Well, buddy, tonight's your chance. This plug will stretch her. Once I fuck her pussy, you might want her ass."

"I'll consider it. What do you say, Cosette?"

"Fuck you!"

"Better watch that, sweetheart. My main man Lenny knows his way around a ball gag. I have to admit, there have been times I could have used one with you."

"No shit!" Lenny twisted the plug, and it went deeper into her rectum. "What does she do, anyway?"

"She's an investment analyst, and she's good! That's how I can afford to pay for half the French restaurant you brought for dinner tonight."

"Why do they call her Ms. Piranha?"

"Her staircase to the top is littered with the carcasses of men she's eaten alive to get there."

"Is that so! Well, Ms. Piranha, you are Cosette tonight. And you belong to me!"

"Fuck you, too."

"Sweetheart, my prick will be in your pussy later. Right now, I'm using this."

Patricia heard buzzing, and knew Lenny had turned on the vibrator. "Shit, man, that damn thing is bigger than either of us!" Marc's comment made her squirm.

"And she'll love it. Just watch." Lenny started to insert the vibrating dildo. The butt plug almost came out. "Listen carefully, my little coquette, you have to resist pushing, and relax. There will be consequences if that plug comes out."

Marc leaned in close to her ear. "He means it. I watched him drip hot wax on the ass of a lady who couldn't keep it in."

"And then I fucked the living shit out of her asshole. She'll never forget that night."

"Neither will I. That's when I first thought about inviting you to have a go with my lady." Marc's revelation startled Patricia. She had no idea Marc had shared another woman with Lenny.

Again positioning the vibrator at Patricia's pussy hole, Lenny pushed the tip into her vagina. Patricia moaned and twisted on the table, scraping the nipple clamps on the wood. "Don't you fucking scratch this new table! Hold on, Lenny. Let me get a towel."

Patricia shouted, "What kind of prick are you? He's fucking me with a goddamn vibrator and you're worried about your table?"

"Exactly right. I'm worried about my table. Lift her up, Lenny, so I can slide this under her tits."

Lenny reached around with one arm and slid it under her belly. With seemingly no effort, he hoisted her up, the ropes tugging at her wrists. Marc slid a towel under her, her breasts pressing into the rough cloth when Lenny released her.

"Okay, man, continue."

"The pleasure is all mine." With no prelude, Lenny shoved the vibrator completely inside of her, only stopping when his hand hit her pussy. Patricia couldn't help it. The butt plug fell out.

"Marc, will you look at this? The plug came out. What do you think we should do?" Lenny pulled the dildo out and rammed it back into her. Patricia squealed.

"Let's ask her, Lenny. What to you think we should do, Tricia?"

Barely able to speak, but not wanting hot wax dripped on her bare ass, Patricia managed to say, "Please, Marc, hold it in, I can't."

"Lenny, should we be generous and hold it in?"

"No way, man! If you're down here with me, you'll work it. Fuck her asshole with it while I fuck her cunt."

Before Patricia could digest what they meant to do, she felt someone push the butt plug back in. Lenny again rammed the dildo back into her pussy, closely followed by the plug ramming her anus.

She squirmed on the table and squealed. The two men showed no mercy, fucking her senseless. Somewhere in the delirium of sensation that fogged her mind, she heard Lenny say, "Easy, Marc. We don't want her to come yet. I want to be in her pussy when she comes."

Marc's voice had a timbre she had never heard, hoarse and harsh. "Then fucking do it, man! I've wanted to see this for as long as I've known her. Fuck her until she can't walk!"

"Play with her tits while I fuck her. Make her squeal, but not so loud that anyone will call the cops."

With the blindfold on, Patricia could only sense Marc beside her. When he reached under her and grabbed the chain attached to the nipple clamps, she winced. Then he pulled the chain, hard. She screamed, louder than she meant to.

She felt Lenny rubbing his bare prick against her pussy. Then she heard something ripping, probably Lenny opening a condom. "Get the gag, man. We can't risk having the cops come."

Paper rustled. Before Patricia could call red, Marc stuffed something the size of a small orange in her mouth and fastened it around her head. Again in a feral voice, Marc instructed her. "Tricia, stay calm and breathe through your nose. Do you understand?"

She nodded her assent. The point where she could have called red had passed. She had to get through this. She hoped she wouldn't pass out.

"All right, she's gagged. Fuck her."

The next sensation made her scream, but only a grunt could be heard through the ball gag. Lenny's cock not only entered her pussy, he pushed his full length in with one stroke. With her legs spread and tied, she became nothing more than a hole to fuck. She couldn't move. Lenny held her hips and slammed into her again and again, his stamina seemingly endless. He pounded her, as she teetered on the edge of her own orgasm.

She felt Marc reach under her and grab the chain again. She couldn't stop him. He jerked the chain, her nipples pulling beyond endurance. She heard Lenny shout, "Fucking hell, man, she's coming. Yank it again!"

Marc jerked the chain again and her torso went rigid. Electricity surged through her body and her nerves crackled as her orgasm seized her. Lenny continued to thrust into her, and then he grunted like a rutting elk. "Fucking bitch, that's it, pull it out of me! Fuck, yes!" Lenny's pelvis hit her ass a half dozen times as he squirted his load into her cunt. With each thrust he grunted, and Marc laughed.

Lenny didn't withdraw his prick immediately, allowing himself to go flaccid inside of her. Patricia went limp on the table, feeling like a deflated party doll. She wanted to gasp for air, but couldn't with the gag in her mouth. She took deep breaths through her nose, until she could finally, breathe normally.

She felt Lenny back away. "Your turn, man. Do her ass, and I promise you, she'll come again. I'm going to have a drink and watch."

Quite unexpectedly, Marc slapped her ass with his hand.

"Tricia, as I remember, one of the men in your dream sodomized you. Well, sweetheart, it's about to become real."

He slapped her again, and massaged her buttocks. "I hope you're ready for this, because I sure as hell am."

Patricia recognized the feel of Marc's penis against her body, only this time, he spread her ass cheeks and poked at her bum hole. When the tip of his cock entered her anus, she nearly cried with relief that it felt slippery. He had applied the lubricant, so he wouldn't be dry-fucking her.

Unable to say anything, she endured the second assault. Marc allowed her time to adjust before pushing in deeper. When he did, she moaned, as loudly as the gag would permit. The involuntary urge to push his cock out caused her muscles to contract. Unlike the butt plug, his cock stayed inside of her.

"Jesus Christ, Lenny, she's tight as frigging hell! Her asshole is grabbing me."

"I told you, man. This one is made for it. Fuck her till she comes. She'll thank you for it and come back for more tomorrow."

Patricia could tell by the way Marc held her hips he intended to do as Lenny said. She wanted to brace herself, but like before, her anus became a hole to fuck. She couldn't move or do anything to prevent the violation of her body.

At that moment, Lenny pulled off the blindfold. She saw his face on the table next to hers. "Doll, I'll take off the gag if you give me a kiss with some tongue."

She nodded her agreement. Lenny undid the gag. "Do her, Marc." With intensity that nearly made her faint, Marc fucked her up the ass. The lubrication on his cock greased her up, and he pistoned in and out of her anus. Her own arousal surged when Lenny kissed her and at the same time, pulled the nipple clamps. She pushed her tongue into his mouth and he tugged the chain again.

Not believing it could be possible, she felt on the brink of another orgasm. She broke the connection with Lenny's mouth and gasped, "God, please, rub my clit. I want to come."

In a commanding voice, Marc shouted, "Lenny, do it! Make her come while I'm in her ass."

Lenny knocked his chair over as he got up. The thick finger that had rubbed her clit earlier found it again. With incredible strength, he lifted her off of the table with his arm and rubbed her, while Marc's prick continued to violate her ass. Lenny had left the ball gag beside her mouth. She stifled a scream and sunk her teeth into the ball as a violent orgasm ripped through her. Marc's fingers dug into her hips as he shuddered and pumped his cream into her ass.

5

Patricia dried herself after taking a long, hot shower. Lenny said it would help relieve the ache in her muscles from being stretched on the table. Marc gave her a robe to put on, a long white one with lace and pearls. It looked like lingerie meant for a wedding night, not for a bondage and discipline scene.

Nonetheless, she happily put it on. Looking in the mirror, she marveled at how it flowed over her body and accentuated her curves. Marc had spent a small fortune on this experiment with her, including all the clothes he had bought. She didn't know what to make of that.

When she came out, Marc stood at the sink with his shirt-sleeves rolled up, washing dishes.

"Isn't that my job? I'm the maid."

"Considering what we put you through, you've earned early release from the role."

"Where's Lenny?"

"He left."

"Why?"

"I asked him to leave. I wanted some time alone with you."

"What is your relationship with him, anyway?"

"He's a friend."

"Did you pay him to be here tonight?"

"Whatever arrangement we have is my business."

"Did you fuck the woman he dripped hot wax on?"

"That is also my business."

"Tell me, Marc, what is my business, besides the fact that the investments I made for you are paying for most of this?"

"Your concern should not be about how I spend my time or money, but about how to get your own life in order. That should be plenty to keep you occupied."

"Do you realize this is the first real conversation we've had since this whole thing started? There are no roles this time, only us."

"Perhaps we should go to bed before we start fighting again. I'm damn tired."

"I'm tired, too, but I don't feel like fighting, or sleeping. I actually feel very relaxed and comfortable."

"Well, there's a shocker!"

"Why the hell are you so testy? I'm the one who just got tied up and gangbanged!"

"Two men isn't a gang bang."

"In my experience, any number greater than one is a gang bang!" Patricia went to the cupboard and surveyed his liquor selection. "Christ, Marc, is whiskey all you drink? There are other choices available."

"There's some Remy Martin V.S.O.P in the back."

"So there is." She picked up a clean tumbler from the dish rack and poured herself a healthy serving. Leaning against the counter, she studied Marc's profile. The hard line of his jaw told her plenty. "Did Lenny piss you off before he left?"

"Why the hell would you ask that?" Marc slammed the dishrag into the water, splashing water on his shirt. "Shit! I should have taken it off before I started this." He undid the last few buttons, took off the shirt, and tossed it over a chair.

"I'm asking because something has you going. For once, I don't think it's me."

"Well, guess again. Lenny said to tell you anytime you need a partner, to come to the club. You'll be his special guest, and he'll show you the ropes privately."

Patricia didn't even try to hide her amusement. "You're jealous of him! I thought so! But seeing as how I got pussy fucked and then buttfucked, I really didn't have time to dwell on it."

"You certainly seemed to enjoy his company."

"You invited him here, I didn't."

"Do you want to see him again without me?"

"Hell, no! Is that what has you tied up in knots? Dr. Forrest, you need a serious reality check!"

"And Patricia Kendall, you need to get a handle on just how fucking sexy you are! Once you start putting it out there, Lenny is just the tip of the iceberg. I may lose you all over again, for a very different reason."

"Not to be trite, but how about if we cross that bridge when we come to it?"

"And when will that be?"

"Well, I suppose we have a few decisions to make before that happens. I think it's still too soon. What if this subversive therapy doesn't work, and I relapse into being a workaholic again?"

"Have you thought about your job or your BlackBerry tonight?"

"Actually, no. You took my BlackBerry. I have no idea where it is."

Marc picked up his coat from the chair and reached into the inside pocket. "Here. Have at it."

Patricia took her BlackBerry and turned it over in her hand. "You know, before this week, I would have been crazy not knowing what might be on this. Right now, I can honestly say I don't give a shit. Whatever is there will still be there on Monday morning." She put it on the counter without turning it on.

"Is that window dressing, Tricia, or is it real?"

"I don't know, Marc. It's what I'm feeling right now, but it took some extreme space to get me there. Will it last? You're the shrink, you tell me."

"I'm not asking as your shrink, and you know it."

"No, you're not, and according to what Dr. Dick told me, you're in violation of the agreement we made."

"Goddamn it, Patricia, his name is Dr. Richards! He doesn't deserve your bitchiness!"

"And I don't deserve your pissy mood! You made up the rules for this little game, and you're the one breaking them! This 'being ourselves' bullshit isn't working. Maybe I'd better get dressed and go home."

Patricia dumped her drink into the sink and turned to go back to the bathroom, where she had left her clothes. Marc grabbed her arm.

"Some rules are made to be broken." He swung her around, wrenching her arm as he did so.

"Fucking shit, Marc, you're hurting me!"

"Isn't that the point, my little love? Doesn't it hurt so good?" He held her tightly against his chest, and kissed her, his whiskers scratching her face. He forced his tongue inside her mouth and held her head still as he roughly licked the moist flesh.

Patricia pushed against his arms, digging her nails into his skin. She couldn't break free, and Marc didn't let go. She felt him tugging at the sash of the robe, which she had loosely tied. It easily pulled free. The robe opened and her breasts pressed against his bare chest. She stopped struggling, the feel of skin against skin placating her anger.

Marc broke the kiss, but still held her tightly. "That's better, Tricia. You don't really want to go, do you?"

Mollified, but still not convinced she could stay without having an argument, Patricia balked. "If I stay, you have to stick to the agreement: no unpacking our baggage and no confrontations. I won't fight with you, Marc. Fuck this red, white, and blue bullshit. I'll walk."

"All right. I'll keep my feelings to myself for now. But, damn it, Patricia, we have to talk about where we are with everything. You know that as well as I do."

"I know, but not yet. I can't, Marc, I just can't. Please, let's do more of what we've been doing. It's working for me."

Marc lowered her robe and kissed her shoulder. "It's working for me, too. I never knew I could get into topping."

"And I didn't know I would like being a bottom."

"You're a natural."

"I hope that's a good thing."

"Considering how this last week has been, I think it is." Marc kissed her neck, and then whispered in her ear. "Are you up for more? It's still early."

"It depends."

"On what?"

"On how rough it will be. I can't afford to go to work with bruises showing."

"I promise, the bruises won't show."

Patricia had to laugh. "You fucking bastard, when did you get so perverted?"

"When I realized how kinky you really are. Your file reads like an erotic novel. Do you know how many times I had to jerk off while reviewing Phil's notes about you?"

"How many?"

"See these calluses?" Marc held up his right hand and pointed to his palm. "They weren't there before I started reading your file."

"Of course, they have nothing to do with your karate classes!"

"Not that I am aware."

"Don't you know that's why God created K-Y, to keep wankers from getting calluses?"

"No, that's why God created pussy. It's a much better solution for the problem."

Patricia picked up Marc's hand and kissed his palm. "If I'm up for more, what do you have in mind?"

"That dream you had, about the servant girl and the master of the house. Didn't she bathe him?"

"Yes, among other things."

"Well, I'm the master of this house, and you've adopted the role of servant tonight. Considering our earlier activities, I should have a bath, don't you think?"

"And . . ."

"And what?"

"And what else?"

"Ah, my pet, that would be telling. Are you in?" Marc emphasized his point by rubbing his hard-on against her bare leg.

"It seems I should be asking you that." She ran her fingers through his thick, brown hair. "In keeping with our agreement, I'm green."

"Excellent!"

"How do you do this to me?"

"Do what to you?"

"Make me agree to things I never thought I would, or could."

"Could it be because we have something special between us?"

"Maybe. But I tend to think it has more to do with how well hung you are."

"Is that a fact?"

"It is indeed a fact."

The smile on Marc's face told Patricia the tension between them had broken. Relieved that the weekend might progress the way she imagined it would, she pushed her advantage. "Do I have any say about what happens tonight?"

Marc gave her a pointed look. "It depends."

"Okay, I'll bite. On what?"

"It depends on if I approve of your suggestions. Remember, in this space, I decide what happens."

"All right. I've agreed to that. But it seems I should at least be able to give some input."

"Tell me what."

Patricia stepped back. Marc made no attempt to stop her. To emphasize her point, she turned around and lifted her robe. "Is my ass red?"

"A bit." When she turned back to face him, Marc couldn't hide his grin.

"Well, Mr. Alpha Male, my ass is still recovering from the other night, and you gave it a few more whacks tonight. If I hope to be able to sit at my desk on Monday, I can't take much more."

"I understand."

"But will you back off with that?"

"It depends."

"Fuck, Marc! On what?"

"On how cooperative you are otherwise."

"What do you want me to do?"

"I don't know yet. Let's start by your drawing my bath. What did you do with the nipple clamps?"

"I left them on the bathroom sink."

"Then let's go to the bathroom. Is there anything else you don't want tonight?"

"Not that comes to mind. My ass is burning like hell. That's the only yellow I'm calling." Patricia suddenly realized yellow had been off limits earlier. "I can still call yellow, can't I?"

"Lenny said no yellow, I didn't." Marc looked around. "I don't see Lenny, do you?"

"No, you sent him back to his dungeon, to torment some other submissive soul."

"So I did. And you're sure you don't want to follow him there?"

"I'm quite sure. I want to be here with you."

"A few minutes ago, you wanted to leave."

"Only because I didn't want to fight. We're not fighting, so I'm not leaving."

"C'mon." Marc took Patricia's hand and pulled her toward the bathroom. He stopped outside the door. "You haven't told me, what do you think of this loft?"

"It has potential."

"Really. What would you do to it that I haven't?"

"A few more chairs, big, oversized ones. There's room. And pictures. Christ, Marc! The walls are bare. You have exquisite taste in art. Why haven't you put anything on the walls?"

"Because until this week, I didn't know if I would keep this place. Things have changed."

"Have they?"

"Patricia, you made me agree not to go there tonight. That being the case, why don't you draw my bath? I believe we have some therapeutic work to do."

"Is that what you call it?"

"Well, it's better than calling it a dom/sub scene, isn't it?"

"I suppose so." With no more discussion, Patricia went into the bathroom. She took her business suit and blouse off of the shower rod and hung them on the bathroom door with the French maid costume. Studying the clothes for a moment, she noticed the incongruity. "Look, Marc. Doesn't that just say it all? My life hanging on a door. It deserves a caption."

"How about, 'I'm all of this, and more.' Works for me."

"Me, too." She took a deep breath, as the full import of what was happening sank in. Assuming the role of the servant girl in her dream, she went back to the tub and turned on the faucet. "Sir, are you ready for your bath?"

"I am, dear heart. Take off your robe. I want to look at you as you bathe me."

Patricia took off her robe and put it on the hanger over her suit. When she returned to the tub, Marc had not yet undressed. Trying to retain the role, she politely admonished him. "Sir, you cannot bathe while clothed."

They stood face-to-face, Patricia completely naked and Marc wearing only his trousers and socks. Pointing to the nipple clamps, Marc also assumed his role. "I gave you a gift and you left it on the sink? Perhaps I don't want such an ungrateful girl in my bath with me!"

Surprising herself, Patricia responded to Marc's stern tone with an apology. "Oh sir, I am sorry! I forgot I left them there."

Without Marc telling her to do it, Patricia picked up the clamps. She fastened the chain around her neck and then carefully attached the clamps to her breasts. She tightened them to the point where she could feel their pinch, and then stopped. When she looked up, it startled her to see Marc stroking his erection through his trousers.

Suddenly realizing the tub had filled with water, she hurried to turn off the faucet. Marc never took his eyes off of her. His intense stare flustered her. She needed a few minutes to collect herself. "Sir, might I get you a drink before we begin?"

The idea seemed to appeal to Marc. "That would be appreciated, my dear. Get yourself one as well."

Patricia left Marc in the bathroom and went back to the kitchen. She retrieved two clean glasses and poured them each some Jack Daniel's. Bolting hers back in one gulp, she refilled her glass. As the warmth spread though her body, she returned to the bathroom.

Expecting to see Marc already undressed and in the tub, she was surprised to see him still standing there, waiting for her. She handed him his drink and set hers on the sink. Forgetting her role for a moment, she asked, "Why aren't you in the tub?"

"I'm waiting for you." He took a sip of whiskey. "I want you to undress me."

Marc continued to sip his drink and watch her. She could see his eyes moving down her body and back up again. She burned inside knowing he wanted her.

Slowly, deliberately, she put her hand on his chest and slid it down his belly. When she reached his waist, she opened his belt and unzipped his fly. Wanting him to suffer the same infuriating frustration as she had to endure, she lowered his trousers with excruciating slowness, and made sure their skin touched whenever possible.

"You have to sit. Otherwise, I can't take off your pants and socks."

Marc sat down on the toilet seat, his erect cock touching his stomach. Dutifully, Patricia knelt in front of him, first taking off his socks and then his trousers. She knew having his bare feet rubbed made him crazy. Before he could stand, she put his foot on her bare thigh and massaged it. His cock twitched as she rubbed.

"Suck my toes."

She had only ever done this once. Marc had ravaged her afterward, fucking her so hard she could barely breathe. Patricia picked up his foot. Bringing it close to her mouth, she leaned forward and licked the bottom. The glass he held nearly slipped from his hand. She stopped.

Marc put his glass on the sink. "Don't stop, Tricia. Do what I asked. Suck my toes!"

One by one, Patricia sucked his toes into her mouth. Before she reached the last one, he put his hand on her head and held her still. She had barely stopped sucking when suddenly he grabbed the chain attached to her nipples and pulled. She groaned as the pleasurable pain shot through her chest. Marc growled, "Help me into the tub."

She did as he asked, holding his arm as he stepped into the steaming water. As he lowered himself into his bath, she saw his cock leaking. Well beyond being shy about his condition, she spoke her mind. "Marc, can you handle this? If I bring you off now, in the tub, will you be able to manage anything else?"

"Don't fucking worry about what I can or can't handle, Tricia. You are here tonight to do as I say. Now, wash my prick!"

"Yes, sir." Even if she couldn't gauge his stamina, Patricia understood she had to relinquish control. This test could well determine her future and her ability to sustain balance in her life.

She knelt by the tub and lathered the washcloth with soap. Apart from the pleasure she would give him, she wanted to make sure she cleaned him thoroughly. If he could manage another erection tonight, she wanted his cock in her pussy. Once his arousal kicked in, he wouldn't even think about the implications of their earlier session.

Leaning back in the tub, Marc closed his eyes. She could tell by his breathing that it wouldn't take much to bring him off. Wanting to give him a chance to settle a bit, she put the soapy cloth on his chest, intending to slowly work her way down.

"Tricia, I said wash my prick!" His abrupt command startled her.

"Don't you want me to bathe you all over?"

Marc cupped her breast in his hand and squeezed. "I want you to wash my prick."

Again, his forcefulness both surprised and excited her. Unlike in her dream, she felt more in control. "Do you want to come or do you want me to stop before?"

"I want to come in your sweet hand, Tricia. If you're worried about later, don't. I'll make sure you're satisfied."

"Do I take that to the bank?"

"Yes, along with the portfolio you put together for me."

Patricia knew they were teetering on the brink of another argument. Not wanting the war of words to escalate, she dropped the washcloth and stood.

Marc sat up in the tub. "Where are you going?"

"Only to get your drink, sir." Patricia retrieved his glass and gave it to him. "You are tense. This will help you to relax." She again knelt by the tub and waited.

Marc stared at his glass and then bolted back the contents. He gave her the emptied tumbler, which she put on the floor. "I'm having trouble doing this."

"Doing what, Marc? I don't understand."

"Holding these roles. I don't want some fantasy servant to jerk me off. I want you to do it."

Patricia fished the washcloth and soap out of the water. "Well, I want you to fuck me, which is why I'm hesitant to do this. You've already ejaculated twice tonight. This will be three. Can you do four?"

"Try me."

Patricia again lathered up the washcloth. "All right, Mr. Stud. Here goes."

She wrapped the cloth around his cock and tightly closed her hand. Marc groaned. With no inclination toward gentleness, Patricia rubbed his prick, both scrubbing him clean and jerking him off. Satisfied she had properly washed him, she dropped the cloth.

Marc grabbed her hand. "Patricia, for Christ's sake, don't stop!"

"I'm not stopping." She had a sudden impulse to get into the tub with him. "Open your legs more."

Marc did as she asked. She crawled into the tub and knelt between his legs. The chain hanging from the nipple clamps floated in front of her as she again grasped Marc's cock. He grabbed the chain and tugged, her tender nipples stretching with agonizing pleasure pain.

Her grip tightened around his prick. "That's right, Tricia. Don't hold back." He jerked the chain again and she nearly toppled onto his chest. "Give me a hand job that's worth writing home about."

Regaining her balance, she hissed at him. "You fucking son of a bitch! You want me to jack you off? You got it!"

She found the soap and lathered up her hands. With speed worthy of a hooker masturbating a john, she pumped his cock. Marc never let go of the chain, holding it as he thrashed in the water. The sinewy veins throbbed as she beat him off, his dick hard and red. She loved how it felt in her hand, actually pulsing with life.

Suddenly he gasped with the desperation of a dying man struggling to breathe. He rasped out, "Jesus fucking Christ!" as semen burst from his penis, spraying her breasts with white cream. She didn't let go, continuing to pump as he spurted and splashed, covering the bathroom floor with water.

6

Marc came out of the bathroom with a towel wrapped around his waist. "I really made a mess in there."

"I know you did. Thanks for cleaning it up."

"Technically, I suppose I could have made you do it. But that hardly seemed fair."

"Excuse me, but I didn't know fair came into play with a dom/sub scene."

"I think we might have gone beyond the scene, don't you?"

"I know we did, and I'm glad about that."

"You are? Why?"

"Because the role playing only goes so far. There reaches a point where we have to come to terms with being ourselves."

"I thought you didn't want to go there tonight."

"I don't, at least not into the emotional part. It seems whenever we get close to the bone, we fight, and I can't fight anymore, Marc. The sniping and blaming are over, no matter how this all plays out."

"Then tell me what you do want."

"Do you think we can be this way with each other without the roles, and without arguing?"

"I don't know. With no setup, all we have left is the raw need to be dominant and submissive. Can you handle that?"

"I can be the puppet if you can handle pulling the strings."

Marc opened her robe and tugged the chain still attached to her nipples. "Just call me Geppetto."

Patricia looked up at the mezzanine overhead. "The bed is up there?"

"That's where I had them put it. It took four Teamster types to get the bedroom furniture up there. The two delivery guys had to call for reinforcements."

"How the devil do you get up there?"

"With the ladder, of course." Marc reached up and grabbed a handle, which Patricia hadn't noticed before. A ladder slid down to the floor. "The person who originally built this loft bedroom used the fire-escape ladder as inspiration. Unfortunately, they didn't finish it. As you can see, they left it an open platform, with no outside wall."

"And what happens if you're drunk and have to pee during the night?"

"You either hold it, or you be mighty damn careful coming down."

"Can't we have some stairs and a guardrail built for it? I don't want either of us to break our necks."

"We?"

Patricia smiled sheepishly. "I'm sorry, Freudian slip."

"Actually, it's good to hear you use the 'we' word again. I'll see what I can do about it. In the meantime, the ladder can double as a torture rack."

"What a comedian."

"Patricia, I'm not joking."

Marc's firm tone and somber expression made her shiver.

"What do you get out of this, Marc? Why are you so into seeing me helpless?"

"Why are you so into being helpless, Patricia? It seems the dynamic works both ways."

"It's about power, isn't it? Controlling and being controlled are two sides of the same coin."

"It's also about pleasure, Tricia, and about my being able to lead you into a place where you can't go alone. By allowing me control, you're giving yourself the freedom to let go and feel. I watch you feel, and I get off."

"You really enjoy it, don't you?"

"More than I ever expected to." Marc pointed to the ladder. "We'll start here, at the ladder, and then move up to the bed."

"Just like that?"

"Just like that. Take off your robe. I want you naked."

Patricia untied the sash of her robe. "Remember, no bruises."

"Correction, no bruises that show. Now, take off the robe, go to the ladder, and put your hands over your head."

Marc went to the closet and came back with a shopping bag. He took out a pair of leather handcuffs. "These are lined with fur that will protect your wrists."

"You've thought of everything, haven't you?"

"Lenny told me what works and what doesn't. So far, he's spot on."

Patricia tossed her robe onto the sofa. She leaned against the ladder and put her hands over her head. Marc wrapped the cuffs around a rung, and then fastened them around her wrists with Velcro tabs. She wouldn't be going anywhere until he released her.

Marc took off his towel. Much to Patricia's amazement, he again had a full-blown erection dangling from his groin. "Well, Mr. Stud, it looks like you are good for another one."

"Yes, I am, Ms. Piranha, but not until I'm ready." He stood

in front of her and stroked his cock. "You're fucking hot, Patricia. Too damn bad I don't have my digital camera here."

"What the hell would you do with pictures? Post them on the Internet?"

"It could mean a whole new career for you if I did."

Lenny had left the blindfold and ropes lying on the table. "I won't tie your ankles unless I have to, but I think I will use the blindfold. It's better if you can't see what's coming." Marc stretched the elastic around her head and covered her eyes. "Lights out, Tricia."

Patricia could see nothing, but she could hear Marc rummaging in the shopping bag. "You really are a merciless motherfucker, aren't you?"

"But Tricia, isn't that what you want?" Before she had a chance to spit out a retort, a flash of pain took her voice. Marc had smacked her pussy with something, she didn't know what. Another swat connected and she yelped, her knee pulling up in an involuntary defensive posture.

"Patricia!" She recognized the near growl in Marc's voice from their night at Lenny's dungeon. "Keep your legs down, or I will have to tie them to the ladder."

Practically panting with pain and desire, she gasped for air. "I don't think I can!"

"Oh, but pretty lady, you will!" The next thing she knew, Marc had pulled her legs open and lashed them with rope to the ladder. "Now they will stay open."

"My God, Marc, I can't stand it!" He didn't answer. "What the hell are you doing? Where did you go?" Panic welled up in her at being left bound and helpless.

"Steady, pretty lady, I'm just turning on some music." Marc put on some blues. The music calmed her, until he told her why he put it on. "This will cover any noise you might make, so I don't have to use the ball gag again."

"Marc, you're scaring me."

"Are you calling red?"

"No. At least not yet." Patricia took a deep breath. "Could you do what you did the other night? Give me a shot of whiskey. I'm shaking."

She heard the cupboard door open and knew Marc had gone for the Jack Daniel's. After taking a few more deep breaths, her heartbeat started to slow down.

The cool edge of a glass touched her lips. "I'm going to tip it now, Tricia. Swallow all at once, so you don't choke on it."

Marc poured the whiskey into her mouth and she drank it in one gulp. The heat of the liquor spread through her torso. "One more, please?"

He poured another shot into her mouth. This one melted some of the fear, and she began to relax.

"Is that enough?" Marc's voice had a hint of concern.

"It's enough. I'm all right. And I'm still green."

"Lenny really did call it before he left. He said you are one ballsy bitch."

"What an inspired quote! I'll have a tapestry commissioned on Monday."

Marc laughed. "If you can make jokes naked and tied to a ladder, about to be pussy whipped, you are definitely all right."

"Was there ever any doubt?"

"No."

The flash of pain hit again and she yelped. Her whole body tingled with the ripples of sensation.

Again struggling to breathe, she gasped for air. "What the fuck is that, Marc? It stings like hell!" She barely got the words out before he swatted her pussy again.

"It's a cat-o'-nine-tails, my little love. I do like the leather toys." The lash that followed connected with her upper thighs.

With each successive swat, Patricia went deeper into the

zone, that luscious, forbidden place where pain becomes sweet pleasure. When the leather bit into her skin, she moaned and trembled. Each time Marc swatted her pussy, her body ached for release. She lost track of time, and the number of times he lashed her. Dazed, she again felt the edge of a glass against her lips.

"Patricia, drink this. It will bring you around."

She drank the whiskey he gave her, coughing after she swallowed. Then she moaned. "Marc, I need to come. I'm throbbing with wanting it."

"Do you want me to fuck you until you come, Tricia? Say it! Ask me to fuck you until you come."

Patricia nearly sobbed. "For God's sake, yes! I want you to fuck me until I come. Please, Marc, put your cock in me and fuck me so hard."

She felt him pulling at the ropes around her ankles, untying her. Her knees felt rubbery, and she had trouble standing. "Patricia, I have you." Marc took the blindfold off. "When I unfasten the handcuffs, lean on me so you don't fall."

He didn't have to tell her to lean on him. When he released her wrists, she went limp. He caught her before she went down. "It's all right, sweetheart, take some time to get your land legs back."

Patricia flexed her fingers, working the circulation back into her hands. "We have to climb that damn ladder, don't we?"

"Yes, unless you want me to fuck you on the floor."

"Help me get to the bathroom. I have to go before I get up there."

Marc supported her as they walked together to the bathroom. He didn't leave while she used the toilet, waiting until she finished. His erect cock bobbed close to her face as she sat. She desperately wanted that hard rod inside of her.

She finished and washed. After a glass of water, she felt able to continue. "All right, I'm ready."

"Can you walk by yourself now?"

"I think so." She wobbled a bit when Marc stepped away. Steadying herself, she left the bathroom with no help.

Marc coached her about using the ladder. "You go up first, and I'll follow. Take it slowly, putting both feet on each rung. You're still shaky. I don't want you to fall."

She did exactly as he said. When she reached the top, she crawled onto the mezzanine on her hands and knees, with Marc close behind. "You fucking have to have stairs made for this damn thing! I feel like I'm climbing into a hayloft, not a bedroom!"

"I don't know. I rather enjoyed the view from back here."

"Very funny! Is there enough room to stand up?"

"Just. You'll be fine. My head almost hits the ceiling."

Patricia stood and looked around. "While you're at it, how about having that railing made? If I get trashed up here, I really will break my neck."

"You plan on getting trashed?"

"I hope so!"

"Well, then . . ." Marc took her hand and led her to the bed. "I bought this hoping we would share it."

Patricia trailed her hand over the footboard. "Where on earth did you find a leather bed?"

"It's leather and mahogany, with matching mahogany pieces. This is New York. You can find anything you want here."

Patricia picked up a leather strap with a buckle hanging on it from the side of the bed. Each corner had one. "And what are these?"

"Accessories."

"Do I need to ask what for?"

"Lie down, Patricia. Allow me to demonstrate."

"It's amazing!"

"What is?"

"This." Patricia brushed the tip of Marc's cock with her finger. "You're still hard, even after having three orgasms in a few hours. Are you taking Viagra or something?"

"This is all me, sweetheart! I don't need no stinking Viagra! And I'm ready for more." Marc took the strap from her hand. "Lie down and put your hands over your head."

"You're going to strap me to the bed, aren't you?"

"That's exactly what I'm going to do."

"Well, at least I won't fall down if I'm on the bed!" Patricia crawled on the bed, not caring that Marc had a bird's eye view of both her ass and her pussy. She stretched out in the middle, with ample room left on either side. "This is a fucking big bed!"

"I told you, it's a king, just in case we ever have company."

"Like Lenny?" She knew that one would hit a nerve.

"Actually, maybe I should get the name and number of that cutie he used as a candlestick. She likes the dripping-wax thing."

Patricia flexed her legs and arms, prepping for being immobilized again. "I'll bring my popcorn and watch, thank you very much."

"Where's your sense of adventure?"

"My sense of adventure is alive and well in an East Village loft, thank you very much! Hot wax leaving me cold doesn't mean I'm not adventurous!"

"Well, let's see how daring you are!" Marc wrapped the leather strap around her ankle and then buckled it. After doing the same to the other ankle, he adjusted the tension of the straps. He did the same to her wrists. When he finished, Patricia lay spread-eagled, bound hand and foot to the bed.

Patricia realized Marc hadn't thought to bring the blindfold. Grateful for the freedom to see, she watched Marc's cock as he walked around the bed. He had sustained his erection since before he tied her to the ladder. Without question, he would fuck her. Her cunt burned with wanting him inside. She waited for him to get on the bed with her. He didn't.

"What are you doing? Aren't we going to fuck?"

"Eventually."

"What the hell does that mean?"

"It means eventually." He reached under the bed and pulled out a plastic box. "Let's see what we might have in here."

"Marc!"

"Yes, Patricia?"

"I can't take much more!"

"Oh, I think you can. I made sure this box would be slow, sweet torture." Patricia groaned. "What, you don't want to be teased?" Marc took a feather duster out of the box.

"Shit, Marc! You know how ticklish I am!"

"Yes, as a matter of fact I do." He brushed the feathers between her breasts, down her belly and then lightly tickled her pussy.

Patricia squirmed and pulled at the restraints. "Damn it, Marc! I would rather be spanked than this. I can't stand it!"

"Stop resisting, Patricia!" Marc stopped, his jaw drawing a hard line across his face. "Let me give you some advice."

"A message from the oracle! I can't fucking wait to hear this!"

"You are hardly in a position at the moment to piss me off, sweetheart! I would watch your mouth if I were you." Marc leaned in close to her ear. "Now listen closely."

"Do I have a choice?"

"No, actually you don't. When we met for our first session on Monday, you said something that impressed me. You said, 'I just want to turn off my mind and feel.' Well, Tricia, that's what this is about. I'm giving you that opportunity. What you do with it is up to you."

"And what are you doing Marc, besides getting your rocks off?"

"I'm feeling with you, possibly for the first time since I've known you."

The seriousness of Marc's comment silenced Patricia. During the last week, the wall between them had begun to crumble. Unless she wanted to risk rebuilding it, she had to check her sarcasm at the door.

"All right, you win. I'll do what you tell me to do, as long as you promise to fuck me." Marc's cock dangled close to her face, like a carrot in front of a donkey. "I want your prick in me. What do I have to do to get it there?"

"All you have to do is relax. Give yourself permission to feel. Don't resist, don't struggle, and more than anything, don't think. Focus on the sensations, nothing else."

"Now you sound like Dr. Ruth. Next thing you'll be telling me is that an orgasm is just a reflex, like a sneeze!"

"Well, it is. She's right."

"It's been hours since I've had one, I don't remember."

"I promise you Patricia, before I take off those leather shackles, you will be royally fucked and you will have an orgasm." Again the tension between them had broken without a fight.

"So, what else do you have in your Pandora's box?"

"Since you asked, let me have a look." Marc rummaged though the box and pulled out a small red bottle. "Let's see if this works."

Patricia strained to see. "What is it?"

"The description says, 'Feel the heat. Hot warming lubricant is the perfect addition to a night of passion.' Sounds like just what the doctor ordered, doesn't it?"

"Oh, God!"

Marc squirted a dollop onto his hand. "Smell that! It's cherry.

Says on the bottle it's edible." Marc cupped Patricia's vulva in his palm and massaged the lotion deep into the soft tissue. Watching her closely, he added, "Considerate of them to flavor it. Makes me want to eat your pussy."

Marc squirted more of the warming lube directly onto her clitoris. The initial cool sensation quickly warmed as he continued to rub her. She had the impulse to raise her hips off of the bed to meet his hand, but quickly stifled the urge. Marc noticed.

"Tricia, what are you feeling?"

"I don't know."

"Yes, you do. You suddenly tightened up. Tell me why."

"I want to cry."

"Why?"

"You don't remember, do you?"

"Remember what?"

"You touched me like this the first time we made love." She almost sobbed, but forced it into a laugh. "Of course, I wasn't tied to the bed that night with horse liniment making my clit hot."

"Your clit was plenty hot. I remember everything about that night."

"You do?"

"Of course I do. That was the night I fell in love with you."

Patricia couldn't stop the tears from sliding down her cheek. "You're fucking killing me."

"No, Patricia, I'm fucking keeping you alive."

The sob that broke from Patricia's throat rang in her own ears. Something shattered inside her heart, the icy wall that insulated her from the world and froze Marc out of her life. The cherry red heat seemed to travel from her groin into her chest, its warmth melting the disintegrating ice.

She continued to cry. Marc did not stop rubbing her clit, and the effects of the lotion became more intense. "Shhhh, Patricia, it's all right. This is the release you need. Allow yourself the space to feel. That's all there is, just the feeling. Whatever it is, it's all right."

Marc's voice soothed her. Even though the tears continued to run down her cheeks, her focus shifted to the incredible heat building in her belly. It wasn't just the lube, something else had kicked in. In a fluid motion, her hips undulated underneath Marc's hand.

He stopped rubbing her and held his hand still. She masturbated against his fingers, her movement limited by her bondage. Even with the leather straps holding her ankles and wrists, she could tilt her pelvis and rub.

"That's right, pretty lady, make it feel good. I know you want to come, but you haven't told me how much. How much do you want to come, Tricia?"

Marc's hypnotic monotone lulled her, and calmed her. "Marc, I want to come so bad, but I want to come with you inside me. Please, fuck me and make me come. Dear God, please do it now!"

"First, let's clean your face." After grabbing a wad of tissues from a box by the bed, Marc wiped Patricia's nose and dried her cheeks. "There, that's better. And let's take these off." After unhooking the chain around her neck, Marc opened the screws on the nipple clamps and gently pulled them off of her breasts. He tossed them into the box with the other toys, and then leaned over and kissed her breasts. "You are so fucking beautiful, Tricia."

Patricia started to speak. Marc put his fingertips on her lips. "Yes, I remember. I said the same thing on that first night. It's just as true now as it was then."

Opening her mouth, Patricia licked Marc's fingers, the same fingers that had masturbated her a few minutes ago. She tasted her own juice, tinged with cherry. Marc did not pull his hand away. She closed her mouth over his fingertips and sucked them, the way she had sucked his cock earlier that night.

Marc stretched out on the bed. He slid his fingers out of her mouth and traced a line across her lips. Then he kissed her. His lips barely touched hers at first, the softness of the kiss belying the growing fire. When Marc rolled on top of her, she didn't expect it. She moaned into his mouth as he kissed her harder, his tongue licking her own.

She lay helpless on the bed as he probed between her legs, his cock sliding against her clit. When she felt his tip begin to penetrate her, she pushed upward as hard as she could. The force of her thrust buried his cock in her cunt.

Marc gasped, breaking the kiss. Patricia knew the deep penetration caught him by surprise. She squirmed against him, hoping he would fuck her the way she wanted to be fucked. Through clenched teeth, she hissed, "Fuck me, Mr. Stud. Fuck me and make me come."

"Oh, yes, pretty lady. I'm going to fuck you so good!"

Patricia did not anticipate Marc's ferocity. He pulled out and drove himself back into her like a pile driver. Spread-eagled and pinned to the bed, she could do nothing to blunt the force of his thrusts. She squealed as he pounded her, the music not nearly covering the sound. With her pussy stretched wide open, Marc's prick sunk into her cunt up to his balls with each lunge.

His face contorted with lust, Marc growled at her, "I'm going to fuck you until you come, just like you asked me to do." She knew he meant it.

As he fucked her, the heat of the lube mixed with the juice in her cunt. She knew Marc had to feel it too, the burning sensation increasing with the friction. With all the concentration she could muster, she focused on the feeling, the tingles a warning that her climax would be soon. As the tingles became spasms, her orgasm shook her body, and she screamed.

"That's it, bitch, come for me! Come hard for me!" Patricia convulsed underneath Marc as he continued to pound her. "Oh, yeah, your cunt is so hot, Jesus Christ, yes!" Marc pumped his climax into her belly, the same way he had that first night.

Marc didn't move for several minutes. Patricia had the overwhelming urge to hold him and stroke his hair. But she couldn't, still being strapped to the bed.

"Marc?"

"Yeah, Patricia, I know, I have to get off of you."

"And you have to undo these straps."

Marc smiled down at her. "Now why would I want to do that?"

"Marc Forrest, you'd better damn well let me loose!"

Marc kissed her nose. "Or what?"

"Or you had better be ready to fuck me again PDQ."

"I surrender! You win this one. Four is it tonight. You've drained me dry."

"It's about goddamn time! Your balls will need to be rehydrated after tonight!"

"It's good to hear you've recovered your voice." Marc got up and unbuckled the leather straps. "Do you need to use the toilet before we go to sleep?"

"As much as I don't want to tackle that ladder, I probably should. I smell like a fresh-baked cherry pie! I need to wash."

"I should, too. My dick is still hot."

"I'm happy to know you shared the joy." Patricia looked over the edge of the mezzanine. "If I jump, do you think I could hit the sofa?"

"I wouldn't recommend it. Let me go down first. I'll help you."

Marc steadied Patricia as she climbed down the ladder. After they both used the toilet and washed, Marc poured them each a Remy Martin. "May I toast our evening before we go to bed?"

"I would like that."

Marc raised his glass. “To be in love is to be with you.” He clinked his glass against Patricia’s. “Thank you for your trust in me.”

“Thank you for giving me another chance.” They drank their nightcap, and then climbed the ladder, together.

7

When Patricia woke up, she smelled coffee. It took her a moment to remember where she was. When she did, she touched the pillow beside her and whispered, "Marc." She sat up, and saw her new robe lying on the bottom of the bed. Marc had obviously been awake for a while.

She got up and put on the robe. Looking down into the living room, she saw Marc on the sofa drinking a cup of coffee and reading the *New York Times*. "What time is it?"

Marc glanced at his watch. "It's twelve-thirty."

"Jesus! Why didn't you wake me up?"

He turned around and looked up at her. "Because you needed to sleep. Do you need some help with the ladder?"

"Maybe. Let me try it." Like she had the night before, Patricia got down on her hands and knees. Then she carefully lowered one foot onto the ladder. Pulling herself upright, she put the other foot on the rung. "I think I've got it. Getting on the damn thing is half the battle."

She slowly climbed down, making sure she didn't step on the bottom of the robe. Marc grabbed her around the waist as she reached the bottom. "That robe is lovely, but I enjoyed the view last night much more."

"I'm sure you did. By the way, thank you for this. It's beautiful."

"I thought you would like it. I remembered the other one you had once upon a time."

"I thought you did. I noticed it last night."

"How do you feel today?"

"Great! I slept like a baby, as you already know."

"No dreams?"

"None that I remember. I think my subconscious is on hiatus, probably conjuring up more demons to be released."

"Given your inclination for sexualizing your demons, your nontraditional therapy may have to continue for some time."

"Do I need Dr. Dick's . . ." Patricia stopped herself. "I'm sorry, I mean Dr. Richards' permission for that?"

"No. He already told me you're too damn smart for traditional therapy. It didn't work with you. You played it like a chess game. He told me you outmaneuvered him every time."

"I couldn't help it. I didn't want him in my stuff."

"At least you told him enough about 'your stuff' to let me know what the hell was going on. Why didn't you tell me about all of this, Patricia? Lord knows I asked often enough."

"Could I have some coffee before we go there? And I could really use some food."

"All we have is leftover French. You have your choice of beef bourguignon, coq au vin, quiche Lorraine, and I think some scallops provencale. There are also appetizers and desserts left."

"Lenny really did buy one of everything, didn't he?"

"He certainly did. We put away a substantial part of it last night, and there is still a heap of food left."

"How about the quiche Lorraine? At least it has eggs in it."

Patricia helped herself to some coffee while Marc heated the quiche in the microwave. He also put plates, silverware, and napkins on the table. "Tricia, can you bring the carafe of coffee and some milk? I need a refill."

Patricia brought the coffee and refilled his cup. "I'm getting used to your calling me Tricia. That's been a hard one for me."

"I know it has. I've always liked it."

"Dr. Richards helped me realize why I'm so sensitive about it."

"Did he? I don't remember reading that in your file."

"That's because I never told him. After a session where I talked about my parents, I remembered a conversation I had with my father. He always called me Tricia. We had a fight about my majoring in business management and finance. I remember distinctly what he said. 'Tricia, you'll never amount to anything in business. Investing money is a man's world. You'll end up being somebody's secretary.' I became Patricia that day. I never used Tricia again and I've never looked back."

"When I called you Tricia, you heard your father, didn't you?"

"I suppose I did." Marc held her chair as she sat down. "It's a bitter pill to swallow, finding out I've spent my adult life trying to prove my father wrong."

"Well, you sure as hell have!"

"And my emotions went into a cryogenic freeze because of it."

"Why didn't you tell Phil about the connection you made about your name? Your therapist should be told those things."

"You're talking like a shrink now, Marc. This isn't the kind of shit I talk about. You know that."

"You told him about all of the sexual turmoil. That's pretty damn personal, Tricia!"

Patricia sipped her coffee and smiled. "He's such a conservative stuffed shirt! I did it mostly for the shock value. I couldn't tell if he squirmed because I made him uncomfortable or if it turned him on. Maybe both."

"Well, that conservative stuffed shirt is responsible for your being here, and for this." Marc got up. He went to the bookshelf under the mezzanine and picked up an envelope. After giving it to Patricia, he sat back down.

"What's this?"

"Open it."

Patricia unclasped the envelope and looked inside. "Marc, I don't understand. I signed these and gave them to my lawyer months ago. He told me he sent them to your lawyer. I thought you had signed them and filed them."

"I meant to. But Phil convinced me that we shouldn't get legally separated until he had a chance to work with you some more. Then he came up with this unusual version of marriage counseling."

"But if you haven't filed them, the clock isn't ticking yet. We have to be separated on paper for a year before we can file for a no-fault divorce."

"And what if I told you I want to come home?"

Patricia put her coffee cup down, her hand visibly shaking. "But you told me you wanted out, that you couldn't live with me anymore. You made that very clear when you left me."

"I said that before you went into therapy, and before I understood what you've been holding inside."

"When Dr. Richards told me you were willing to work with me, I thought you were just making sure I would be all right, I mean, all right without you. I didn't know you were considering coming back."

"I didn't either. Not until this week. But goddamnit, Patricia, I still love you. I never wanted to get divorced, but I couldn't reach you. You shut me out emotionally and physically. I couldn't live like that anymore."

Tears slid down Patricia's cheeks. "I couldn't help it. Once they made me a partner, I knew they were watching my performance. I had to make the grade, Marc, I just had to. I didn't mean to freeze you out, it just happened."

Marc handed her a napkin. "You know, this is twice in two days you've cried. I don't remember the last time I saw you cry."

"I cried when I signed those damn papers! I cried myself to sleep for a week after I sent them back to my lawyer."

"I didn't know that."

"How could you? And how could you know how many nights I hugged your pillow before I went to sleep, and how many times I picked up the phone to ask you to give me another chance?"

"For God's sake, Patricia, why the fuck didn't you?"

Patricia swallowed a sob. "Because I didn't think you loved me anymore. And honestly, I didn't blame you. Who could love Ms. Piranha?"

Marc took her hand. "I could. And I still do. Patricia, you've made it. You are a success. You don't have to prove anything to anyone, not to me, and certainly not to your father."

Even with the tears, Patricia laughed. "What about Dr. Dick?"

"Phil will no doubt miss your sexy stories, but you owe him no explanation. Our reconciliation is enough."

"Are we reconciling?"

"If you'll let me move back home."

"But you already have an apartment. And what about this place?"

"The apartment I have is a sublet, which is almost up. I meant to move into this loft, now that I've decided to keep it."

"What happens to the loft if you're coming home?"

"I'm still keeping it. It's our special place. I can't let it go."

"Can we afford to keep two apartments in Manhattan?"

"Patricia. Of course we can! We're doing it now."

"I'm all fucked up. You're right. The value of both properties will only go up. If we keep them for a few years, we'll stand to make a huge profit by selling them."

Marc laughed. "Your BlackBerry is still on the counter. Do you want it, Ms. Piranha?"

"Fuck, no." Patricia sipped her coffee. "All I want right now is more coffee, and some more of this quiche."

"And all I want is you." Marc refilled her cup as she ate. "We have to also agree on something else."

"What?"

"That we will continue playing, and maybe visit Lenny's once in a while."

"You like all of this, don't you?"

"More than I ever thought I would. When Phil first suggested it, I'm sure he thought it would be no more than some spanking and perhaps some light bondage, something to suggest your dreams. He wanted us to have some common ground, where we could work through our problems."

"He really is a stuffed shirt. When I first told him about my dreams, he kept clearing his throat. Every session after that, he kept a glass of water and some throat lozenges by his chair."

"He is old school, Patricia, and Freudian. You presented him with a challenge, which I think is why he initially consulted with me. Once we talked, he came to the conclusion that I could handle your inclinations much more than he could."

"No shit!"

"Let me ask you something?"

"And what would that be, Dr. Forrest?"

"What do you still want to do? I've arranged a sampling of scenes from your file, and added a few personal touches to keep you guessing. If we're going to go on this way as a couple, I need to know what you want."

"One thing has been missing that I wanted this week."

"What did I miss?"

"An over-the-knee spanking. Did Dr. Richards record my tutor/schoolgirl fantasy?"

"In great detail. I think he liked that one. Do you want to do it?"

"Another time we can do the whole thing. Today, I just want it to be you."

"Meaning?"

"Meaning . . ." Patricia stopped and took another sip of coffee. "Jesus, I can't believe I'm actually going to say this."

"Say it, Patricia. You've got to get used to talking to me about what you want, and what you are feeling. Whether or not we can make this work depends on it."

"If you remember, in the fantasy, the tutor spanks the girl for being naughty, or for not having her homework finished, or for any number of other transgressions."

"I remember very well."

"If you read it, you know what happens."

"Tricia, you're talking around it. You're still not telling me what you want."

"All right. I'll say it! Once you come back home, I want you to spank me when I get out of line. If I'm being a bitch, pull up my skirt, pull down my panties and wallop my ass!" Patricia closed her eyes and squeezed Marc's hand. "If you play with my pussy while you spank me, and then fuck me, that would be even better."

Marc guided Patricia's hand to his lap. She felt his erection. "I think I can agree to that."

"It feels like you've recovered from last night."

"Have you?"

"Quite nicely, thank you."

Marc stroked his hard-on with Patricia's hand. "Have you been a naughty girl, Patricia?"

"I have been a very naughty girl, Dr. Forrest."

"Do you think you should be disciplined for being naughty?"

"At least several times a week, here at the loft. If I'm being a very bad girl, I may need to be disciplined every night at home, before bed."

"We will have to agree on some rules for being at home. Even if you don't break any of them, there will need to be ongoing lessons in obedience. Is that understood?"

"Understood." Marc moved his hand. Patricia continued to stroke his cock. He touched the lapel of her robe, and then let his hand rest on her breast. "When I saw this robe, I remembered the one you wore on our wedding night. It looked like this."

"I still have it."

"You do? I haven't seen it in years."

"I stored the robe and negligee with my wedding dress."

"When I thought of our wedding night, and seeing you in that lingerie, I had to buy this. I'm glad you like it."

"I do. I feel like we had our wedding night all over again last night."

"In a peculiar way, I think we did." Marc pulled the robe open, exposing her breasts. He cupped the soft flesh in his hand. "Christ, I love your tits. I always have."

"It used to embarrass me when you would stare at them. It doesn't anymore."

"Patricia, men like tits. It's just the way it is."

"Then you won't mind if I want to wear the biker babe costume again? It was the first time I've ever gone out dressed like that. It turned me on to have men look at my chest."

"We'll wear those clothes when we go to Lenny's." Marc pinched her nipple. "Who's your daddy?"

"You are."

"And who decides the scene we're playing?"

"You do."

"Are you ready for some discipline, Patricia?"

"What do you want me to do?"

"I want you to tell me why I should spank you. How have you been a naughty girl?"

Patricia wanted to hit a nerve. "I liked it when Lenny fucked me. I want him to fuck me again." She saw Marc's jaw tighten. Bull's-eye!

Marc's demeanor changed. She could feel it. "Is that so? What else do you want Lenny to do?"

"When we go to his place, maybe he could join us in the dungeon and teach you more of his tricks."

"I know plenty already, Tricia, enough to keep you happy for a good long while." He grabbed her hand and pulled her to her feet. "Come here!"

She didn't really walk to the sofa, Marc pulled her there. He sat down. "Take off your robe and lie across my lap."

Making sure she stood directly in front of him, Patricia opened her robe and let it fall to the floor. Before she could lie across his lap, Marc stopped her. He opened his pants and unzipped his fly. After exposing his prick, he patted his lap. "Lie down, Tricia."

She lay down on her belly across Marc's lap, her breasts dangling over his leg. The rush of freedom she felt in that moment made her heady. Her exhilaration increased even more when Marc said, "Spread your legs wide open, Tricia. When I tell you to get naked and lie across my lap at home, you will always spread your legs wide apart so I can play with your pussy. Do you understand?"

"I will, I promise."

"Good." Anticipating the first swat, Patricia tensed. "Relax, sweetheart. You know this is for your own good." Marc slapped her with the palm of his hand, the sting unexpectedly hard. She winced. Before the second smack came, he tickled her pussy lips. The surge of heat moved from her ass to her clitoris. "Do you like that, Tricia?"

"Yes, very much."

"I'm going to teach you how to enjoy being spanked." He slapped her ass again, and then rubbed her pussy. "It won't be long before your libido makes the connection between being spanked and being turned on. Once I'm home, we will work on giving you an orgasm from just being spanked."

Patricia could hardly believe this fantasy come true. Marc wanted to do this as much as she did. She whispered, "Thank you."

"What did you say?"

"I said thank you."

Marc pushed his cock into her side. "That's good, Tricia, that's very good. That shows a willingness to be disciplined." He pushed two fingers into her cunt. "Thank me again and tell me why."

She squirmed on his lap as he finger fucked her. "Thank you, Marc, for topping me. Thank you for disciplining me. And thank you for loving me."

Marc slapped her ass again, this time not pausing to play with her pussy before the next smack. The sting from the slaps came so close together, she lost track of how many times he smacked her. She found the zone quickly this time, and relaxed into it. She lost herself in the sensation. When he reached under her and pinched her nipple, she jumped.

"Patricia, I told you to sit back on the sofa!"

"I'm sorry. I didn't hear you. She obediently stood, and then sat down beside Marc. Marc knelt in front of her. "Spread your legs. I wanted to eat your pussy last night, and never did. I want to do it now."

Patricia slid forward and opened her legs, her bare ass sinking into the leather sofa. Marc immediately put his hands on her inner thighs, opening her legs even wider. After spreading her pussy lips open with his fingers, he leaned forward and sucked her clit into his mouth.

"Fucking Christ, Marc, that's good!"

He licked and sucked her clit avidly, even voraciously. She pushed against his face, wanting him to suck her harder. When she did, he bit her, the way a cat nips at the hand of a beloved owner when playing. It didn't hurt, but the pressure of his teeth made her groan. He stopped and lifted his head. "Did I hurt you?"

"Fuck, no! It feels wonderful!"

Patricia remembered how much she wanted to hold him the night before and couldn't. She sat up. "May I take off your shirt? I want to touch you."

Marc's smile gave her the answer she wanted. She leaned forward and unbuttoned his shirt. She rubbed his chest with both hands, and then slid her fingers through his hair. He kissed her arms, and then buried his face between her breasts. More than anything, she wanted him inside of her. She whispered into his ear, "Marc, please, let's make love like we did on our wedding night."

Marc stood. He took off his clothes, his naked body shining as the sunlight from the window streaked across the room. She lay down on the sofa, pulling her knees up to her chest, completely opening herself for his entry.

He mounted her, pushing his cock into her. He kissed her deeply, passionately, and then, again, consummated their marriage.

FIT TO BE TIED

LISA G. RILEY

Acknowledgments

Thanks to my mother, Gloris B. Riley (1938–2000), for always encouraging me. I love and miss you, Mom. Thanks to Dyanne Davis for always reading when I needed you to and for laughing and being silly with me. By the way, you might *think* that your love scenes aren't all that steamy, but they are!

LGR

1

From beneath thick lashes, Chloe Johnson Carnegie trained her eyes on the man sitting next to her at the bar, and just as quickly took them off him again. He was still staring at her. Every time she did her little thing—played peekaboo—she found his intense brown eyes trained steadily on her. His bold, unflinching stare excited her beyond belief. And she knew that he knew it. She felt his eyes travel insolently and leisurely over her body for what could have easily been the tenth time in as many minutes, and suppressed a shiver when her nipples suddenly hardened and pushed against her bra. She had to stop herself from looking at him in dismay, while she prayed he didn't notice the evidence of her arousal. What was he doing to her? She closed her eyes and took a deep breath.

This is ridiculous, she thought as she picked up the disgustingly sweet wine cooler and took a sip. Men have stared at you before. Pull yourself together. Normally, she would have glared a man down until he looked away, or if he were entirely too bold, a soft-spoken insult would send him on his way. But not tonight. Tonight was different. Tonight she was going to go buck wild and she'd promised herself that no matter how difficult it was, she'd do it.

"So what brings you to our neck of the woods?"

Startled, Chloe looked up to find the grizzled old bartender looking at her in question as he cleaned a glass. "Pardon?"

"If you'll excuse me for saying so, miss, you don't exactly look like the type of person who would come in here."

"Oh. Umm." Chloe quickly thought of a lie. "I just wanted to try it, that's all. I mean, my office is just a couple of blocks from here and I've never been in. I just thought I'd stop by for a drink after work."

"Well, what do you think of the place?"

Uncomfortable, Chloe tried to think of something nice to say about the bar. She heard a snicker to her right and turned to look at the man next to her. "I'm sorry, do I amuse you?"

The man took his time answering. He took a drink of his beer, put the bottle down on the bar, and turned to look at her. "Yep."

"And why would that be?" Chloe's back was up. She couldn't stand to be laughed at, even if the man doing it was sexy and drop-dead gorgeous.

"Because you don't belong here. You ordered white wine, which Clancy doesn't stock. This is a beer-drinking crowd, lady. You don't belong here any more than white wine does."

Chloe looked him over disdainfully from his head to his scuffed boots. "Mind your own business." The order was succinct. She ignored the man's smirk and turned back to the bartender. She smiled at his laughter and asked, "Are you Clancy?"

"Yes, I am."

"Well, *Clancy*," she emphasized his name to make it clear that she was talking only to him, "Now that Mr. Know-it-All is minding his own business, I'd like to say that I think your place is perfect. Perfect for what I need right now."

"Thank you, miss," Clancy said with a smile. "Here, have some peanuts." He pulled a large bag of peanuts and a bowl from beneath the bar. "Let me know if you need anything else," he finished and, after topping off the bowl, he went down to the other end of the bar.

"Will do," Chloe murmured. She sighed and for at least the fifth time, looked down at the man's hands from the corner of her eye. She couldn't help herself; the sexy masculinity of them demanded her attention again and again. The palms were wide and strong looking with ridges of calluses, and the fingers . . . *God, the fingers!* The long, thick bluntness of them almost made her weep from edgy excitement.

Her bottom lip went between her teeth in jealous anticipation when those fingers wiped away the condensation on his beer bottle. The moan that wanted to hurl itself between her lips was swallowed back as she imagined that each brush was a stroke against her needy, greedy flesh. The shiver, however, refused to be repressed this time and it flowed hard through her body. The slight movement sent her skin into hypersensitive overdrive as it brushed against her clothing, and she almost ran her own hands over her body just to find some relief from the torture.

When the man rubbed his fingers against the bottle one last time before gripping the long neck to lift it to his mouth, her breath caught on a loud sigh as she followed the bottle's ascent. It came out in a deflating whoosh when he drank. Needing a drink herself now, she picked up her wine cooler and drained the bottle. She was so caught up in her own lust that she didn't even realize that she had turned on her barstool so that she was completely facing him.

But he did.

Logan hid his "gotcha" smile behind another drink of beer and looked at the woman. It was obvious from the near orgasm she'd just had after he'd deliberately teased her by playing with his beer bottle that the lady had a hand fetish. *Little freak.* She hadn't been able to keep her eyes off his hands for longer than a few minutes since she'd sat down. He'd noticed her as soon as she walked into Clancy's, and she looked way too classy to even be in the neighborhood, let alone in the long, narrow, smoke-filled room optimistically called a bar.

The middle corner of the wraparound bar where he sat gave him a full view of the door, which was to his right and down a short hallway. When customers walked in, what they saw first was the right side of the bar until they turned and walked farther in and saw the four small table-and-chair sets behind the bar. Clancy's was hidden and discreet and nobody minded your business, which was exactly why he liked it. So when she'd walked in, he'd automatically looked up to see who it was. He would have gone back to his drink, except she seemed so out of her element. And she'd looked so uncertain as she'd stood hesitantly near the door that he hadn't been able to take his eyes off her.

She'd stood there for long moments, giving him a chance to check her out. She was short but built, and the expensive slacks and blouse didn't hide the fact. She wasn't quite the brick house Lionel and the rest of the boys had sung so gleefully about, but she had more than enough for a man to hold on to while he sank gratefully into her. She was damn near perfect, was what she was. Plump breasts, small waist and rounded hips—hell, she *was* perfect! And he just knew that with a front like that, the back of her would be a treat all its own. Long experience studying the intricacies of women's bodies told him that her behind would definitely have some heft to it. It just had to. The laws of physics demanded it, damn it.

He'd sized up her body in a few seconds and lifted his gaze to her face and got lost in her eyes. Tawny brown orbs had peered at him from beneath dark lids surrounded by long curly lashes. They were a little shy, a little nervous, and seemed to be almost pleading with him for help. Curious, he'd lifted a brow, but just as he was preparing to rise to go over to her, she'd broken eye contact, licked her lips, took a deep breath, and started walking toward his side of the bar. The lady was on a mission. After her eyes had moved away from his, he took in the rest of her pretty features. Dark smooth skin stretched over a pert nose, a stubborn little chin, and high cheekbones. The short cap of straight black hair that stopped just short of her ears showed off her face perfectly.

When she'd walked past him to take the stool next to his, he'd gotten a good whiff of her. She smelled as expensive as she looked. Clancy had hurried over to take her order and her soft, cultured voice had requested white wine. Logan had noticed her embarrassment when Clancy had told her that he didn't carry it. When Clancy had offered her a wine cooler instead, he'd heard the relief in her voice when she'd accepted. Just as he'd noticed the expression of distaste when she'd taken her first sip from the bottle . . . and the way she kept peeking at him, each time with a little more boldness. He knew that she was trying to make a decision.

He'd noticed everything because he couldn't take his eyes off her. He knew it was bold and rude, but when he wanted something or someone, he didn't make a secret of it. And he wanted her. At first he thought his staring might make her uncomfortable, but when her nipples poked against her silk shirt trying to see the light of day, he didn't think about it anymore. And all bets were definitely off when she practically came just from looking at his hands. That criminally sexy, helpless little shiver she gave at the end put the cap on things and screwed it tight, as far as he was concerned. But she would come to him. He knew that she wasn't the kind of girl who usually picked up men in bars, so he would let her decide what to do, but that didn't mean he couldn't help her make the right decision. *It's on, little lady.*

He finished his beer as he stared at her some more. Her eyes were on his hands again, so he lifted one to his face and rubbed the tips of his fingers first across his top lip and then across the bottom one. He followed that up with a slow lick of his tongue across the rim of his bottom lip. He heard her breath catch and tried not to grin. *Your move, sweetheart.*

Chloe let her eyes follow the trail of his tongue in painful, hungry silence. Jesus God, the man was dangerous. Should she do it? *Stop stalling, girl*, she silently chided herself. *You know you want the man. And it's pretty damn obvious that he wants you. It's an easy answer. Imagine all of that . . . that . . . manliness spread out* na-ked *on top of you . . . and covering every little inch*. Her breath shuddered and so did she. Absently, she turned back to face the bar. She had to admit to herself: he was fine as all get out.

Surreptitiously, she studied the muscular ranginess of his body that was noticeable even under the jeans and work shirt he wore. He had a lean muscularity that made her want to strip him bare of that shirt and undershirt and let her fingers do the walking. She *knew* he had a set of those washboard abs, the kind that fingers could press into and bounce back from because they were so hard and defined. Still keeping her head turned slightly toward him, she let her eyes travel up to his face.

It was handsome enough, with the fullest lips she'd ever seen on a man, a prominent jawline, and the usual Roman nose that had a slight bump on the bridge that signified a break at some point. His eyes were thickly lashed and a deep, dark brown that made a nonswimming woman want to willingly drown in them. She ought to know because she'd already had to stop herself from taking that suicidal dive several times since she'd gotten there. The short, thick, brown hair on his head made her want to run her fingers through it—right before she used it as leverage to snatch his head to her body where that wicked tongue of his could work its magic.

The parts of her body that she referred to as her three home-girls (because they were always there and always, *always* on the lookout for her pleasure) clamored to full attention when the thought of his tongue exploded into her head. The two up top were so hard now that it was almost painful. Chloe looked at him again. And found him looking right at her. His brow was lifted in challenge, as if to say, "*Bring it on.*" Chloe turned to fully face him again and stood. *That's it,* she thought resolutely. *Girls, let's go have some fun.*

Logan watched her take the few steps necessary so that she was standing in front of him. He looked into her eyes. Some of the bravery of seconds before had faded, but not all of it. He let his brow lift again in question and watched as her chin went up a notch. *Atta girl,* he thought with sneaky glee, *show me what's what.*

"Have you got condoms?" he heard her say and almost reared back in surprise. Well, what a way to take the bull by the horns.

"Yes, I do. And your name would be . . . ?" He was sorry to see her falter. Just for a few seconds, though.

"I'm sorry. I've never done this—"

No shit.

"Well, never mind. You don't need to know all of that. It's Trixie. My name is Trixie."

Yeah, right.

Logan held out his hand. "It's nice to meet you, ah, did you say . . ." The name was so clichéd he could barely get it out without laughing. " 'Trixie?' "

"Yes, I did," she said in a determined voice.

"Well, if you're Trixie, then I'm Rod," he said and watched

her lips twist in disbelief. He looked down at her left hand. There was no ring. He frowned. The line where a ring had once been was still quite visible. He looked back up into those soft, amber eyes. "Are you sure you want to do this?" he asked her.

"What? Of course I am."

"All right, then. I've got you for the entire night," he told her.

She frowned. "I didn't say I'd be your prostitute."

He laughed. "I know you didn't. I just want to take my time with you."

Chloe smiled. "Sounds like a plan to me."

"All right, then. There's a hotel down the street," he said as he threw money on the bar. "Let's go . . . Trixie."

2

"Wait," Chloe said when he began to stand. She stepped between his thighs, settling her hands on his shoulder. "I've been wanting to do this all evening," she whispered and bent her head. Her tongue slipped out to lick his lips a few times before she got her teeth into the act, biting and nipping gently at the middle of his top lip that protruded slightly.

He moaned and Chloe, feeling completely seduced now, covered his mouth with hers and swallowed the sound. Reaching down, she lifted his hands and placed them on the sides of her torso so that they were resting near the undersides of her breasts. When she felt his fingers squeeze and caress her skin and brush against her breasts, she sighed in relief and joy, her knees buckling so that she fell into him.

Logan gripped her tightly, his fingers digging into her as every single one of his senses greedily took her in. He pushed his tongue against hers and pulled and sucked it into his own mouth, making her slump against him with a soft little sigh of surrender. She moved in closer and he nestled himself in the vee of her thighs, groaning when she widened her stance a bit to enclose his jeans-covered, already hard dick and thrust her hips at him. He transferred his hands from her rib cage to her ass, where he gripped her tightly, his fingers alternately releasing and sinking into the plentiful flesh. Near the end of his control, but unable to help himself, he squeezed and pulled her closer, grinding her against him again and again. Common sense finally got through, telling him that as much as he wanted to, he couldn't actually fuck her in the bar.

Reluctantly, he broke the kiss and gently pushed her back away from him. She was looking up at him with wide, surprised eyes, her breaths coming in quick, shallow pants. Her tongue shot out to lick his lips and he couldn't resist kissing her again. He rested his forehead on hers, giving himself a chance to catch his breath.

"Let's go," he growled.

Chloe stood in the middle of the hotel room, barely remembering how she had gotten there. Everything was sort of a blur, but she vaguely remembered holding hands with "Rod" and almost running to keep up with him as his long, quick strides ate up the distance to the hotel in record time. He'd checked them in (all the while using one finger to caress her between her butt cheeks while she leaned into him and tried to stifle her moans). And now she stood in the middle of the hotel room as he closed the door behind them, trying to remember how she'd gotten there. His hands had been all over her in the elevator, stringing her out so skillfully that she thought she'd explode from the tension. Her body still burned and tingled where his hands had been.

Chloe came out of her daze and started noticing her surroundings. The mauve curtains and the bedspread covering the queen-sized bed were nice, she thought—right before he grabbed her and pulled her into his body.

He ravished her mouth, biting and sucking on her tongue

until she was straining against him, her teeth clicking against his as she tried to appease her hunger. The kiss was purely carnal, but was not enough to even begin to take the edge off. Chloe moved in closer, wanting to lose herself inside him as the heat burned a huge trail through her body. The kiss simply was not enough. She needed to feel him pushing inside her. She needed to ride. "The bed," she begged into his mouth. "We need the bed. Now."

"The first time is going to be hard and fast," he said as he unbuttoned her blouse and stripped it from her body. Her bra was next.

"Good," she said and finished unbuttoning his shirt to pull it off him. She began to undo his belt buckle and froze when she felt his mouth on her breast.

"Keep going," he told her through a mouthful of nipple as his hands went to her slacks.

Chloe struggled to finish unbuckling his belt. "Ahh," she moaned and unbuttoned and unzipped his jeans. Eyes closed and her head thrown back because he'd begun to use his teeth, she slid her hands into his boxers and started pushing both them and his jeans down his thighs. She felt him push her slacks and panties down so that they fell around her ankles and off. She screamed when he pushed a finger into her. "Oh, God!" Her thighs opened wide and her hands went to his arms, where she held on for dear life.

"Reach into my back pocket and get my wallet," he said as he continued to work her mercilessly with his fingers—one pushing inside while another one stroked her clitoris.

Chloe opened her eyes and looked down at him. His eyes were narrowed in concentration and his mouth was still on her breast. Had he said something? "Wha . . ." she stopped to catch her breath and gather her thoughts when he used his thumb to press on that little bundle of nerves while two of his fingers now slid in and out . . . in and out. "What?"

Logan felt her cream spill out to drench his fingers and made a guttural sound in his throat, the need to feel himself moving inside her riding him hard now. He lifted his mouth from her breast, pulled his hand away, picked her up, and carried her over to the bed. "Reach into my back pocket and get my wallet," he said again.

Chloe obeyed him this time, feeling like a dose of cold water had been splashed on her face. His mouth was gone. His fingers were gone. What the hell?

"Very good, Trixie," Logan said when she pulled out the wallet. "Now get the condom out and push my jeans down just a little more." When she'd done that, he sat on the end of the bed and placed her astride his thighs.

Chloe looked down at the huge, thickly veined cock that was standing at attention, waiting just for her. She licked her lips. It was perfect for a hard ride. Completely anxious to fill herself with him, she ripped the package with her teeth and pulled the condom out. He was slick, hot, and thick against her sensitive palms and her labia clenched fitfully in anticipation. She used his shoulders as leverage and lifted herself to her knees, groaning and squirming helplessly when his hands went to her butt—fingers digging, palms pushing. Her thighs shook as she lowered her body just enough to take in his pulsing tip and her eyes slowly fell shut. *Ahh, so good.* He felt so good. Opening and stretching to receive him became the goal of the moment, and unadulterated greed and satisfaction could be heard in the sounds she made in the back of her throat as she sucked him in.

His hands grasped her waist and slammed her down upon him so that his long, thick length was filling her to the hilt. He slid in wetly and smoothly, squeezing into the tight, hot moistness and leaving an explosion of heat wherever he touched. Chloe went insane. Broken, untamed cries escaped her throat as the intense heat roared through her body and she rode the storm, bucking wildly on his lap. It was over for her before he could pull out and thrust and she uttered one last shriek before falling against him.

Logan opened his mouth, catching her nipple when it brushed against his lips. He sucked her hard, biting and laving until she was squirming on his dick again, mewling in near agony at the renewed, intense pleasure. She tried to regain some sense of sanity, but couldn't as he controlled her every movement with his hands, furiously slamming her down as he drove up into her.

Chloe couldn't help it—she screamed, over and over again, as a second orgasm forcefully tore through her in shocking pleasure. His hands tightened on her waist with bruising force, and he slammed her down and held her there, his penis lengthening inside her as he came. Hard and long. She knew she'd be sore and bruised later from the rough treatment, but she couldn't care as she clamped him securely within her body.

Logan let her rest against him for a few seconds before he lifted her over his head so that she was lying face down on the bed. "Don't move," he said.

"A bomb couldn't blast me from this bed," Chloe said in a weak voice as she prepared to get comfortable for sleep.

"No." Logan's voice was implacable as he held her in place. "I said don't move."

Chloe turned her head to look at him. Shit. What had she gotten herself into? She thought this even as the little jerk of fear sent a little thrill down her spine. "Excuse me?" She tried to turn over, but he held her ankles.

"No, don't move," he told her again, this time much more gently. Chloe looked in his eyes. He looked calmly back at her, his eyes unflinching and she let herself be reassured. She turned her head back around.

Logan sat on the bed to take off his boots and the rest of his clothes. "You have the most incredible ass," he said and reached out to rub and caress it. He felt her shiver. "In fact, I love your entire body." As he spoke, he used both hands to fondle her ass cheeks. He then trailed his hands down to her thighs, pressing his fingers deep into tender flesh and eliciting a gut-level groan from her. "Feel good?"

"God, yes."

"Good." He continued to massage her body, concentrating more on a specific area when she moaned in satisfaction. Her calves received special attention, as did the arches of her feet. By the time he was finished, she was just how he wanted her—completely relaxed. Her slow, steady breathing told him that she was close to falling asleep.

"Now," he said with a light slap to her ass, followed by a kiss to take away the sting. "Crawl up to the headboard and get on your knees."

Panting in excitement from the slap to her ass and from wondering what was going to happen next, Chloe obeyed. She felt the bed dip with his weight as he got fully on it and moved toward her.

"Open your thighs and hold on to the headboard." As he was talking, he was adjusting her himself. Chloe blindly obeyed. She helplessly mewled her surrender when the heat of him surrounded her as he knelt behind her and his bare chest pressed against her back. She pushed back against him and to her surprise felt his dick—full and hard again—against her ass. Wantonly, she made small movements so that his cock was sliding up and down the crease between her butt cheeks.

Logan was enjoying it as much as she, but knew he had to stop her before he did something she may not necessarily be ready for. "Hey," he whispered in her ear and stilled her motions. "Slow down—reel it in, Lady T. I'm not wearing a condom and this ass of yours is giving me definite ideas. Kinky, dirty ones."

It was hard, but Chloe made herself stop. "Just hurry up!" she demanded breathlessly.

"Well, you know what they say," Logan began as he lightly licked the back of her bent neck from her hairline to the first round bone pushing against her skin. "Patience is a virtue," he finished right before he bit down on that bone, causing her to jerk in his hands and let out a brief scream. He smiled against her skin and put his agile tongue to further use, sliding it slickly down until he had reached the bottom of her spine.

He stopped. He could feel her holding her breath, waiting for what he would do next. When her breath shuddered out, he held her by her hips and pressed open-mouthed wet kisses across her lower back, growling when her body released her essence to burst forth into the air. Her smell invaded his nostrils and he greedily sucked it in as he bathed the two dimples at the top of her butt with his tongue. He licked and sucked at her and couldn't get enough of the clean, sweet taste of her skin.

His mouth worshipped at the altar of what he'd come to think of as "the great ass." Each scrape of his teeth, each lick of his tongue, every whisper of his breath against her taut, sensitive skin was homage to the needy, voracious lust that had grabbed ahold of him the moment he saw her, and it rode him still. There was no appeasing it and he gladly let it take control, biting down fiercely on one butt cheek and making her buck against him and moan her surprise and impatience.

The heady, musky smell emanating from between her thighs beckoned him until his face was pressed between her thighs and he was licking her anywhere his tongue could reach. It wasn't enough and abruptly he pulled away to lie on his back so his face was beneath her body, directly in line with her quickening mound.

"I need to taste. Lower yourself," he demanded and wrapped his arms around her upper thighs to do it himself. His mouth was already open when he forcefully slammed her down on his face. She cried out and he suckled harder. The taste of her just made him want more, and the more she bounced, squirmed, and moaned, the tighter he held her. Her thighs were quivering, her voice was getting hoarse, and he was getting hungrier. He craned his neck to follow the rise and fall of her body, eating her out and gulping down every drop of cream that leaked from her body. His hunger would not, could not be satisfied and he let it have its way.

The pleasure was close to unbearable. Chloe clutched at the headboard and tried not to claw her way through the wood. She fell forward and felt his hands tighten on her thighs and spread them even further apart. His tongue and teeth seemed to be everywhere at once and she couldn't get ahold of her senses. She was in agony, riding his face and listening to the slurping sounds he made as he devoured her. She actually felt her toes curl when he tongued the sensitive insides of her labia, first one and then the other. She felt on fire and the heat only intensified as he feasted, sucking her clitoris to the roof of his mouth and grazing it with his teeth. And God help her, she fed herself to him, blindly grinding herself into his face. Working on self-motivated instinct, she closed her knees around his head, ensuring that she got as much of the intense pleasure as she could.

When he gently bit down on her labia and opened his mouth wide enough to suck them entirely inside, sucking and slurping while his tongue worked its way into her opening, she gladly said good-bye to her sanity. It was too much . . . too intense . . . too perfect to take and she struggled to get away.

But he held her securely in his grip, licking, sucking, lapping, *drinking* until she had gone even beyond wild and her mind emptied of everything but the insanity of the moment. Her thighs shook, her arms quivered under the strain, and she rode his mouth and screamed until she couldn't do either anymore.

Logan felt her weight fall away from his body and released her from his grasp. She didn't make a sound and he knew she was exhausted. He took her by her waist and gently laid her on her back on the bed, smiling when she said a tired "thank you."

"Don't thank me yet, baby," he said roughly, right before he opened her legs and buried his rock-hard penis inside her in one swift motion. "That's right, sweetheart," he encouraged when she wrapped both her legs and arms around him at the same time. "Hold on tight."

3

Logan held "Trixie" in his arms and thought about the night he'd just had with her. Four times. They'd made love four times and he still wanted more of her. He'd been greedy and sometimes a little rough, but she'd been right there with him, even initiating it herself the last time. He stared into the darkness. Not for the first time, he wondered if she'd let him in enough to really get to know her, or if they would go back to their normal lives when morning broke.

She murmured something in her sleep and he focused his attention on her again. He lifted her hand to kiss her long, tapered fingers and was reminded that he was annoyed. He rose naked from the bed and stalked over to the desk where she'd dropped her purse earlier in the evening. Picking up the small, expensive bag, he opened it and rooted around inside until he found what he wanted.

He walked back to the bed and sat near her hip, turning on the lamp and adjusting it so that the light was shining directly in her face.

"Hey!" Chloe came out of a deep sleep. Artificial light was

always the one thing guaranteed to wake her up. "Logan!" she protested.

In answer, he said three words. "Put them on."

Chloe looked at the marquis diamond ring and matching gold band he was holding out to her (practically shoving them in her face, actually) and then looked back up at his face. It wasn't happy. She took the rings and slid them back on, pouting all the while because she knew she was in for a fight. "Now, be reasonable, Lo—"

"No. There was no reason to take them off in the first place."

"I disagree. I wanted the game to be authentic, so I couldn't very well walk into Clancy's with my rings on. Then you would have known that I was married."

"Well," Logan began calmly. "Seeing as you're married *to me,* there was no way I couldn't have known."

Chloe's bottom lip poked out even farther at that bit of logic. "Oh, you know what I mean, Logan. Stop being obtuse."

"You know I'm right, Chlo. Just don't ever take them off again. I don't care what game we're playing."

Now Chloe smiled. "But you have to admit, the game brought a whole new level of excitement to the mix, didn't it?"

He leaned in to press a kiss to her mouth. "Yes, it was exciting. But then again, I get excited just looking at you. It's been that way for a long time—from the minute I met you, in fact."

"We only met seven months ago," she reminded him.

"Exactly, and I've been excited ever since."

She chuckled and put her arms around his neck, rubbing her nipples against his hairy chest. "I'm so glad you're back."

He held her waist. "And I'm glad to be back. Now behave and stop tempting me. You know you're not ready to go again."

"I know, but I missed you," she said plaintively and kissed his chin.

"I missed you too, baby," Logan said and kissed the top of her head. "Right now we're going to bed," he said.

Chloe released him to lie back down. She was sore, yes, but she still wanted him between her thighs again. She had a healthy sexual appetite. Truth be told, she was just an under-cover freak, but not many people knew that. Not even Logan, really. He knew that she loved sex and that she wanted to have it as frequently as possible, but he didn't know about her secret desires. Tonight was the first time she'd given him even a glimpse of that side of her.

"So, were you completely shocked when you called from Cleveland and I asked you to play this game with me?" she asked him once he was lying beside her in bed.

"Shocked isn't really the word," Logan said. "Surprised is a better one."

"Really? I didn't shock you?"

"No, I know what a complete sex fiend you are. Now, I can't say that I was expecting you to call with the idea of pre-tending to be strangers—clichéd as it was—but it isn't a com-plete surprise that you wanted to play a game."

"Clichéd! Huh, I thought it was creative."

"Oh, come on, Chloe. Picking up a stranger in a smoky dive isn't clichéd to you?"

"Hmph. Whatever, Logan. It made you hard," she reminded him.

"Even clichés have their uses," he said with a wicked grin.

Chloe sighed. That darn grin of his always made her hot. It was pure sin. Logan knew it, and was unapologetic about it. All he had to do was flash it at her and she was clenching her thighs together so her "homegirl" below wouldn't attack him. This time Chloe ignored her and laughed at the grin. "I knew you'd love it."

"Oh, yeah. It was definitely hot. Even your nervousness and then your sass turned me on. And I just loved the name Trixie," he said so that she understood that he didn't. He laughed when she frowned.

"Well, you weren't much better, *Rod*. How original."

"I was just trying to show you that I could be just as uninspired as you."

"Ha."

"So, why'd you do it? What made you come up with the idea in the first place?"

"I thought of it after you'd been gone for two days. I was inspired by the fact that I missed you and I thought it would be great for both of us."

"Well, it certainly is different from what I'm used to getting when I come home from a trip," he said. "It beats the hell out of a simple ride home from the airport."

"I thought it might."

"Putting some of my old work clothes in the backseat of the car so I could change when I landed at the airport was a stroke of genius."

"It added to the appeal of the game: *Wealthy woman picks up unknown, blue-collar man in bar.* Just the forbidden feel of it made me hot."

"Little liar. You're almost always hot," he teased.

"True," she admitted with a sigh. She studied him from beneath her lashes, wishing she could share everything with him. He had loved her idea tonight, but she didn't know if he'd be ready for, or accepting of her secret. She'd never even thought to be ashamed of it until she'd met Logan's boss. She sighed. It was all about perception, and she didn't want to jeopardize her husband's job.

Logan felt the sudden tension in the quiet. "What is it, sweetheart?"

Chloe looked into his eyes and then away again. She couldn't do it. What if he didn't understand or couldn't forgive her? "Hmm? Nothing."

Logan hid his disappointment. He knew that there was

something she was keeping from him and it bothered the living hell out of him.

"Anyway, how was Cleveland?" she began. "Did you get the contract?" He was the vice president of one of the largest building firms in the country and for the past few months, he'd been courting the city government of Cleveland for a multi-million-dollar complex the city wanted to build to draw in more tourists.

"It went well, I think. It's just a matter of convincing city planners that an out-of-town firm is a better choice than a locally owned one."

"When do you expect a final decision? They've been putting you guys through hoops for weeks now."

"It should come within a month or so."

"Oh, that would be awesome. If you get this contract for the firm, you'll be a shoo-in for the presidency."

"Carter hasn't officially announced his retirement—it's just a rumor so far. And besides, even though Carter is ready to retire and I've been one of his right-hand men for at least two years, I know the fact that I'm only thirty bothers him. He's old school and believes that youth equals irresponsibility."

"That can't be true, otherwise he wouldn't have trusted you for the past couple of years," Chloe pointed out.

"Trusting someone to help run the company is not the same as trusting someone to run the company itself," Logan said and yawned.

"And I suppose your meeting and marrying me all within four months doesn't help the situation, does it? He probably thinks you're really irresponsible now."

Logan saw that she was really worried and kissed her forehead. "Actually, sweetheart, you don't know this, but at the wedding, he took me aside and told me how pleased he was that I bit the bullet and did the right thing by you and married you."

Chloe frowned and leaned on her elbow to look at him. "Come again?"

"He thought you were pregnant."

"No way!"

"Yep, I'm afraid so. He went on and on about how rare it is these days to see a young man like myself stepping up and doing the right thing."

"Well, I know you set him straight on the matter."

"Damn right, I did," he said with a definitive nod. "I told him that I couldn't do anything less. Of course I would marry you when you were three months preg—" The rest of what he was going to say was cut off by a mouthful of pillow.

"Don't play, Logan. You better not have told him that."

Logan laughed as he removed the pillow. "Relax. I'm just kidding. Of course I told him the truth."

"And that is?"

"That I fell in love with you almost the second I saw you, and the only reason we weren't married any sooner is because I had a hell of a time convincing you not to be so conventional."

Chloe leaned over to peck him on the lips. "And aren't you lucky that your powers of persuasion are so powerful?" she teased.

"Yes, I am," he agreed in all seriousness as he pulled her back down in his arms, where she put a leg over his thighs and rested her head on his chest. He caressed the back of her leg from knee to butt.

"Mmmm, that feels good," Chloe murmured sleepily as the effects of the day caught up with her once again. "Logan?"

"Hmm?"

"Are you sure that marrying me so quickly won't affect your career? I mean, Mr. Carter is so cautious and conventional himself—ten times more than I am."

"Don't worry about it," he reassured her. "Everything will be fine."

"I hope you're right. I'd hate to be the cause of any trouble for you."

"You're not, and even if you were, it wouldn't change how I feel about you. I love you, Chloe." Again Logan tried to reassure her, hoping she'd tell him what the big secret was.

"I love you, too." Chloe yawned and closed her eyes.

Long after she'd fallen asleep against him, Logan remained awake thinking. He knew Chloe was keeping something from him. He'd known that since he'd met her. He could have found out long ago what it was, but he wanted her to tell him. He knew that she worried about appearances, especially when it came to his relationship with his boss. He'd told her from the beginning that his boss was a conservative stick-in-the-mud and she also knew how hard he'd worked to get to the current position he held now. She was always the proper, little conservative wife in public.

She was wild in bed, but he suspected that even there she was keeping something from him—something he'd never find out unless she told him. But it wasn't just that that kept him up. He had a feeling that she was hiding something from her past. She always threw out little hints that she was. He knew that she was testing him to see what kind of reaction he would have. He was tired of that, too. If there was something to tell him, then she should just tell him.

He could seduce it out of her or get it out of her by sheer persistence, or he could have her investigated, but he rejected all of those methods. She had to tell him on her own, and she would. It was a matter of trust.

Logan pushed through the double doors of Carter Building and Contracting.

"Oh, Mr. Carnegie, hi. Welcome back."

Logan smiled at the receptionist. "Thanks, Kara," he said

and made his way through the maze of cubicles back to the part of the floor that held the executive offices.

"Good morning, Liddy," he greeted his assistant, who also happened to be his wife's first cousin and best friend.

"Good morning, Rod . . . uh, I mean Logan," she teased.

Logan stopped in his tracks to give her a stern look. "So the Johnson party line has already been activated this morning, huh?" He made a point of looking at his watch. "Hmm, and it's already a quarter to eight. You guys are slipping."

"Not. We talked just after you woke her up at the ungodly hour of six to check out of the hotel. You were in the shower at the time."

"Lydia, I will always be grateful to you for introducing me to the woman I love, but," he cautioned her when she grinned her satisfaction, "make no mistake: you need to stay out of my business."

"Oh, pooh." She dismissed his demand with a wave of her hand. "The girl never gives me any dirty details. All I know about last night is that she was 'Trixie,' you were 'Rod,' and you left the bar and went to the hotel and had a long, satisfying night. The spigot of knowledge was cruelly shut off after that."

"You should know, Lydia, that that doesn't exactly comfort me," he told her with a frown.

"Why? You know I would never tell anyone."

Logan just looked at her for a moment. She looked genuinely perplexed. "I trust you not to tell anyone, Liddy; that's not the issue. I love you like a sister." He put his briefcase down and leaned on her desk to emphasize his point. "However, there are certain things a man doesn't want his sister to know, and that includes information about intimacy with his wife. Get it now?" he asked when she couldn't contain a sappy grin.

"Oh, you're so sweet. And what a coincidence because I think of you as my honorary brother."

"Yeah, okay. I'm talking to the wrong person, anyway. I'll have to talk to Chloe."

"You're not mad at her, are you? I swear to you, it was harmless; just a little girl talk."

"I know, Liddy. Do I have any messages?"

"Aside from the ones I gave you yesterday when you called in, you have one other message," she said as she handed him the messages. "It's from Mr. C. He's already here and he'd like to see you at nine."

"Right," Logan said with a dismayed shake of his head.

Liddy laughed at him, knowing what he was thinking. "Let's face it, Logan. You're never going to beat him in in the morning. The man is a human dynamo. He's already here when I get in and I'm here by seven every morning."

"Seven? I know I keep you busy, but you don't need to get here that early, do you?" He winced when she only lifted a brow. "You do, huh?" When she nodded, he said, "Dear God, why?"

"You work hard, so I work hard." She shrugged. "I have to get here at seven if I want to beat you. You're a workaholic, and I want to be here in case you need me. You know as well as I do that today you're actually late."

Logan frowned, feeling guilty. "Then I'll have to slow down, won't I? And from here on out, I don't want you in here before eight, unless it's something out of the ordinary."

Liddy only smiled and turned back to her computer. "I'd better get back to work. Since you were out of town, there's bound to be a barrage of stuff today and I still need to finish up other things."

Logan lifted a brow at her back, knowing that she wasn't listening to him. "I mean it, Liddy—eight o' clock, not a minute earlier." He turned toward his office. "And since you're in so early, I want you to leave early. Take off at four."

She turned back around. "I'll think about it."

Logan shook his head and went into his office, shutting the door behind him. The woman was stubborn. He put the thought out of his mind as he crossed the width of his office to get to his large mahogany desk. He sat down in his chair and did what he did every morning before starting work. He turned and looked out the window that stretched the length of the back wall of his office.

From where he sat, he could see both Lake Michigan and the Chicago River. As usual while looking at them and ritzy Michigan Avenue, he reminded himself how he'd started his career working in a hard hat and work boots. It had been a long, hard road from there to having an executive office. The reminder always humbled him and made him feel proud at the same time. It kept him focused on his goal.

He turned back to his desk just as the phone rang. It was his private line. He answered. "Hi, sweetheart. I was hoping you'd call."

"You were?" Chloe asked. "Why?"

"Because I wanted to know if that wicked mind of yours had come up with any other debauchery to welcome your man home with." She chuckled low in her throat and he imagined her warm, naked, and waiting for him.

"You plannin' on taking another trip between now and tonight that I don't know about, man of mine?"

"No, but I'll be coming home from a long, hard day of work. Isn't that enough?"

"I'll be coming home from work, too. What do you have planned for me?"

"You're the little woman, both literally and figuratively. It's your job to make your man happy."

She laughed again. "If that's *my* job, then what do you call what you did for me last night?"

"Mutually satisfying," he quipped, making her laugh even harder. "Anyway, Chloe. What's up?"

"Nothing. I just wanted to hear your voice. After all, it's been all of an hour since I last saw you."

He laughed. "Do you think this honeymoon period will ever wear off?"

"Oh, yeah. Soon I'll be calling you to yell at you about leaving the toilet seat up or something else stupid."

"What are you going to do for the next few hours before going into the station?"

"I thought I'd take another look at swatches and maybe go visit that antique store again." Chloe had recently landed a position as host of a children's television show for a local television station. She taped at one o'clock.

"Okay, have fun. Just remember not to let it stress you out," he reminded her. They'd recently closed on a new house and were decorating. She'd gotten so frustrated that she'd fired the decorator.

"That decorator deserved to be fired," she said and he heard the sulk in her voice. "He kept insisting on that chrome and steel, techno-looking crap when we told him that we didn't like it."

"You don't have to convince me; I know he needed to be let go. Anyway, sweets, I've got to go. I'll talk to you later. I love you."

"Love you back. Bye."

Logan sat in John Carter's office waiting for him to complete a phone call. He studied the older man, wondering what he'd do once he retired. Carter Building and Contracting was his life and, besides that, people rarely retired at the age of fifty. John was fit and trim and despite the head full of gray hair and years of putting in long hours building his company, he still looked much younger than his actual age. Lines bracketed his eyes, but that was really it.

"Sorry about that, Logan," John said and stood. "The call couldn't be avoided."

"Not a problem, John. What's up?" Logan hid his smile at the other man's restless movements. The man was always full of energy. Even now he was imperceptibly rocking back and forth on his toes and his eyes were snapping with vitality.

John clapped his hands and rubbed them together. He started pacing back and forth behind his desk. "There's been a lot of talk lately about my retirement. I'm sure you've heard it, just as I'm sure that you've been with me long enough to realize that rumors around here are usually made up of bullshit. You ever heard the phrase 'believe half of what you see and some or none of what you hear?' "

"Yes, in one or two versions of 'Heard It Through the Grapevine,' I believe," Logan answered quietly. His eyes continued to follow John as he paced.

John stopped and looked at him in surprise. "What do you know about an old song like that? That's good music—real music. I didn't think anyone of your generation would recognize it."

Logan lifted a brow. He was being tested again. "I prefer Marvin Gaye's version myself."

The surprised approval in John's eyes was unmistakable. "Well, all right then. Anyway, as I was saying, the rumors are true. I plan to retire in the next year or so, at least semiretire, anyway. You know that I have a daughter, but she isn't interested in taking over and she has absolutely no experience. And so I'll have to pick someone from within the company. That leaves you or Winston. You're not as old as Winston and you haven't been with the company as long, but I like your work ethic and you're good at bringing in new accounts. You also have a background in construction, so that's a plus."

"Thank you, John."

"You're welcome, but just as I told Winston, you're being *considered* for the presidency. You haven't won it yet."

Logan left John's office with a light spring in his step. All his years of hard work were paying off. He'd had to deal with his father's disapproval because he'd chosen to take a job on a construction site when he was eighteen instead of going to college, and he'd had to put in years of backbreaking work to prove himself. College had eventually beckoned, because he'd figured out that the only way to advance was to get a degree. He'd never liked school, but he struggled through it and came out on the other side in the top ten percent of his class. He'd worked forty hours a week, had taken a full course load, and had graduated in three years.

Yes, it had been a struggle, but now here he was thirty years old with a corporate presidency dangling in front of him. He wanted it, he wanted it bad, and was confident enough to believe that he deserved it. He also knew that he had stiff competition, but it didn't concern him. He'd just continue to do what he'd been doing.

He smiled as he thought about how happy Chloe would be for him.

4

Chloe smiled one last time for the camera and hoped that this would be the last take. She had a headache and she knew that the toddlers she worked with were just as tired and cranky as she. Unlike them, however, no one would coddle her if she suddenly threw herself to the floor and had a crying fit or crawled into a corner and snuck a few winks of sleep.

"Okay, boys and girls. We'll see you right back here tomorrow. Have an eye-opening day, and make sure you learn something new! Goodbye! Adios! Au revoir! Ciao!" Chloe repeated her lines for the fifth time and silently prayed that the little bladders of the children around her held tight. They'd already had three potty accidents on set in the past hour. She waited with bated breath to hear those six words that were magic to her ears.

"All right, everyone. That's a wrap!"

Chloe cheered. "Yes!" She lifted one of the children off her lap and prepared to make her way to her dressing room.

"Bye, Ms. Chloe," the children chorused and Chloe leaned down for her usual swarm of hugs.

"Bye, babies. It was good to see you today. I'm glad you came," she said around the kisses that were being pressed all over her face. "You guys be good, okay?"

"Yes, Ms. Chloe."

"'Kay, Ms. Chloe!"

"Love you, Ms. Chloe!"

The high-pitched voices followed Chloe as she left the studio to head for her small dressing room. She sat down at her vanity. "Phew. Another day and another few little minds—at least one or two, hopefully—nourished and opened to learning."

As she removed the makeup from her face, she again thanked God for her current employment. She loved her job. She'd always loved children and had studied child psychology in college. After getting her master's degree in sociology, she'd worked as a social worker with the Department of Children and Family Services, but dealing with abused and neglected children, and feeling powerless to do anything, quickly burned her out and she'd quit within the year.

Her next job was as executive director of Tomorrow's Child, a Chicago-based nonprofit organization that developed educational materials for preschool children. It was after her appearance on a public affairs show at her current station that she was approached by the director of children's programming to help develop programming for preschoolers. She'd accepted the position and it had led to her current one as host of the block of shows for children under five that ran every morning from seven to ten.

Her life had changed so much in the past seven months. First she'd met Logan and then she'd gotten her dream job. Perfect man, perfect job—her life was better than it had ever been. She wouldn't say that she'd fallen in love with Logan the first time she'd met him, but she had fallen in lust and had wanted to get to know him. There was just something in his eyes that drew her.

After a couple of weeks of getting to know one another, they'd slept together. And after a couple of months of trying to spend virtually every waking moment with each other, they'd moved in together. She'd had no idea that her cousin's begging her to come to the company's Christmas party with her would turn into something so wonderful. The only reason she'd gone with Liddy was because her cousin had only been at the company for a month and hadn't wanted to attend the party alone.

Within ten minutes of her arrival, she and Logan had noticed one another. Within fifteen, they were off in a corner talking and had stayed that way for almost the entire night. It had been a whirlwind romance, yes, but she didn't regret one minute of it. She looked down at her rings and smiled tenderly. Logan was the best thing to ever happen to her.

"Still can't believe it, huh?"

Chloe looked up to see her director standing in her doorway with a teasing smile on his face. She smiled back. "Hi, Steve. What's up?"

"Nothing much. I just came by to give you the revised schedule for tomorrow's taping and you also have messages that Jill asked me to drop off." He walked into the office and handed everything to her.

"Oh, okay, thanks. I wonder why she didn't just transfer the calls to my voice mail."

Steve shrugged. "I don't know. But you might want to check your phone anyway. That red light is flashing for a reason." He laughed when Chloe looked embarrassed.

Chloe rolled her eyes. "God, I didn't even notice."

"You're too happy to notice anything so practical. See you later."

"Wait, Steve, before you go, tell me how your niece is doing." Steve had started working at the station the very day that she had, so they had a special bond. One day he'd looked so distressed and had made so many mistakes that she'd taken him aside and asked if there was anything wrong. He'd told her that his four-year old niece had a really bad asthma attack and had to be hospitalized.

"Oh, she's much better, Chloe, thanks. She's back at school three days a week and bragging to all her friends about how Ms. Chloe from the TV came to the hospital especially to see her. Thanks again for doing that, by the way. She was thrilled. She'll never forget it. Neither will my sister or her husband."

"It wasn't a problem. She's so sweet and adorable. And besides, Steve, you've done a lot for me. Your being here made this job easier than it might have been. I'm not used to being in front of the camera and you've made it comfortable for me. But anyway, you should have gotten your niece on the show. Why didn't you?"

"You sound like my sister, and I'll tell you what I told her: auditions were closed by the time I thought about it," Steve answered.

"Well, what the hell kind of uncle are you?" Chloe asked in phony outrage. "A good uncle would have had her here the first day!"

Steve smirked. "Again, you sound like my sister. She's high maintenance too—"

"Hey!" Chloe protested.

Steve laughed. "I gotta go. Don't forget to check your messages. See you later."

"Bye, Steve, and thanks," She laughed and turned to her phone, thinking again that she was lucky he was her director. She pressed in her password, leaving the receiver in its cradle so she could go through her paper messages while she listened to her voice mail. The first voice mail was from her dad checking to see if they were still on for Sunday dinner. At the same time that she listened, she read a message from an old college roommate. The next one was from that same woman and so was the next one. Frowning, she deleted her dad's voice mail so she could hear the next one.

The voice that came out of the machine was a jolt from the past: "Hi, Chloe, it's Mary Pasik, remember me? Well, I was Mary Tanner when you knew me. Anyway, I was watching TV with my kid today and who should I see but little old you. You could have knocked me over with a feather! I said to myself, 'Give her a call, Mary, and see if you and your old best friend can get together for lunch.' Remember all the fun we used to have together? Especially that one incident in particular—" Mary laughed and Chloe cringed because the laughter managed to be both grating and sly. "You know what I mean, don't you? God, that was a wicked time! Anyway, you look good, Chloe, and good for you for getting such a high-paying job. I'm so impressed! Call me, okay? Here's my number."

Out of habit, Chloe scribbled the number down on a piece of paper. In a sort of daze, she deleted the message and listened to the next one. It, too, was from Mary and it was pretty much a repeat of the first one. She sat back in her chair and sighed. Mary Tanner. She hadn't heard from her since they were nineteen and Mary had dropped out of school. "Well, shit," Chloe said. "Not now." What was she going to do? The one person she didn't need in her life right now had actually called her. She could ruin everything.

All of her energy and excitement from moments before gone now, Chloe slumped down in her chair and dialed her cousin's number.

"Hi, Liddy."

"Hey, Chloe. What's wrong? And before you say 'nothing,' just know that I can hear the 'something' in your voice, so give."

If Chloe hadn't been so upset, she'd have laughed. "I wasn't going to deny it. You're not going to believe it, but Mary Tanner called me."

"Mary Tanner? That bitch roommate of yours from college?"

"Yeah, her."

"What does she want?"

"She didn't really say in her message, but I can tell it's not going to be good for me. She said something about an incident and I can only assume she's talking about the picture I took. She tried to laugh it off like it was a joke, but I can tell that she doesn't really think it is." Chloe stopped herself because the anger she was feeling wouldn't be contained. "Frigging hell, Liddy!" she said. "Why did she have to contact me now? Damn it!"

"Do you think she'll try to use it against you?"

"Yeah, of course. She's Mary. And besides, she's left me five messages in the space of a few hours. That doesn't bode well."

"Shoot," Liddy breathed. "You're right, this is bad. What are you going to do?"

"I thought about calling her back and cursing her out—making her admit that she's up to no good. I could totally preempt her."

"Sounds like a plan to me. Why don't you do it?"

"Because I don't want anything to do with her. She just brings back such bad memories. I can't believe I let her fool me for so long."

"Which bad memories? You mean when she slept with your boyfriend? Or was it the part when she told all your friends that you got all your good grades by cheating?"

Chloe grimaced. "All of it," she answered and thought about the girl who had been her roommate during their freshman year of college. They'd become fast friends from the first. They'd done everything together. They were so close, and Chloe had been so trusting, that it had been months before she'd realized that Mary was really a sneaky little worm of a girl who drew people in with her charm. Chloe had realized the hard way that Mary wasn't really a friend but a user, and she'd stopped dealing with her. But not before they'd had their one little, youthful indiscretion together. However, Chloe couldn't even blame Mary for that, for she'd done it freely. She'd just thought it would be fun. Now it was back to bite her in the ass. She sighed.

"Anyway, Liddy. Even if Mary weren't the one person in the whole world who I regret knows my secret about the picture, I wouldn't want to talk to her. I haven't spoken to her in at least ten years."

"I know, but hey, it may not be as bad as you think."

"Oh, yes it will. Crap, I made one mistake as a nineteen-year-old that I'm apparently not going to be allowed to forget, thanks to Mary. I wouldn't care so much if it were just her, but this secret could affect Logan's career as well as mine. And you know, I'd never thought of what I'd done as a mistake and I've never regretted it. Until now. What the heck am I going to do, Liddy?"

"It sounds to me that you already know what you need to do. And you need to tell Logan. So what you posed for a lousy picture? He won't care. He's a good guy. Give him a chance."

"I know, I know. But what do you think Mr. Carter would say?"

"What?" Liddy's voice was shocked. "Who gives a flying fig about what Mr. C would say? He's got nothing to do with this. It's none of his business."

"It's too bad that other people's opinions have to count so much," Chloe said resentfully. "It really shouldn't matter. I didn't do anything wrong. It's my body; I didn't commit a crime. It's nobody's business what I did with my body. It is so unfair that I should even have a dilemma here. Why should it matter to other people at all? Why should they care what I did before I met Logan, or even what I do while I'm married to him?"

"Look here, Chloe," Liddy interrupted her tirade. "You

need to calm down. You're imagining things that may not even happen. Just call that evil heifer back and see what she wants. And remember, no matter what, I've got your back."

"You've *always* had it, Liddy," Chloe reminded her with a soft, grateful smile. "Thanks. I appreciate you."

"You're welcome. Now, go handle your business."

Chloe hung up with Liddy and stared into space. She tried to imagine what Logan's boss would say if he ever found out and she groaned out loud. She covered her mouth with her hand in dismay. "Oh, God, Logan. I'm so sorry. You married me and you don't know all the details. What am I going to do?" Mr. Carter was such a traditionalist and such a stickler for proper behavior that she was sure Logan wouldn't get the presidency if the old man ever found out about the picture.

It was that thought that made her pick up the phone and dial. She waited for her call to be answered and smiled when the familiar voice sounded. "Hi, Daddy."

"Hi, Sweet Pea. How's my favorite girl today?"

" 'Favorite girl,' my foot," Chloe teased. "I happen to know that it's that old mutt Ginger that you love best."

"Well, she does keep me company every day and she brings me my slippers. What have you done for me lately?"

Chloe's laugh was startled. "Dad!"

Robert Johnson grunted. "You started it."

Chloe laughed again. "I guess I did at that." For as long as she could remember her father had been this way: dry-witted and no nonsense. The only parent she'd ever known, he never failed to make her smile. "Anyway, what's up?"

"I don't know. You tell me. You're the one who called."

"I'm just calling to see how your day is going, that's all." Chloe stalled and chose not to remind him that he'd left her a message. "How are the plans for your trip coming?" He and two of his retired, widowed friends were planning a six-week trip through the capitals of Europe.

"Fine, just fine. My passport is current, I've got a clean bill of health from the doctor, the kennel is ready to board Ginger, and you and that husband of yours agreed to check on the house every once in a while. So, I'm good to go."

"Good, but I told you that Logan and I would take Ginger. It wouldn't be a problem at all."

"No, no. I don't want to trouble you two. Besides, your house is too new and too big. Ginger wouldn't know what to do with herself, especially when the two of you are at work. You're away from home too much."

"I only work a few hours a day, Daddy. I'm home most of the morning and you know that. What's the real reason you don't want me to keep Ginger?"

"Look here, little girl. Don't pester me about it. You're not keeping Ginger, and that's final. Besides, have you even talked to your husband about it?"

"No, but I'm sure Logan wouldn't mind."

"You can't be sure of that, Sweet Pea. Listen, you're so used to being by yourself and doing whatever you want. It can't be that way anymore. You're married now. You can't make decisions like this without discussing them with him."

Chloe was surprised. Her father was right. "You're right, Dad. I didn't even think about asking Logan before telling you I'd take Ginger. I guess I'd better."

"Don't bother. You're newly married. Spend some time together alone. The last thing you need is some rowdy dog running around, tearing up stuff. Aside from that, she's got horrible dog breath."

Chuckling some more, Chloe shook her head. "All right, Daddy. Have it your way." She fiddled with the phone cord. "Uh, tell me about your friends. Are they all set to go?"

"Roscoe and Charlie are grown men. If they ain't ready, that's their problem. I know I'm ready. They paid their money just like I did. If they want to waste it by not being prepared, it's their business."

"That's my dad—always concerned for others."

"Um-hm. And now that we've talked about everything under the sun, are you ready to tell me what you really called about? What's going on, baby girl?"

"Oh, Dad. You know me all too well."

"Yes, I do. Start talking."

"Do you remember Mary Tanner from college?"

"That loose gal who used you and talked you into doing things you had no business doing? That Mary Tanner? Chloe, I could never forget that child."

Chloe sighed. "She didn't talk me into anything, Dad. I've told you before that it was my idea."

"Anyway," he said in a tone that said he still wasn't convinced that what she said was true. "What about that harlot?"

Chloe's eyes widened and she tried not to laugh. "Dad!" His silence told her that he wasn't going to waste time defending his word choice, so she continued. "I haven't seen or talked to her in years, but she saw my show and tracked me down here at the station. She's left messages."

"Damn. What did she want?"

"Dad! You cursed."

"You've heard me curse before, Chloe Anne Johnson, most recently Carnegie. Stop stalling and tell me what she wanted. Does it have anything to do with that stunt you pulled a long time ago?"

"She didn't exactly say, but she asked me to call her back."

"Are you going to?"

"I don't want to, Dad, but I feel like I have to."

"I don't think you should call her. I think you need to tell Logan what happened, but I've been telling you that since you found out that his boss is so conservative."

"Now you sound like Liddy. It didn't even occur to me to

tell him at first, because I didn't think it was a big deal. But now that I know other people might . . ."

"Well, now it is a big deal—a huge one. You'd better tell him before he finds out some other way. I'm sure the actual act won't bother him, but what might bother him is that you were scared to tell him. And while you're at it, you might want to tell your boss, too."

Chloe's heart pounded frantically and she felt a trickle of sweat slide between her shoulder blades. She knew her next words would make her sound like a daddy's girl, which she was, but she couldn't help it. She whined them anyway: "But, Daddy, I don't want to."

5

Logan let himself into their new home. He was dead tired. He took off his coat and hung it on the antique wooden coatrack Chloe had found on one of her many shopping excursions. He yawned and put his briefcase down. He knew it was late, but he'd had a shitload of work to catch up on because he'd been out of town. He looked at his watch. It was after ten and he still had more work to do.

He guessed that Chloe would have eaten dinner and would be asleep by now. She liked to go to bed early and sleep late. He pictured her cozy, warm, and naked underneath the covers. She preferred to sleep in the buff.

His stomach growled and he was faced with the dilemma of going to the kitchen to satisfy his hunger or going upstairs to satisfy a hunger of another kind. Again, he pictured Chloe naked and welcoming, her body sleepily opening to him, and it was an easy choice. He turned toward the stately staircase that lead up to the second floor and to his wife, and spotted a piece of paper hanging from the newel post of the staircase. He walked closer. The paper was held in place by an apple, which he promptly grabbed and bit into.

He glanced down at the paper and slowly stopped chewing. The back of a bent neck—dark, delicate and smooth-looking with glossy, soft, black hair ending in a vee right at the bend—was showcased. The perfect picture of vulnerability and submission. He wanted a taste. A caption underneath read *Take Me, I'm Yours*. The piece of apple lodged in his throat from lack of saliva. His mouth had gone completely dry. He looked farther down on the paper and saw an arrow pointing upward, so he started walking up the stairs. In his haste he was actually jogging. On the tenth step, the sound of paper crunching beneath his foot reached his ears and he looked down.

It was another picture. Beautiful, full, sensual lips puckered around a slender, tapered finger. Chloe's lips. Chloe's finger. The apple was forgotten as it fell to the floor. He read the caption: *Come get a taste.* Heart pounding with a new surge of adrenaline, Logan rushed to the top of the staircase. And stopped dead in his tracks. All he could do was stare. Pebble-hard, dark nipples peeked at him from behind frothy, sheer black material. His dick began to pulse and keep time with the beat of his heart. His breath caught in the back of his throat as he continued to stare and automatically, he started undoing his tie. "Jesus," he muttered, completely unable to look away.

He made his eyes travel to the bottom of the page. *Wanna play peekaboo?* The obvious answer was "yes" and Logan wasted no time going to their bedroom. He took off his suit coat and let it drop to the floor, stepping on it as he rushed. The buttons to his shirt were carelessly ripped out of their moorings to go flying every which way in the hall. He could not be controlled. The door to their bedroom was only a few feet away and he rushed toward it, only to be denied entrance. It was closed. There was another picture posted.

The sexual frustration rolled off him in waves and he almost ignored the last picture. It didn't matter to him what was featured in the picture—it could be her damn toenail—he didn't need to see anything else. If he got any harder, he'd be in pain. But he couldn't help it, he looked. His eyes narrowed and he stepped closer. A glimpse of the hem of the same frothy black material from the other picture; clean-shaven, plump labia nestled between smooth brown thighs. There was no caption.

Before he realized it, Logan's hand had gone to the zipper of his pants. His cock sprang free, and as he continued to stare at the picture, his fingers began to stroke. Chloe was not usually clean-shaven, but he knew it was her because he recognized the small birthmark tattooed on her soft inner thigh. He growled low in his throat.

"Logan?"

Her voice was soft, seductive, and expectant. Logan opened the door. The room was dark except for a soft light that shone from the bed area. The bed was huge, custom made to be larger than even a king-sized one. It rested on a platform and was piled high with pillows, while purple and blue silks hung freely from the four posters. In the center of it all, a naked Chloe looked like the prized, pampered concubine in a sultan's harem. Logan strode over and stepped onto the platform.

Her eyes traveled over him and widened in surprise when she saw his exposed balls and penis. There was no other way to put it: she purred. "Ooh, I see you brought a few of my favorite things with you," she whispered as she began to crawl towards the foot of the bed and him. *Both Julie Andrews and Diana Ross had forgotten a few things when they sang that song,* she thought as she continued to crawl, her eyes focused only on the prize.

Logan stood still, wanting her to come to him. She looked like a cat on the prowl as she crawled slowly toward him, her heavy breasts swaying and dipping with the pressing of her knees into the mattress. Even as he watched, she licked her lips in hungry anticipation and he felt his penis preen, stretch, and strain upward some more, as if it were proud of her approval. He watched her eyes narrow as she saw it perform, and then she smiled. The smile was purely feline.

That's right, baby: show me whatcha workin' with, Chloe paraphrased rapper Mystikal's song in her head when Logan's penis stretched under her stare. She licked her lips again. She couldn't wait to taste his salty essence, to feel that heavy weight in her mouth, that long length pushing toward the back of her throat and slipping and sliding against her tongue. As if she'd expressed her thoughts out loud, a stream of pre-cum began to ooze out and slide heavily down the side of his penis.

Having arrived at the foot of the bed, Chloe sat on the edge and let her legs hang over the side. She still had not focused her eyes anywhere besides his penis. Her fingers flexed in preparation. "Can I, Logan? Please?"

Logan's answer was to cup her chin in his hand and pull her face toward him while simultaneously pushing himself toward her mouth.

Sounds of greed escaped Chloe's throat as she finished undoing his pants and pushed them and his boxers over his butt and down his thighs. Her hands massaged their way back up his thighs to cup and squeeze his ass. Slowly, she pushed him toward her open mouth. Starting from the top, she licked her way down one side of his penis, ravenously scooping up the pre-cum in her path and making him grip her shoulders tightly in his hands.

Teasingly, she licked her way down his thigh, tasting and kissing the salty skin and feeling his muscles tensing with each stroke. Slowly, she began licking the inside of his knee, her face completely between his thighs now. She held him steady with her hands on his outer thighs when he jerked from stimulation. She made sure her hair brushed softly against one inner thigh while she tenderly licked her way up the other one. Though he hadn't said a word, his hands were in her hair now, pushing her, urging her, *begging* her to do more.

His knees were locked, his thighs were tense, and Chloe grinned wickedly when she felt that he was even holding in his ass tautly. Not for long, she thought, just before she gently sucked one of his balls into her mouth. "Oh, yeah," he moaned and she found the little seam running up the center of his testicle and followed it with the tip of her tongue. She closed her eyes in her excitement as the heat already pooling in her stomach flamed hotter at the salty taste and light weight of him against her tongue.

Careful not to let her excitement get the best of her, she gently teased the other testicle with the soft pads of her fingertips, controlling it so that it rolled back and forth between her fingers and her thumb. She felt her own breathing accelerate in excitement and she released the ball from the hot, humid depths of her mouth, giving it one last lick as she did so.

She looked up at him, making sure her eyes stayed connected to his as she went in for an ice-cream-cone lick, giving his dick a long lick from the base to the top, watching his eyes narrow in anticipation. At the last second, she opened her mouth in an "o" and slid it completely over the top of his erection, taking in as much of it as she could. This was her favorite part and Chloe went at it with gusto, holding the bottom of his penis with one hand and sliding her mouth up and down over and over again.

The lusty sounds coming from the back of his throat and hers only made her want more and she slid her hand up and down his shaft in the wake of her mouth, repeating both movements over and over again. She watched as he clenched his teeth and threw his head back, the tendons in his neck straining against his skin. She squeezed her thighs together to stem the flow of her own excitement, pushing her rock-hard nipples against his thighs for self-stimulation.

His time for orgasm was getting closer and Chloe wrapped her arms around his waist, bringing him flush against her face where she sucked harder and faster, wanting all of him, never wanting to let him go. The huge, swollen head pushed against the back of her throat and she reveled in the feel of it, contracting her throat muscles and pulling in her cheeks as she sucked.

She heard him say her name urgently, if a bit weakly, and looked up at him. His face was ravaged with desperation and hard-won control. She knew what he wanted and almost cried in disappointment. He loosed her arms from around his waist and she released his penis. Eagerly, she stood on the bed and jumped on him, knowing that he would catch her. "Hurry, Logan," she said and wrapped her legs around his waist.

Logan turned, stepped off the platform, and backed her up against the wall, shooting his penis into her with one quick thrust. Her own juices made the penetration smooth and sure. Neither moved at first, each of them savoring the feel of the other. Panting and harsh breathing were the only sounds heard in the large room.

Chloe felt his warm breath on her neck and pressed a kiss in his hair, prompting Logan to lift his head and look at her.

"You're amazing," he told her before bending his head to kiss her. He kept his mouth closed, simply rubbing his lips back and forth against hers. After a few seconds of this, he parted his lips slightly to slide the tip of his tongue through, flicking it gently across the surface of her lips.

Chloe closed her eyes and enjoyed his gentle loving, allowing her tongue to tangle with his and trace the rim of his lips. He was soon slowly thrusting his tongue into her mouth, allowing her to suck on it once in a while, but otherwise, just leisurely plunging it in and out. She was crazy with need for more of him.

When she squeezed her internal muscles around his shaft, he began to match the thrusts of his penis with the thrusts of his tongue. Again, taking it slow, teasing and tempting her with some, but not all. "Logan, please," she begged after she had broken the kiss.

Ignoring her, he took her mouth again, feeding her his tongue, allowing her to suck it in, but only for a moment. She squirmed against him, grinding herself onto his dick, trying to keep it inside her. But he continued to tease her, one moment plunging in deeply to the hilt and the next pulling out until she only cradled the tip within her body.

Chloe became a mass of emotions, at turns pleading with him to take her harder and faster and then demanding that he "man up" and do what the hell he was supposed to do. He ignored her, and eyes closed, arms holding her up beneath her thighs, he continued to push slowly into her. Push in . . . pull out . . . push in . . . pull out, the wet sounds her flesh made as it tried to hold onto him driving Chloe mad.

Beyond desperate, she grabbed at his butt and tried to control the speed that way. When that didn't work, she tried everything from nibbling on his neck to sucking his earlobes to nuzzling his chin. But nothing swayed him. He controlled both her body and his need.

"Please, Logan." Chloe was crying now, she was so strung out. He had begun to play with her nipples, alternately biting and sucking first one and then the other.

Logan switched his mouth from her breast to her mouth, driving his tongue inside over and over again. He grabbed her hips, his fingers digging as he began to plunge his penis furiously inside her.

Chloe tried to catch her breath as she gleefully rode him

hard, matching him thrust for thrust, her mound clenching and unclenching in ecstasy as he rammed her against the wall. She came hard, quickly and in one long rush. She held onto him while his orgasm slashed through him, loving the rare feel of his hot sperm spurting inside of her.

The bed beside him dipped and swayed some more and Logan looked over at Chloe. She'd been moving restlessly about almost from the moment she'd fallen asleep thirty minutes before. Wondering what could be on her mind, he rubbed her back until she settled again. He went back to his laptop, studying the architect's designs for the project in Cleveland.

"Please, Logan."

Logan heard Chloe whisper. Her voice was beseeching and seductive at the same time. He looked over at her again. She was still asleep, but more than a little intrigued now, he continued to stare at her.

"Yes, Logan. I'll behave. I promise. I'll be good. Just tie it a little tighter, please."

Logan's brow shot up in shock and curiosity . . . and he leaned in closer in case she had more to say.

"Logan, *please*. That isn't tight enough."

"Hot damn," he whispered in wonder with an eager, hopeful smile. "Logan, you are one lucky bastard!" He looked up through the skylight of their ceiling and saw heaven . . . literally. "Thank you, God," he said fervently.

Still asleep, she sounded so turned on that she was making him hot. A wicked thought crossed his mind and after putting his laptop on the nightstand he leaned even closer to her. "Just how tight do you want it, baby?" he growled in her ear.

Still asleep, Chloe moved sensuously against the sheets and smiled sexily, but didn't say anything.

Unable to resist, Logan pressed his mouth to hers, at the same time that he slipped his hand between her thighs. Lucky for him she was just full of surprises, he thought as he began to gently fondle her clitoris. His last thought as she opened her eyes, dug her nails into his arm, and began to moan was that it was a man's job to make his wife happy and give her what she wanted. And if she wanted BDSM, then he'd just have to be man enough to give it to her.

6

"I'm so glad that tomorrow is Saturday," Chloe said later to Logan in their kitchen. After their last round of lovemaking, they'd realized that they were hungry and had decided to find something to eat. Dressed in a short robe, she stood at the counter. She lifted one of several Ritz crackers from a plate and spread butter on it. She looked up in time to see Logan frown in distaste and deliberately shoved the whole thing in her mouth. "Mmm, yummy," she stated. "You should try them sometime."

"No thanks, I prefer to die of natural causes rather than high cholesterol," Logan said from the stove as he flipped over a couple of pancakes on the griddle. He wore his boxers and nothing else. "Don't load up on those crackers. I've made a boatload of pancakes here."

"Trust me, I'll have enough room," she said and she bit into another cracker, this one without butter. "So, anyway, what do you want to do tomorrow?" Her eyes traveled to look out the window. It was still dark, but the sky would be turning light soon. "Actually, I guess I should be asking what you want to do today. I have the whole day free. What about you?"

Logan thought about his answer as he put the last pancake onto the platter and turned the burner off. The dream he'd overheard her having earlier was still on his mind. *Perhaps it was the day to make it come true,* he thought when a couple of ideas flashed in his head. Oh yeah, he could at least make part of it come true. He answered her with a big smile. "I've got to go into the office for a couple of hours first thing in the morning, but I'm all yours for the rest of the day. What did you have in mind?"

"Nothing, really." Chloe grabbed the syrup, butter, napkins, and silverware and walked down the couple of steps that led to the small breakfast nook in the corner. "I would love to just do nothing. No shopping for furniture, no looking at color swatches, no paint shopping, no work, no anything," she finished as she set the condiments down on the little round beechwood table and arranged the silverware on the napkins.

She took the plates he carried in one hand and set those down as well. "Water, juice, or milk?" she asked as she walked toward the refrigerator.

"I'll have juice, thanks," Logan called and put the platter of pancakes in the middle of the table. "Apple if we have it."

Chloe came back to the table carrying two bottled waters under her arm and a glass of apple juice in each hand. "I brought both water and juice," she said unnecessarily and handed off the glasses of apple juice. Setting a bottle of water at each place setting, she smiled. "There, now let's eat. Thank you, honey," she said when he pulled out her chair. She waited for him to seat himself before serving herself two pancakes.

The next few minutes were filled with the clinking of silverware against china as they tacitly decided to forego conversation to take the edge off their hunger.

"These are great, Logan," Chloe said appreciatively after she swallowed a mouthful. "Gosh, I'm starved! I really worked up an appetite," she finished with a saucy wink and rubbed her toes against his bare leg.

"Thank you. My dad and I used to make these pancakes for my mother on Sundays," Logan said and put three more pancakes on his plate. "And you helped to work my appetite up, too. You blew me away, especially with that freshly shaved yoo-hoo of yours."

Chloe smiled at his euphemism. "It's not a chocolate kiddy drink, Logan. But I'm glad you like it this way. I'd always wanted to try a Brazilian wax, so I'd thought I'd treat you and myself."

"Well, all I can say is bless you, my lovely wife. Bless you and the Brazilian who came up with the concept."

"Before you start genuflecting," Chloe said in a dry tone, "I didn't just do it for you; I like it too."

"Whatever your reasons, I thank you. Just as I thank you for the wonderful, mind-*blowing* experience when I first got in. You've done well, Grasshopper."

She laughed. She'd only ever been in two serious relationships before meeting Logan and despite her love of sex, she'd rarely performed it orally. But after she met Logan, she wanted to do it all the time. She'd actually begun to crave it. So he'd told her, in great detail, what he liked. "I always was a fast learner. Besides, I was inspired."

"I can appreciate that, and speaking of inspiration, let's talk about what inspired that show last night."

Chloe looked over at him with a confused frown. "What show? What do you mean?"

"I mean that elaborate seduction plan you set up. As much as I loved it . . ." he paused and his eyes took on a faraway look before he brought himself back. "I mean, *really* loved it, I also know that something must have happened yesterday to make you plan it. Something happened that you want to forget and you planned last night to take your mind off it."

Chloe avoided his gaze. "I don't know what you mean."

"Don't you? Okay, I'll give you an example. When we were on our honeymoon and our luggage was lost for a couple of hours, the first thing you did when we got to the hotel was to jump me. We were barely inside the room before you were stripping my clothes off me. There was also the time your secretary at your old job accidentally sent an annual report to the wrong address. You were on me so hot and heavy when I picked you up from work that night that I actually had to pull over to the side of the road."

Chloe was quiet as she squirmed uncomfortably in her seat. Damn. He did know her well. "Not that you minded," she tried to say wryly.

"Oh, hell no, I didn't mind. But sweetheart, you can also *talk* to me about things that are bothering you. I'm always ready to listen when you want to talk. I enjoy the avoidance sex, as I've come to think of it, but I don't want to be used for my body. I've got a brain, too," he said.

Chloe thought about Mary's phone messages and wanted to tell him, but she just wasn't ready. She did what anyone who feels cornered would do. She went on the defensive. "And I didn't know you were taking notes," she said.

"I didn't have to take notes to notice a pattern," he stated calmly and waited for her to answer. When she didn't and continued to look away from him, he reached across the table and lifted her chin so she'd have to look at him. "Now, tell me, Chlo. Did something happen yesterday?"

Chloe stared at him, wanting to tell, but unable to make the words leave her mouth. She sighed. "Yeah, something did happen, but I can't tell you. Not yet. I'm just not ready to talk about it. I'm sorry."

Logan released her chin and didn't bother to hide his frustration. "Does this have anything to do with the secret you've been keeping from me?" When her eyes widened in surprise, he scowled. "Yes, I know you're keeping a secret from me. I've known for a long time. Even if you hadn't been dropping hints, I would know. I didn't ask you about it, because I didn't want to pressure you. I figured it's something that happened before we met."

There's your perfect opening. Tell him, Chloe, she thought to herself. But when she opened her mouth, the words just refused to come. "Yes, it did happen before we met and I want to tell you. It's just so hard to do it."

"Why is it hard? You're supposed to trust me."

"I do," Chloe hurried to assure him. "It's just that . . . well, I don't want to see your reaction. It's just one more thing that if people knew it about me, they'd be shocked by it. It shouldn't be a big deal, but to certain people it will be."

Shocking? Now Logan was even more curious. "You think it will be a big deal to me?"

"I don't think so, but it might."

"Why don't you let me be the one to decide that?"

Chloe shrugged. "I'm not really ready to talk about it yet."

Logan tried to figure out what it could possibly be, which was almost impossible since he had no idea where to begin.

"Is it really that bad?" he asked. When it was clear that she wasn't going to answer, he sighed and said, "This is the first and only time I'm going to ask you about it. You'll have to come to me. I won't ask again."

Relieved, Chloe nodded quickly. She stood and walked over to sit in his lap. "I will," she whispered and kissed his neck, grateful when he wrapped his arms around her. "I promise."

Caught in that hazy place between sleep and wakefulness, Chloe stretched, yawned, and opened her eyes. She turned to look at the clock on the nightstand. It was a few minutes before eleven. She smiled and bounced out of bed, thinking that her husband should be home in at least a couple of hours. She grabbed the remote control and turned on the television that was positioned on the wall about five feet away from the foot of the bed, flipping through the channels until she found one of her favorites—one of the cartoon channels. She still loved Saturday morning cartoons, and thought that some of the ones made today were so sophisticated and witty that they just had to have been written with both children and adults in mind.

"Oh, good," she said absently, as she picked up her robe from the foot of the bed and put it on. "*Jimmy Neutron* is on."

She walked into the bathroom to take care of her usual morning ritual and contemplated taking a bubble bath in the sunken tub. "Maybe after *Jimmy Neutron,*" she murmured. She emptied her bladder, washed her hands, and grabbed a toothbrush and toothpaste. It wasn't until she was looking in the mirror that she noticed a note taped to it. She read it out loud: *Good morning, sweetheart. I have a surprise for you. After you're finished in the bathroom, I want you to press play on the DVR and watch the recording that I made for you.*

"Oh, a surprise. He's so sweet," she whispered with a sappy grin. She hurried through her morning hygiene and rushed back into the bedroom.

Sitting on the bed, she picked up the remote and did the necessary things to get her to the recording. She blinked in surprise when the actual image to come on screen was of Logan himself. He sat in one of the end chairs from their nineteenth-century dining room set, looking stern and imperious. Intrigued, she leaned close to hear what he was saying.

"*Chloe, did you know that you talk in your sleep? I listened closely last night and it seems my little wife has a deep, dark fantasy. We're about to live out your fantasy, darling.*" Chloe's heart rate accelerated upon hearing this as she wondered which one.

"That's my man," she whispered because her voice was too dry from excitement for her to speak any louder. She realized she'd missed some of what he was saying and pressed rewind.

"Listen carefully." (his voice became more forceful and domineering, and her fingers clenched the duvet cover). *"Follow my directions to the letter. On top of your dresser, you will find a bag. I want you to get that bag—not yet,"* he commanded and Chloe anxiously sat back down on the bed, her toes curling into the carpet with nervous, energy. *"In that bag you will find a special toy and a DVD. Do not open it until you're sitting back on the bed. Get the bag now, Chloe, and come back."*

Chloe's lips twisted in disbelief and her brow lifted. "Okay, I can see I'm gonna have to rein you in some. This little bit of false power has already gone to your head," she murmured, but she did as ordered because she was still turned on. She grabbed the bag and hurried back—just in time to hear him start talking again.

"You may open the bag and pour everything in it onto the bed."

She did. Her mouth dropped open and it was quite some time before she gathered her wits enough to close it and then press the pause button so she could examine what she found. It was a vibrator, but it was unlike any vibrator she'd ever seen before. The first thing she noticed about it was that it had little nodules all over it, so that wherever it touched her, she would be stimulated. She picked it up and almost dropped it in surprise. It was soft and bendable. "Oh, my," she breathed, starting to pant from the lusty thoughts running through her mind.

After repeatedly bending it and watching it bounce back into shape, she continued to study it some more, her heart pounding so loudly in her ears she imagined it filled the whole room. The vibrator was at least seven or eight inches long, purple and battery operated. Noticing that, she looked back to the other stuff that had fallen on the bed. Yes, there was a pack of batteries. She breathed a sigh of relief. "Put down the vibrator, Chloe," she told herself, thinking that maybe saying the words aloud would help slow her down.

She put it down and studied the other things. There was a lubricant and a DVD. She picked up the DVD, but there was no label. Picking up the remote control again, she pushed play. She rolled her eyes when the first words to come out of Logan's mouth were: *"Put down the vibrator, Chloe."* She stuck her tongue out at him.

"Are you excited, Chloe? Does having that vibrator in your hot little hands make your clit hard? What about your nipples? Have they turned into those hard little pebbles that I like to suck into my mouth and roll against my tongue? Are you wet, Chloe? Do you want to come? Do you want to ride that vibrator, sliding it in and out of your body until you come so hard that you can't see straight?"

Transfixed, Chloe was nodding her head yes to all of his questions.

"I know you are, but you can't touch yourself. Do you understand, Chloe? You are not allowed to touch yourself. This is what you're going to do: You're going to take your robe off and lay naked on the bed with the covers over you. You're to stay like this all day until I get home. You're going to put the batteries in the vibrator and put the vibrator in that beautiful, greedy, slick opening of that lovely pussy of yours. Do not put the setting on anything higher than low vibration.

"Take the DVD I've given you and put it in the player. You will watch the DVD until I get home. If it ends before I get home, then start it over. You keep watching it until I get home. No deviations. Remember: do not touch yourself to relieve your horniness. Your body is mine and only I will give it pleasure.

Again, Chloe's brow lifted in disbelief and stayed that way throughout his next few sentences.

"And you will not have an orgasm until I give you one. Do not come, Chloe. If you do, you'll be in trouble when I get home.

An involuntary, excited "oh, my" escaped her mouth.

"You may begin."

The screen went blank, but Chloe was already on her feet, the tension and excitement having brought her to them like a puppet long before he'd finished talking. Her palms slick from excitement, she took the DVD by its edges and inserted it into the player. She took off her robe and climbed naked to the center of the bed, taking everything with her, including the remote control.

She was already wet, but she put lubricant on the vibrator anyway and slowly inserted it into her body, moaning when the nodules rubbed against her sensitive inner walls. She carefully turned the switch on low . . . and fell straight back onto the bed from sensation overload, little squeaks escaping her throat as the vibrating nodules sent her straight to the edge.

"Oh, hell," she despaired, knowing it was going to be difficult not to come. Automatically, her legs closed tightly around the vibrator, but, eyes grown big from discovery, she quickly opened her thighs wide when that only increased the sensation.

She made herself sit up. Even moving very slowly, every millimeter she moved proved to be torturous so that she was catching her breath and moaning every step of the way. She crawled under the covers where she lay on her back and looked at the remote like it was a poisonous snake ready to attack. She was almost afraid to see what was on the DVD.

7

"Oh, God, I'm going to kill him," Chloe sighed when their candlelit bedroom appeared on the screen. She didn't want him dead because he'd taped them without telling her. No, she wanted him dead because he had known that watching them make love would turn her on like nothing else would. "Evil bastard," she moaned. It almost sounded like an endearment as she watched him carry her into the bedroom.

She remembered the night perfectly. It was the night before he was scheduled to leave for Cleveland. They'd been all over each other because they'd known it would be days before they saw each other again. Her bottom lip between her teeth, Chloe studied the screen. He was fully dressed, but she only wore a towel. He'd just given her a bubble bath and he'd washed her from top to bottom, not leaving one part of her body untouched.

She'd begged him to get in the tub with her, but he'd refused, preferring to tease her. And the only reason he was carrying her was because she'd been too weak to stand after twenty minutes of his special Logan bath, as he'd called it. "The jackass didn't let me come then, either," she murmured. She shivered now as she remembered and then she moaned because the movement reminded her body that it was fully aroused. She closed her eyes and fought for control, trying not to move at all.

Her eyes opened and went back to the screen. He sat on the side of the bed with her in his lap, and was kissing her while his hand was under the towel, feeling her up so skillfully that she curled into him, groaning her pleasure into his mouth.

Her hand went to his shirt and slid inside to fondle his nipples. He broke off the kiss to sit her on the bed and stood up to take off his clothes. "You really are a freak," Chloe told herself as she watched her hands grab and dig into Logan's bare ass to pull him closer to her. She imagined the musky, heady scent of him and closed her eyes, curling her toes into the sheets . . . and tensed when her muscles clenched around the vibrator in reaction.

She took a deep breath and watched as he removed her hands from his behind and bent down on his knees. She'd missed seeing him take her towel off, but she saw her naked body as he bent his head to press kisses down her writhing torso. Chloe sucked in a breath when her DVD self let out a long, drawn-out whimper, threw her head back, and leaned back onto her arms, arching her torso into Logan's face.

As his face went lower and lower and her image's body bucked harder and harder, Chloe found herself playing with her nipples, pinching and squeezing them hard between her fingers. When Logan's head reached its destination between her thighs, she watched as he splayed her legs wide open for the camera, his large hands completely swallowing her knees and his fingers pressing into her thighs. His mouth moved to kiss along her inner knee and thigh and, thoroughly entranced, Chloe bent her knees and opened her thighs wide open for real when she saw how swollen and wet her on-screen labia were.

One of her hands inched its way down her torso, just as her on-screen hand did, and her other hand played with her nipples, just as on-screen. She writhed in time with her on-screen self and let her hand keep moving insistently downward, completely uncaring now about Logan's edict that she not give herself an orgasm. "Forget him," she moaned, as her hand finally reached the vibrator, just as her hand on television reached the back of Logan's hand and pushed it into her cleft.

Logan began to feed and Chloe could hear the hungry, slurping sounds he made, just as she heard the high-pitched sounds she made as she tried to find satisfaction, both on screen and off. Grinding her body against the vibrator was as natural to her now as grinding against Logan's mouth had been when the recording was made. Her legs tightened around the vibrator, just as her television legs tightened around Logan's head.

The vibrator was drenched and slippery, but she held it firmly and rode it as the orgasm started at the base of her toes and thrashed itself through her body, making her hips buck wildly and her legs shake uncontrollably. As the orgasm took complete control of her, Chloe screamed, "Yes, Logan! Oh, yes!"

She didn't realize that her on-screen image screamed the exact same words. She opened her eyes when she heard Logan's voice. It was the hard voice and she realized that he must have added this to the recording that morning.

"*You've been a naughty girl, haven't you, Chloe?*"

Chloe snorted. "So what if I have?" She asked defiantly.

"*I know you have because I know you,*" the recorded Logan continued. "*You just couldn't keep your hands off yourself. Get ready for your punishment. I'm looking forward to it. You're going to get it when I get home, little lady.*"

Chloe actually felt a little thrill shoot down her spine when he said the last couple of sentences and she shivered with excitement. "Bring it on, big man," she whispered and her voice shook. She rewound and finished listening to him speak.

"Watch the DVD again, Chloe. Watch it and do not touch yourself again." The screen went blank.

Chloe was slowly pushing the vibrator inside her body again, concentrating on the sensations. "Shows what you know," she said haltingly as she started to fly over the edge again. "I don't need to watch the DVD again. Your voice will do just fine."

Chloe took her eyes off the television when Logan appeared in the doorway. She froze, the tone of voice he'd used on the recording meshing in her head with him standing there looking big and fierce and just staring at her. She found herself feeling a little nervous.

She watched as he sniffed the room with exaggerated motions and said in an intentionally intimidating voice, "I smell you. You came, didn't you, Chloe? You touched yourself and you came."

Chloe gulped, and to her surprise, found herself a little nervous and trying to explain herself! "Well . . . I . . . uh . . . kinda did, yes. I couldn't help . . ." She got distracted watching him walk into the room and step onto the platform. She wondered what was in the bag he carried. When the bag rattled, she weakly finished her thought, ". . . myself—I couldn't help myself."

Her eyes remained riveted to the bag as he began to open it. She barely heard him say, "How many times, Chloe? How many times did you come?"

"Two, no, three—I came three times," she said in a weak voice.

She watched as he began to remove long pieces of silk from the bag. She licked her lips. "Logan? What are you going to do?"

"I'll ask the questions," he said sternly and reached into the bag again to bring out more lengths of material. There were four in all and they looked to be at least six feet long.

Chloe had her answer and, if at all possible, her heart picked up even more speed. She finally looked up at him when she realized that there wasn't anything else to pull out of the bag. She found his eyes focused entirely and intently on her. She shivered again. This domineering, demanding Logan was almost scary.

"I told you what was going to happen if you were a bad girl, Chloe. Now turn over."

Barely able to contain herself, Chloe flicked off the television and did as he said. The unknown and the idea that she was about to live out a fantasy she'd had for so long had her obeying without complaint.

She felt air hit her bare, sensitized skin when he threw the covers off her. "You've been really bad, Chloe, so that calls for extra punishment," she heard him say in a hard voice as he gently stroked her from back to ass. The contrast between the two was devastatingly sensual.

"Scoot down so that you're in the middle of the bed," he commanded. She did so.

"Give me your hand," he said. She obeyed and felt him slip the silk over her wrist. She felt a small tug as her arm was pulled so he could loop the other end of the silk over one of the posts.

"Stick out your foot."

Again, Chloe blindly obeyed so he could tie her foot, just as she did when he walked around to the other side of the bed to give her other leg and arm the same treatment. After he'd finished tying her arm, he leaned over and whispered, "Your safe word is 'oranges.' "

What the . . . ? Oranges? Chloe had the insane urge to giggle. Lord, he was such a dork, but he was a sweet dork and he was all hers.

"If it gets to be too much and you want me to stop, all you have to do is say the safe word, okay, baby?" Logan asked.

She nodded and smiled because his voice was heavy with lust, but gentle at the same time. His hand was just as gentle when he took it over her hair, and she nuzzled her head into the caress.

She could only imagine what she looked like, all trussed up and wide open for his pleasure. She felt his finger trail down her side from shoulder to hip.

"You had three orgasms while I was gone, huh? Oh, yeah, you've been very bad," he said softly as he kneaded her behind and then kissed it. Which is why she was completely caught off guard when the palm of his hand connected with her flesh. Hard.

"Ow!" she said and whipped her head around to look at him with an angry scowl.

He looked back at her, his brow lifted in question and she knew he was asking for her permission to continue. Through her surprised anger, she felt heat pool from her stomach to her clit from the pain, but she shook her head no anyway. She wasn't quite ready to go down that road.

Logan rose and continued the game. "You must be punished, Chloe."

She felt him reach between her thighs and pull the vibrator out. Her body suctioned around it fiercely and she made a sound of protest, already missing the feel of it stretching and teasing her.

"You liked this a little too much," he whispered as he thrust the vibrator back into her and turned its setting up a couple of levels. Chloe screamed from the sheer sensation. She felt him pull it out and push it in again, this time twisting and turning it so the little nubs scraped against every inch of her vaginal walls.

She bucked and pushed back against it, grateful that he'd left leeway in the ties. But she could only bend her knees so much before she was snapped back into place. It was pure torture—satisfaction was just within reach and she couldn't get it. She tried again and felt him push the vibrator in a little further. She pushed her hips down, straining to get the vibrator to touch just where she needed it. *Almost there . . . I'm coming, I'm coming . . . yes . . . yes . . . yes—*

"No, no, no," Logan chastised right before he pulled the vibrator completely out of her. "No more orgasms for you. Not yet."

Chloe's head whipped around again and she panted. "You . . . bastard."

Logan grinned. "I'm afraid name-calling is grounds for more punishment, my naughty wife," he said and plunged the vibrator back into her labia.

Chloe's whole body strained against the ropes as the scorching heat ripped violently through her. She would have screamed, but she couldn't. All energy was concentrated on withstanding the heat because she knew there would be no immediate fulfillment.

She relaxed when he pulled the vibrator out again, only to go taut once more when he pushed it back in. It had to be on full throttle now, she thought warily as it pulsated so strongly inside her that she thought she felt the vibrations drumming even in her head. He was kneeling between her legs and one hand slipped beneath her body to pull and pinch her nipples in tandem with the thrusts of the vibrator. Oh, God, he was killing her!

It went on like this for minutes . . . hours? She was so overcome with frustration and pleasure that she was delirious and couldn't tell. "Please, Logan, please . . ." she begged.

"Please what?"

"Please . . . let . . . me . . . come!" she said between pulses of the vibrator. When there was only silence, she stretched out fully again, widened her legs some more and began stretching her body and then infinitesimally pulling it back in so that her aching clit could get stimulation from rubbing against the sheet. Stretch and pull back, stretch and pull back, stretch and pull back. She did this over and over again until . . . until . . . "Oh, yes!" she shouted, hoping and praying that Logan wouldn't figure out what she was doing. She went as fast as she could, the heat that was twisting and building in her urging her on.

The vibrator disappeared and the next thing she felt was his body lying on top of hers, covering her entirely and effectively stopping her frantic attempts to satisfy herself. She felt his penis hard and heavy against her back and fleetingly wondered when he'd gotten undressed.

He took her ear between his teeth before kissing away the sting and growling, "The only way you're going to come is with my dick inside you. Understand?"

Shocked and thrilled into stillness by his complete dominance of her, she could only nod her head once, before meekly whispering, "Yes, Logan." She waited for his next move.

When it came, she came close to fainting from the utter bliss that filled her. He kneeled, lifted her hips, and sank his dick so deep inside of her that she felt savaged in the attempt. He plundered her fiercely, making her cry out time and time again. She tried to rise up farther, but couldn't because of the silk. "Untie me, Logan," she demanded shrilly, wanting to participate more fully. "Oranges, Logan . . . *oranges*!"

He released her and hurriedly leaned down to slip her wrists through the loops. Chloe rose to her knees and rested on her forearms and immediately felt the full effect of his thickness ramming into her. She pushed back against him three times quickly and came viciously and multiple times, each time lasting a little longer than the one before it. Logan lifted her torso so that her full weight rested on her knees, thereby enabling him to penetrate her depths completely. When his orgasm ripped through him, causing him to shout and grip her hips tightly, the effects of it rippled through her and she came again.

"Okay, Logan," Chloe chuckled later as they lay in bed. "Why was my safe word oranges?"

He grinned and looked sheepish. "I couldn't think of anything else. There you were all sexy, and open and dying for satisfaction. And you were mine for the taking. My mind was fried with the thought of it and all I could come up with was 'oranges.'" He shrugged.

"Oh, yeah, that reminds me," Chloe began. "Don't you think it went a little overboard to say that my body was yours and only you could bring it to orgasm?"

"Hey, you wanted what you wanted, and I gave it to you. I did the best I could. From listening to you talk in your sleep, I knew you wanted to be the submissive and me to be the dominant one. I don't think I was too far off the mark with that comment."

Chloe hid a smile. He seemed to be insulted. "No, you weren't," she said in a placating voice and pecked him on the mouth. "You did good, baby. My boo knows his BDSM!"

"This 'boo,'" he began wryly, "also knows you had a hell of a time. And he certainly knows when he's being patronized."

Chloe grinned unashamedly. "It was obvious, huh?"

"Yes. On both counts."

Chloe laughed in sheer joy and then became serious. She kissed him again, this time leisurely and gently. "Thank you, darling. You always try to give me what I want. You spoil me."

"It's not hard," Logan said.

"Where did you get the vibrator?"

"I bought it in Cleveland. And before you ask, I made the recording because I'd planned on giving it and the vibrator to you as parts of your gift on our three-month wedding anniversary in a couple of weeks."

"Oh, Logan," she said in a dreamy voice. "You're just so sweet!"

He grimaced, but said, "Show me just how sweet you think I am." He lifted her in his arms for another long, slow kiss.

"Will that do?" she asked when they were finished.

"Oh, yeah," he affirmed.

"Did you have the camera hidden in the bookcase in the anteroom?" she asked, referring to the small room that was still in the bedroom, but was separated by a set of three stairs. They'd set it up as a small library with a sofa, a small desk and chair, and a couple of bookcases.

"So, when do you think we can make my fantasy come true again?"

Logan studied her eager face and shook his head. "God, you're a greedy little wench!"

"Uh-huh, whatever," Chloe agreed uncaringly. "When?"

"Whenever you want."

"Oh, goody." She clapped her hands. "I might even let you spank me next time," she tempted with a smile.

"Oh, that would definitely be a treat," Logan teased and playfully rubbed his hands together.

"Hey!" she said with a poke of her elbow. "Don't look so eager!"

"You offered." He laughed when she poked him again.

Chloe settled her head on his chest and began to toy with his fingers. "Darling?" she asked after a while.

"Hmm?" Logan kept his eyes closed.

"Are we trying to get pregnant? I mean, today's at least the third time since you've been back that we haven't used a condom," she explained when he opened his eyes and looked at her.

"I thought about that, too. I know we said we'd wait, but

what do you think about trying to get pregnant now? I'd love to see our baby growing inside of you."

Chloe smiled tenderly. "I want that, too," she said and lifted her mouth for his kiss.

"So, it's settled then," Logan whispered against her lips. "We're going to try for our first baby. No more birth control."

8

Logan rose from his chair as he watched his mother follow the maitre d' to his table. He tried not to show his concern as she moved gracefully through the room, her strawberry blond hair bouncing softly as she walked. She had recently fought off a bad case of the flu and, already small and delicate, she'd lost weight she couldn't afford to lose. None of these thoughts showed on his face as he hugged her and kissed her cheek. "Hi, Mom," he said and pulled her chair out. "You look good."

"Oh, I look terrible, and you know it," Madeline Carnegie chastised with a playful frown as she studied him. He had her eyes and his father's hair, coloring, and build. She couldn't have been more pleased. "But no need to worry," she murmured and looked in his eyes. "I get better every day." His eyes were practically sparkling with good cheer—so much so that she had to smile herself. "You look happy," she commented.

"Do I?" Logan asked with a quirk of his brow. "I suppose that can be attributed to the fact that I am," he said with a smile.

Madeline chuckled. She simply couldn't help it; his smiles

had always been contagious. She shook her head fondly when he remained quiet. "Well, are you going to tell me why, or are we going to play Twenty Questions?"

"Oh, it's nothing and everything. Both my professional and personal lives are right where I want them to be."

"Well, that's wonderful, son," Madeline told him. "What's going on with work?" She decided to hold off talking about Chloe for as long as she could because discussions about her never ended well—at least not when Madeline was involved. She still believed that they should have gotten to know each other better before getting married.

Logan knew that his mother not asking about Chloe was deliberate, and he decided to play along with her—for the time being. "Oh, work is going really well. I think we're going to get the Cleveland job, so I'm excited about that."

"Congratulations in advance, then. Will it mean a lot of traveling for you?" Madeline tried not to frown in concern. If he were gone all the time, how were they going to make this fledgling marriage of theirs work, she wondered.

"Yeah, I'd have to be in Cleveland at least weekly in the beginning to make sure things are going well on the site."

"And how does your new bride feel about this?"

Logan shrugged. "Well, of course she wouldn't be happy, but she understands. And besides, she could fly up sometimes if I'm ever gone too long."

"That's true, I guess," she agreed, but she still worried. "And is there anything else going on at work?"

"Yeah. It turns out that the rumors about Mr. Carter retiring are actually true."

"Really?" Madeline asked and then smiled at the hovering waiter. She gave him her order without looking at the menu. She and Logan lunched there often. As Logan gave his order, she studied him some more. His father had wanted him to follow in his footsteps and go into advertising, but her boy had always liked working with his hands and she'd fought with his father in private about letting him do what he wanted to. He was her only child and all she wanted was his happiness. "Tell me more about this retirement," she demanded when the waiter had left. "How do you know the rumor is true?"

"Because Mr. Carter told me himself, that's how. He says he's retiring in the next year or so, and that I have a shot at the presidency."

"That's great, Logan. Congratulations again. This is exciting news! Wait until I tell your father, oh, and that braggart Louise Anders! She's always going on and on about how her son is the head of his division, but president of a national company by the age of thirty-two—you can't beat that!"

Logan laughed at her excitement. "Let's not get ahead of ourselves, Mom. I'm not the only one in the running."

She dismissed his competition with a wave of her hand. "Oh, pshaw! Who else is up for it?"

"Jamal Winston. He's been at the company longer than I have, but we match up pretty well on just about everything else. I'm a little ahead of him when it comes to bringing in new business, but he is older by twelve years and you remember that I told you Carter is old school."

"Yes, but maybe you don't have to worry about that so much. What can you do to pull yourself ahead of this Winston fellow?"

"Nothing but what I've been doing—work hard and do my best."

"That's right," she said with an approving nod.

Logan smiled. "You ready to hear about Chloe now?" he teased.

Madeline flushed at being caught. She gave him an apologetic look. "Now, I like Chloe, Logan, you know I do. She's a sweet girl."

"Yes I do, and yes, she is."

"But I just wish you two had waited to get to know each other better before you made such a huge commitment."

"We didn't need to, Mom. We love each other," Logan's voice was firm and sure.

"Yes, I know, but—"

"But nothing, Mom," Logan insisted. "You know I never do anything rash or stupid. You also know that I've always had the ability to know what I want when I see it. I've always known what was right for me. You know that's true."

Looking into his eyes, Madeline had to admit that it was. "Yes, it is."

"Well, Chloe is right for me. I knew it almost the moment I saw her. So stop worrying about it so much, and be happy for me."

"I am happy for you, Logan." Embarrassed, she was unable to look at him, so she looked down at the table. "It's just that . . ."

"What, Mom?" Logan put his hand over hers and she looked up at him.

"Well, you eloped and I didn't get to see my only child get married! That hurt, Logan. Deeply."

"I'm sorry, Mom. Would it make you feel better to know that Chloe and I have been talking about planning a small ceremony for the fall?"

Madeline's smile was tremulous and sheepish. "I'm ashamed to say it, but yes it would. I know it's selfish of me, but you're my baby. I want to see you get married!"

"Don't worry. You will. Chloe's dad isn't too happy about missing out on walking his daughter down the aisle, either."

"I'll bet," Madeline said. "Why didn't Chloe join us for lunch, by the way?"

"She already had plans."

"I swear, Chloe, if I see that sappy smile of yours one more time today, I'm going to scream," Liddy complained good-naturedly. "Why are you so damn happy? Cut it out, you're making the rest of us poor slobs feel bad," she teased.

Chloe gave her another big, sappy grin. "I can't help it," she said with a shrug. "I am happy."

"What gives?" Liddy demanded and finished off her small salad. The two of them were having lunch before Chloe went in to work.

Chloe smiled again, this time secretively. It had been a week and a half since she and Logan had decided they would have a baby. They tried for one every night and they had experimented with their new game on more than one of those nights. But all she said to Liddy was: "It's just that Logan and I are so happy. I really love him, and it's all thanks to your dragging me kicking and screaming to your office Christmas party."

"My pleasure. It never even occurred to me that you two would be a perfect match, but obviously you two knew right away."

"Yeah, we did," Chloe stated softly. "So, thank you," she finished and reached across the table to pat Liddy's hand.

"Like I said. It was my pleasure. Logan's a great guy and I'm so glad they hired me to work for him, instead of some of the other guys there."

"So you don't miss teaching at all?" Chloe asked and could have bitten off her tongue when Liddy's eyes grew sad. Idiot, she chastised herself and reached across the table for Liddy's hand again. "I'm so sorry, Liddy. I don't know why my brain wants to keep forgetting that you felt you had to leave teaching."

"Had to, or lose my sanity," Liddy joked with a sad smile. She squeezed her cousin's hand. "It's okay though; I'm getting better about it."

"And everything else, too?" Chloe asked cautiously. She studied Liddy. She was a beautiful woman with big eyes the same color as her own. They'd gotten the color from their fathers, who were twins. Her cousin was five years older than she and Chloe had always looked up to her. She was the female voice Chloe had needed in her life since she'd never known her mother, who'd died after giving birth to her.

"I'm trying," Liddy said in answer to Chloe's question. "That part is more difficult."

"I know, sweetheart," Chloe commiserated with her. Liddy just looked so sad and Chloe wished that she could do something to make it better.

Liddy tried to blink back her tears. "God, Chloe, it's just so hard sometimes," she whispered. "I miss them so much."

"Oh, baby," Chloe said sympathetically and moved to the other side of the booth to hold her. Liddy's husband and daughter had died in a car crash eighteen months before and she'd been struggling to get on with her life ever since. "It'll get better, sweetheart," Chloe whispered into Liddy's hair. "It has to, damn it," she said fervently. She'd loved Liddy's husband like a big brother and her child like she'd been her own. But she didn't love either of them as much as she loved her cousin and that's who she cried for now. She looked up as the waitress came over.

"Is everything all right, ladies?"

Chloe's lips twisted in ruefulness. Why did people ask stupid questions? "Yeah, just jim-dandy, honey," she said sarcastically. "And how are things in your world?"

The waitress sniffed and stomped away. But Chloe couldn't be bothered. She felt Liddy's shoulders shake. "It's all right, sweetie," she said and kissed her forehead. "Let it all out."

Liddy straightened away from her and Chloe could see that she was chuckling. She watched as Liddy wiped the tears from her cheeks and said, "I swear, Chloe, you are too much." This observation was accompanied by a shake of her head.

"What?" Chloe queried in pretended surprise.

"You know what. We'll be lucky if that girl doesn't spit in our entrées."

"Humph, and then *she'll* be lucky if I don't kick her ass."

Liddy guffawed. "Go on and get up. Take your crazy behind back to the other side of the table. I'm fine."

"Are you sure?" Chloe asked with a worried frown.

"Of course I am. Now go." Liddy made shooing motions with her hands until Chloe got up. She continued to smile as Chloe sat down. "You always were like that."

"Like what?" Chloe asked as she put her napkin back in her lap.

"A little, opinionated firecracker—the littlest one with the biggest and loudest opinion who always said what she felt and went after what she wanted."

Chloe smiled reminiscently. "I had to be, otherwise I'd have been trampled on—the small ones usually are. And you know my daddy always said that there's no point in being shy with your feelings or your desires 'cause nobody will know unless you tell them."

"I'll bet you Logan loves that about you, doesn't he?"

"If he knows what's good for him; he'd better act like he does, even if he doesn't," Chloe said emphatically. She smiled when Liddy laughed some more, this time even harder. Okay, so maybe I can help, Chloe thought to herself, even if it's just a little bit.

"Tell me what else is going on with you," Liddy said, "How is Uncle Robert?"

"Oh, he's fine. You know he's on that trip to Europe right now, right?"

"Oh, that's right. Mom and Dad were just talking about it the other day. Daddy said that Uncle Robert was being a fool, gallivanting all around and spending his money like it was water."

Chloe laughed. "I'm not surprised, since Uncle Dave always did say that everything worth seeing is right here in the 'good ole U.S. of A.' " Chloe laughed again because Liddy had repeated the old refrain with her.

"Right," Liddy said. "And Mama would come back with, 'Um hm, Davie, and that's why you're gonna be an ignorant for the rest of your life."

"That's right! I loved how she just changed the language to suit her purposes: 'an ignorant.' It's priceless!"

"Yeah, for Mom 'ignoramus' just wasn't strong enough to capture what she was trying to say. He had to be 'an ignorant' or nothing!"

Now Chloe was wiping tears from her cheeks. Her cousin was so good at imitating people and she sounded just like her mother. "God, Liddy, you should be on stage somewhere."

"Oh, whatever," Liddy dismissed the compliment. "You and Logan should come over for Sunday dinner this week since your pops is out of town. Dad and Mom would love to see you."

Chloe smiled. Sunday dinner was a big deal in the Johnson family. When they were children, the families would get together every Sunday after church. She and Liddy were each an only child and Chloe had loved seeing her on Sundays, even though it was likely that they'd already seen each other at least twice during the week already. But Sundays were different. On Sundays, they'd spend all day in each other's company and Chloe wouldn't have to worry about outside interferences like school or friends. She'd have her cousin all to herself because it was rare that anybody else was invited. She sighed at the memories. "I'd love to come, Liddy. It will be fun. I don't think Logan has anything planned."

"What about his parents' house? Do you guys go there on Sundays?"

"Sometimes, but it's not a standing appointment. We're more often at Daddy's house for dinner."

"Oh, okay, great!"

"Do you think Aunt Miranda will make her peach cobbler?"

"All you have to do is ask her, and you know she will. Just like the rest of us, she loves to spoil you. You know that," Liddy chided and smiled when a shameless, knowing grin crossed Chloe's face. "So, what else is new?" she asked. "How's work?"

"Work is going well," Chloe said and leaned forward excitedly. "I just love this new job!"

"I'll bet you do. I finally caught your act again. I TiVo'ed it. It's good. You can tell a lot of thought and planning went into the programming."

"Thank you! We do our best and it's one of those rare jobs: one I don't mind getting up for in the morning. I really like the place. Life is so good, Liddy, that I have to pinch myself sometimes to make sure I'm not dreaming."

Four hours later, Chloe was wishing something as simple as a pinch could wake her up because she felt like she was in the worst nightmare of her life. She sat frozen in her makeup chair, scared to the bone and paralyzed with indecision. "Everything was going so perfectly," she whispered dazedly. "The children made their cues, we only had to do a few takes for each scene, and my husband wants to impregnate me, damn it," she wailed. The confusing jumble of thoughts made her drop her head on her makeup table in despair.

After a few minutes of this, she lifted her head. "Pull yourself together, Chloe. You can't let Mary do this to you. You just can't," she reprimanded herself sternly.

She'd walked off the set and into her dressing room with the idea of removing her makeup and checking her messages. It was her daily routine. The red message light on her phone wasn't blinking, so she'd just taken off her makeup, breathing a sigh of relief because another day without hearing from Mary had gone by. She hadn't heard from her once since that first day she'd called.

As she'd been preparing to leave, she'd had the idea to check her cell phone for messages, just in case Logan had called her. The little display window had indicated that she'd had a voice message so she'd happily checked her voice mail. And that's when she heard Mary's voice. At first she'd been confused because she didn't know how Mary could have possibly gotten her cell phone number. And then she'd gotten scared because Mary hadn't beat around the bush in this message. Even now, at least thirty minutes later, she remembered the message word for word because she'd listened to it so many times.

"All right, Chloe, I've given you all the time in the world to be nice and call me back, but you didn't. So here I am, forced to call you again. This is how it's going to be. I need money, Chloe, and you're going to give it to me. I only need a couple of thousand to tide me over. If you don't, I'll tell everyone what you did when we were in school. You'll probably lose your job. And I hear your new husband's some big muckety-muck. Does he know what you did? This could mess up that picture-perfect life you have, couldn't it?

"Come on, Chloe. I'm only asking for ten thousand. You can afford it. Hell, you probably make that much in one month's work. My deadbeat ex-husband is late with the child support again, and he never sends enough anyway, so now I'm reaching out to an old friend, that's all. Look at it as one desperate girlfriend asking for help from her luckier, more prosperous friend. No biggie, right? You have until tomorrow to call me to find out where to bring the money. You know the number."

Chloe sighed. She stood and grabbed her things. *He never sends enough anyway.* That one comment kept going through her head. It weighed on her more than the entire rest of the message. Because that one comment told her that one payment to Mary would not be enough. She'd come back again and again for money, treating her like she was an ATM. Chloe turned off the lights in her dressing room and left, knowing exactly what she had to do.

9

Chloe rushed into the house, hoping and praying that she would have a bigger window of time than she thought she had. Logan had been coming home earlier than usual over the past couple of days. Normally she loved that, but today she needed him to stay late; otherwise he'd catch her.

"Please, baby, just finish up a report or something or go over building designs a couple of dozen times," she murmured as she rushed down to the cavernous basement where they stored some of their things. Her bins and boxes were stacked neatly in one corner, while his stuff was in the other. Her eyes frantically read the markings on each box, while she kept one ear out for the door.

"There it is," she cried when she spotted the stack that had COLLEGE: FRESHMAN YEAR written on it. She could only pray that the bin really had stuff from her freshman year in it and wasn't just labeled that way. "How cruel would that be?" She pulled the lid off and started rifling through folders and papers until she spotted the beat-up manila envelope she was looking for.

She snatched it out of the bin, and leaving things in disarray, hurried up the stairs as fast as her three-inch heels would allow her to. Next, she went to their bedroom, where she grabbed a duffel bag off the top shelf of her closet. She unzipped it and tossed it onto the bed. Shoes, clothes, and underwear were thrown haphazardly into the bag as she kept one eye on the clock.

She ran into the bathroom, took her makeup bag from under the sink, and started clearing the bathroom sink and then her vanity of her toiletry items. Zipping it up, she took it and sat it next to the duffel bag on the bed. She hurried over to the anteroom, where she sat at the desk and wrote her note to Logan. She agonized over what to say for a moment and then she began to write, her tears falling to leave wet marks on the paper.

Finished, she rose and walked back into the bedroom. She futilely wiped at her tears as she carefully laid the note against his pillow—the place where she thought he'd be most likely to notice it. Her steps slow and miserable now, she picked up her bags and left the room to leave the man who'd given her so much happiness.

An hour later, Logan closed the front door behind him. Surprised at the lack of scent besides all the potpourri and candles Chloe had all over the place, he sniffed the air. There was no smell of food. She usually had something ready for him or, if he beat her home, he had something ready for her. He smiled. She was probably miffed at him because he hadn't called to say he'd be running a little late.

"I'm sorry, sweetheart," he called as he walked up the stairs to the bedroom. "I know I should have called, but I got so caught up in the work. Then when I noticed the time and thought to call, I just wanted to finish without any distractions so I could get home to you as fast as I could." He finished his explanation just as he walked into the bedroom. He frowned.

She wasn't there, but all the lights were on. That wasn't like her. She turned everything off in a room if she wasn't going to be in it. She often fussed at him about his habit of leaving lights on, saying he was going to make their electric bill hit the roof.

I must have missed her downstairs, he thought. She kept a small office to the right of and behind the stairs, so he assumed she was there working. Before he went to search her out there, he decided to get a little more comfortable. He walked into the room and up the platform to sit on the bed and take off his shoes. His eyes fell on the note on his pillow. He snatched it up, read it quickly, his frown getting deeper with each word he read. "What the fuck?" he whispered and read it again to make sure he wasn't losing his mind.

"Is this a joke, Chloe?" he called as he rushed from the room and down the stairs to search her out. "Is it another one of your games to add spice to our love life? Because if it is, it sure as hell isn't working, sweetheart!"

He searched every room in the house and it wasn't until he was in the attic kicking at cobwebs that his brain finally recognized what his heart had been trying to tell him for at least twenty minutes: Chloe was gone. She had actually left him.

Chloe picked up the telephone in her father's kitchen and dialed Mary's number. When Mary answered, she recognized her voice immediately. "Hello, Mary. This is Chloe. Listen carefully because I'm going to keep this short. I'm not paying you. What I did when I was nineteen may have been careless, but it wasn't criminal. You can tell anyone you want and I'll deal with—" She frowned when Mary interrupted her. "Your finances are not my problem, Mary. Like I said, you do what you want to do and I'll do what I have to do." She hung up in the middle of Mary's diatribe.

She rubbed her forehead and sank down in one of the

kitchen chairs. "Fucking monster," she said. "Dad was right. I should have just stayed away from her."

She knew her decision—even though it was the most painful one she'd ever had to make—was the best one she could have made. It solved everything. "Well, almost everything," she murmured and blinked back tears, as she thought about what she had to do the next day. She'd decided to tell her boss her secret, thereby taking the power out of Mary's hands. "I'm not giving that greedy bitch any of my money," she promised fervently. "I'll burn it before she gets one penny of it."

She could make that decision to tell her boss because it was her job on the line, but she couldn't do that to Logan, and that was why she'd left him the note. "God, Logan. I miss you already," she said aloud.

"Well, I'm fucking glad to hear that at least," Logan growled from the doorway.

Chloe jumped. "Logan! How'd you find me? How'd you get in? What are you doing here?"

Logan strode into the room and stood over her. He was livid. How dare she leave him, with no explanation but some cockamamie note that may as well have been written in gibberish, as much as he understood it? He took a deep breath and counted until the urge to shout left him. It almost worked. "Shall I answer those questions in order? Let's see: Once I checked with Liddy and you weren't there, the logical place to check was here. Your father left me a set of keys too, to check on the house—and last, but not least, damn it, Chloe, I'm here because you are! Where the hell else would I be?"

All the tension from her fear, her confusion, and her misery stretched just enough to snap and that combined with him standing there shouting at her—(unfairly, she thought)—made her explode herself and she jumped from her chair to yell at him. "Stop yelling at me! I only did what I thought was best, and if you can't see that, then you're a . . . a . . ." She searched her mind for a word strong enough to convey what she was feeling, and then she found it. "An ignorant! You're just an ignorant!" she said and swiped at the few tears that had escaped.

Logan repeated the oddly phrased term in his head. What the hell? He silently repeated it again, this time moving his lips in tandem, and it still didn't sound right, so he put his thoughts into words. "What the hell are you saying, Chloe? '*An ignorant*?' "

"And don't you curse at me either, Logan!"

Logan was so confused, he almost forgot his anger. Chloe just wasn't the type to cry, nor was she the type to leave the kind of note she'd left him. Frowning, he looked in her eyes and saw the fear. Something was really wrong. Suddenly tired of the fight, he took her by the hand and walked with her into the living room where they sat on the sofa. "Tell me what's wrong, Chloe. I can't help unless you do."

Chloe sighed and let her head fall on his shoulder. "Oh, God, Logan, she's trying to ruin everything," she said and blinked back more tears.

"Who is? Would that be the 'fucking monster' your dad was right about, or the 'greedy bitch' who's not going to see one penny of your money, burnt or otherwise?"

Chloe pulled away to look at him. "You heard me? How long were you standing there?"

"Does it matter? Tell me what's going on, Chloe."

"I already told you. Didn't you get my note?"

"You mean this note?" he asked and pulled it out of his pocket. "Mind if I read it to you? 'Logan, you were right. I was keeping something from you. But the secret has caught up to me and I can't dither about telling you anymore. The envelope under this note holds my secret. Once you look at it—page ten—it will be up to you whether or not you want to be with me. Just call me on my cell and let me know. I love you, Logan.'" He looked at her expectantly when he finished reading.

"Right," Chloe said. "What did you think of it? Will you lose the presidency because of it?" She held her breath as she waited for his answer.

Logan frowned. "Again, I have to ask: What in the hell are you talking about, Chloe?"

"The picture, Logan. The stupid picture! It's what she's using to blackmail me with."

"What picture, Chloe?"

Chloe sighed impatiently. "You know, Logan, you are really starting to piss me off! The picture in the magazine in the envelope!"

Logan had to count to fifty before he was sufficiently calm enough to say through clenched teeth, "What envelope, Chloe? You didn't leave one."

Chloe ran out of steam and slumped back into the couch. "Oh," she said in a small voice with a confused frown. "I didn't?"

Logan shook his head once. "You didn't."

"Then where is it?" she murmured to herself as she thought about it. "Oh! I must have accidentally packed it in one of my bags. Either that, or I left it at the house somewhere." She scrambled from the sofa and started looking through her bags.

Logan watched her speculatively. She looked sexy as hell in a flared miniskirt and silk blouse. He supposed she was going for professional, and she did look that, but she also looked good enough to eat.

"Ha! Here it is!"

Logan broke his gaze from her legs to see her waving an old, beat-up manila envelope under his nose. He took it from her and opened it, pulling out a very thin magazine called *Smart and Sexy*. The cover featured a girl who couldn't have been older than twenty, wearing a bikini and leaning against a car, and it promised to educate its readers on how girls could be smart and sexy. The magazine was amateurish at best. "Hmm. I've never heard of this magazine. When was it out?"

Chloe's response was wry. "From April 1995 to April 1995. That's the only issue," she explained when he looked up at her. "It was only distributed on my college campus. You see, this fraternity had gotten the girls in their sister sorority to pose naked for a calendar that they were selling for twelve bucks. To counteract it, this friend of mine came up with an idea to put out a magazine that showed girls who were not only sexy, but smart as well.

"Yes, it showed us nude, but it also talked about things like our GPAs, our favorite classes and sports, and other things. It was supposed to be a feminist protest, a way to not only show that we had ownership of our bodies, but that we were more than just our bodies. And unlike the frat boys, we gave our magazine away for free."

"How'd it go over?"

Chloe shrugged. "As I said, we only had one issue. We almost got expelled once it got into the hands of the dean, and my friend had only handed out about twenty before that happened. Hell, we only had a print run of one hundred to begin with, and they made her shred all that she hadn't given away. Anyway," she finished with a sigh, "they decided to go easy on us and put us on probation instead of expelling us. They gave those stupid frat boys the same punishment."

Logan went back to looking at the magazine. "Turn to page ten," he heard her whisper and there were nerves in her voice.

He turned to the page as directed. "Hot damn!" he said as he stared down at a naked nineteen-year-old Chloe. "You were the centerfold." She lay on a white rug, with a towel trailing half on and half off her body so that one ass cheek and one thigh were exposed. Her breasts were flattened by her weight, her hair was long, and she wore large, dark sunglasses. "*This* is what you're worried about?" he asked her with a frown.

"I wasn't at first," she admitted. "In fact, I hadn't even thought about it at all until I took my new job and met your boss and realized how conservative he is. I mean, I work on a children's show. I need to be above reproach. And maybe you could lose your promotion, or worse, your job."

"Chloe," he admonished. "You can't even see your face, much more tell that it's you."

"*You* could," she accused.

His grin was wolfish. "Yeah, but that's only because I know your body. Intimately."

"Oh, give me that." Chloe snatched the magazine from his hand. "You're not taking this seriously. Mary Tanner, my roommate at the time who also posed, saw me on the show and called me at the station a couple of weeks ago. I hadn't heard from her in over ten years, since she dropped out right before the semester ended. When I didn't return her call, she somehow got ahold of my cell phone number and left a voice mail today for me while I was on the set. She says I have to give her ten thousand dollars or she'll tell my boss and yours."

"Oh, I see. So that's why you were running scared. Just take the magazine in and show your boss. I'm sure she'll think it's just as silly and harmless as I think it is. But first if you haven't already, you need to tell this Mary person to take a flying leap. You should probably go to the police and file a report. What she's doing isn't legal."

"I've already told her and trust me; she didn't like it," Chloe said and opened his arms so she could sit on his lap. "And I'd already planned to talk to my boss tomorrow. That's not the point. I'll let the chips fall where they may when it comes to my job. After all, I'm the one who posed for the picture. I'm worried about you. I don't want your job jeopardized because of something your wife did eleven years ago."

Exasperated, Logan said, "Damn it, Chloe! You're such a drama queen. A normal person would have come to me to discuss it. But no, not you. You have to go all Dolly Dramatic on me and pack your stuff and leave. Why didn't you just tell me about it?"

Chloe's lips twisted and she was ready to defend her character, but he pressed his hand to her mouth. "Don't even think about it," Logan demanded. "Unless you're ready to tell me why you acted this way, then don't talk." When her eyes narrowed and flashed at him in anger, he sighed. "I mean it, Chloe. Do you have any idea what it felt like to come home and find you gone? And the worst part is, you didn't even give me an opportunity to discuss it. You just walked out."

All of the indignation left Chloe and she gave up. She took his hand from her mouth and held it between hers, kissing his fingers in apology. "You're right, and I'm sorry. I guess I just panicked. I was afraid of your answer. I guess I couldn't bear to be there while you made up your mind."

"Why? The answer should have been obvious."

She was shaking her head before he finished. "It should have been, but it wasn't."

10

"I don't know if you remember this," she began. "But right after we started dating, you asked me to come out to dinner with a new client, Mr. Carter, and some of your colleagues. The client was in town for a couple of days and you guys were squiring her around. You wanted me to come because other people were bringing their spouses. Remember?"

Logan nodded. "Of course. Linda Giles had come into town."

"Right," Chloe said with a nod. "So, anyway, we were having dinner and this young girl walked past our table. She had on this two-piece, barely there outfit. Mr. Carter was disgusted. Do you remember what he said?"

"No, not really," Logan said, feeling impatient.

"I do. He said that it was absolutely shameful the way some people dressed. He said that the girl looked like one of those disgusting centerfolds and if his daughter had ever tried to leave the house dressed like that, he'd have locked her in her room and thrown away the key. It was very clear that he didn't approve."

Logan was confused. "So? What's that got to do with me?"

"I'm not finished. After Mr. Carter's comment, someone started talking about *Playboy*. He said that posing for the magazine was just a stepping-stone for many women—that they did it to jumpstart their careers in acting and modeling. Mr. Carter said that he still found it wrong and disgusting."

Logan was still confused. "I still don't get what that has to do with me. I know I didn't agree with him."

"You didn't disagree, either, Logan. In fact, at one point you laughed—just like everyone else did."

"And what did you do?"

"I said that if a woman were of age, then it shouldn't matter to other people what she did with her body, especially if she wasn't hurting anyone. Mr. Carter looked at me like I was crazy."

"And did I say anything?" Logan asked.

"No," Chloe said and swallowed back a lump because it had hurt her that he hadn't said anything supportive. "But Linda Giles agreed with me."

"Exactly. That much I remember, and then someone else changed the subject."

"And you didn't say anything to back me up," she said in a stifled voice.

Logan looked at her face. She was sulking. "Oh no," he said. "Don't tell me that you've been thinking about that all this time. All you had to do was ask me, Chloe. Would that have been so hard? You could have asked me and I'd have told you that it's no big deal."

Chloe shrugged uncomfortably. "I thought that maybe I wouldn't like the answer, and then where would I have been? I didn't want to lose you, so I didn't tell you. And I didn't want you to lose your job—"

"I wouldn't have left you over something like that, Chloe,

even if I didn't agree with you posing for the magazine. That's just stupid. Besides, how could he have ever found out about it?"

"Well, since I'm on television I'm recognized—not a whole lot, but enough—and I thought that there might be a chance that someone would realize—"

"And this Mary person did," Logan interrupted. What a freaking mess. He sighed and kissed her forehead.

"Yes. I never even thought about the picture until that conversation in the restaurant. I don't want you to lose your job because of something I did."

"Chloe, if Carter would fire me over something as trivial as this, then I don't want to work for him."

"But, Logan, you worked so hard to get where you are, and I—"

Logan put his hand over her mouth again. "Be quiet. I'm not going to let this job be more important than you or our marriage. There are other jobs if it should come down to it. What bothers me is that you didn't make the same decision when it came to this mess. It should have been a simple choice, Chloe: talk to me or run scared. I can't believe you chose to run."

Chloe couldn't look at him. "I guess I didn't think of it that way. You're right. I should have trusted you. I let my fear get the best of me. I'm sorry."

"Well, all right then. I guess there's not much more to say about it. But don't ever let it happen again." When she nodded in agreement, he continued, "Now, let's talk about this Mary woman. How do you think she got your cell phone number?"

"I've been trying to figure that out. I thought maybe from the Internet, but I don't know how she would have done it. It's a new cell phone number. You remember I lost my cell in Hawaii."

"Right," Logan said thoughtfully. "Is your cell phone number on a list at the station? You know—as a secondary contact?"

"Yes, but I don't see how—" Chloe cut herself off when she realized where his thoughts were headed. "You're thinking that maybe someone at the station gave it to her."

"Exactly. Maybe it was the receptionist just trying to be helpful."

Chloe was shaking her head. "No, the list is only used internally."

"So maybe your old friend Mary knows someone who helped her out."

"Or she could have paid someone," Chloe said. "But I don't see what this has to do with anything. Knowing how she got my number is beside the point. It doesn't help me get her off my back."

"No. Only you can get her off your back. You have to do that by coming clean with your boss—just as you should have come clean with me," he told her sternly with a pinch to her thigh.

"I know, and I feel awful about it," she said. "I'm sorry. Will you forgive me?" She nuzzled his chin with her head.

"I don't know. It depends," Logan said as turned her so she was sitting astride his lap.

"On what?" Her voice was distracted. The relief that everything was going to be okay was almost overwhelming.

"On whether or not you'll let me love you in your daddy's house," he challenged right before he slipped his hand under her skirt to cup her behind.

"Logan!" Chloe protested, but she twined her arms around his neck and opened her thighs wider to rub against his thickening penis.

Logan grinned and got ready to settle in for the night.

* * *

Chloe sat in front of her boss's desk and nervously clasped her hands in her lap. Her boss, Maria Castanza, had been looking at the magazine for at least two minutes. She hadn't said a word—not after Chloe explained the situation and not since she'd given her the magazine. Chloe tried not to think in the negative. Just because Maria was deathly quiet and had a frown on her face, didn't mean that she was going to lose her job. *She's just thinking,* Chloe told herself consolingly.

Logan had offered to come with her that morning to give moral support, but she'd turned him down, thinking it wouldn't look professional to have her husband there fighting her battles. He hadn't looked at it that way. He'd looked at it as having her back. Now she wished that she'd taken him up on his offer.

She'd come in early that morning, hours before her show, so she could talk to Maria without fear of running late for taping. And she'd thought that if Maria wanted to fire her, then she could just leave before the rest of the crew for her show came in. She watched as the other woman slowly closed the magazine and tapped her finger on it.

"Well, that was interesting," she finally said.

Chloe wanted to roll her eyes. Was that all she had to say?

"It looks like you guys had a good idea that just didn't pan out."

"So, uh, does this mean that I'm not fired?"

"Fired? Why would I fire you, Chloe? This picture was taken over a decade ago, long before you started working with us. Now, if it were the Pee-wee Herman scenario," she began and paused when she saw Chloe frowning. "You don't remember it?"

"No, I'm afraid not. I mean, I know who he is, but I don't know what scenario you're talking about."

"You remember he had a Saturday morning show, right? Well, it was somehow found out that he had been in a theater watching a porno and masturbating. My God, there was so much hoopla over it. Parents were up in arms saying that they didn't want their children watching a show that featured him. He eventually got canned, and that, my dear, is what I refer to when I say the Pee-wee Herman scenario."

"Oh, okay," Chloe said hesitantly as she thought about it. "I'm remembering it better now that you mention it."

"So, anyway. Your contract only says you can't do anything untoward while you work with us. It says nothing about the past. And besides that, you can't even tell that it's you. Who is this woman trying to blackmail you again?"

"Uh, her name is Mary Tanner, I mean Mary Pasik. It was Tanner before she got married."

"Pasik. I thought that name sounded familiar. She's a friend of Steve's. Steve Henderson," she elaborated when Chloe didn't react.

"My director?" Chloe was stunned. "Are you sure?"

"I'm positive. I've met her before."

"I can't believe it," Chloe said. "Steve is working with Mary to blackmail me?"

"Let's find out for sure, shall we?" Maria said and picked up her phone.

Chloe walked into her house, her mind still reeling from all that she'd found out.

"Hi, sweetheart."

Chloe turned in surprise. Logan stood just a few feet away from her. She accepted his kiss. "Hi! What are you doing home?"

"I wanted to be here, just in case the news was bad. Was it?"

"What?" Chloe said distractedly. She looked at him again. "Oh, no, I didn't get fired if that's what you're asking."

"Then what's the matter?" he asked and took her hand and led her into the living room. He sat and pulled her down beside him.

"Steve Henderson."

"Your director? What about him?"

"He's the one who gave Mary my cell phone number. It turns out that they'd been dating each other, and when she saw me on television, she realized that he was my director. When I didn't return her calls that first time, he gave her my cell phone number. They thought it would be more effective. He's also how she knew that I'd married 'some big muckety-muck,' as she described you."

"Wow," Logan said. "What a small world. He's been fired, right?"

"Wait, I haven't gotten to the best part. When Maria called him into her office, he not only confessed, he told us that Mary didn't even have a copy of the magazine—that they were hoping that just the threat of telling would be enough to get me to pay up. And yes, you were right; he was fired, effective immediately."

"Excellent on both counts. Now that you know she doesn't actually have a copy of the magazine, she can't hold it over your head as a threat anymore."

"Yeah, I know," Chloe said with a tired. "What about you? Did you tell Mr. Carter about the picture?"

"No. It's none of his business."

"But, Logan—"

He placed his hand over her mouth. "It's none of his business what my wife did ten years ago, Chloe. Hell, *my wife* is none of his business."

His tone brooked no argument and Chloe decided it was best to leave it alone. She took his hand in hers and pressed a kiss to the palm before rising. "I'm going to go change and try to get some rest before work."

Logan watched her walk away, frowning at her slow, dejected steps. He rose and followed her. "I'm sorry, sweetheart and I know you're hurting, but the good news is that you don't have to worry about it anymore."

Chloe stepped onto the first stair and turned to look at him with a sad smile. "Yeah, I know, but I still can't believe Steve did this to me. I mean, even though we haven't known each other very long, we worked closely together every day and I thought we were friends."

Logan bent and kissed her brow. She just looked so miserable. He picked her up and began walking up the stairs. "I'll beat him up for you. Just tell me where the bastard lives, and I'll take care of it. He'll rue the day he ever messed with Chloe Carnegie!" he said in low, dramatic tones.

Chloe's smile was wan, and she didn't say anything.

Logan had made it to their bedroom where he placed her on the bed. He started undressing her. When he got to her shoes, he took them off and began to massage one foot; pressing deeply into the center and making her jerk and moan. He looked up at her. She looked back.

"Your husband commands you to forget about Steve," he stated softly as he treated the other foot to the same massage and then crawled up her body. He lay between her legs. "Let's get started on making our baby. If you're good, I might even let you tie me up."

Chloe studied him some more. He was such a good man. She had a good life, and there was really nothing to complain about. She decided to take his advice and forget about Steve—and everything else about the outside world. For the next couple of hours, it would just be her and Logan.

"Oh, yeah?" she asked in answer to his proposition. She

wrapped her arms around his neck. "Well, since you're being so good to me," she whispered seductively, her body already clenching in anticipation of what was to come. "I'll let you spank me."

"Yeah?"

"Oh, yeah," she said softly and bit his chin. "And not once will I say oranges!"

1

"Hi, Shawn. I'm the woman who was wearing the short red dress, standing on the corner—"

Damn.

Cringing at the words she'd just blurted, Sharice jabbed the pound key on the cell phone keypad to delete the voice mail message she'd just recorded. As the digital voice walked her through the instructions to rerecord her message, she stared out the windshield of her Lexus, idly noticing the after-eleven crowd in line in front of Club Maxwell's. Defying the chilly October air, the women wore their spaghetti-strap tops and tightest skirts, while standing proud in their three-inch strappy sandals.

She tried again.

"Hi, Shawn. . . . This is Sharice. I met you outside of Maxwell's last Friday. I was talking to my friend when you shouted your number out the window. . . ."

My God. Are the pickings for a night of sex so slim that I have to resort to this? Just hang up.

". . . and . . ."

Hang up.

". . . well . . ."

Hang the fuck up.

But, damn, that man had been on her mind all week. It was once again Friday evening, and she somehow found herself cruising down the street in front of the club where they'd met. Her favorite song played on the radio—Jamie Foxx, crooning about how she needed a "G" like him to beat it, and Twista rapping about giving it to her in an elevator—and got her all hot and horny.

The same song had been playing softly from the depths of Shawn's Lex that night, too. Surely, that must be a sign. Just as the fact that his gleaming red car, identical to hers, was a sign. A sign that, unlike her last boyfriend, Darrell and his 1990 Honda Civic, Shawn might actually treat her to dinner, instead of always crying broke. And Shawn's voice, as he'd practically begged her to call him, had sounded like liquid sex. That had been another sign.

The voice was a definite positive for a night of hot sex. For, if his technique was sad, she could just ask him to talk—and that sweet, slow, sexy tone would make up for any lack of finesse.

Sharice paused, about to delete her message again, when the song faded out on the radio and Tommy "Dr. Love" Jones came on.

"Now, that's a sinful song, isn't it?" He laughed. "It's definitely telling you to go out and sin, though not necessarily the way I'm advocating. I'm urging you, KPSX listeners, to go out and go for what you want, sin. Your happiness is just a sin away . . ."

Dr. Love was right. It was about time she "sinned." That is, do something she'd never done before. She turned her attention back to the phone.

". . . Give me a holler at 510-555-1201," she finished.

Sharice clicked her phone off and tossed it onto the passenger seat, surprised to feel herself shaking from surplus adrenaline. How ridiculous that something as simple as calling a guy would spark the fight-or-flight response. However, maybe it wasn't so ridiculous, since she *never* called men first, period. She always waited for them to call her. Hell, she was no fool—she lived by the book *He's Just Not That Into You,* which was coauthored by Greg Behrendt.

Hence, she was committing a double sin—she was calling a guy first and she was calling a guy she hadn't even really met. And the only reason she'd broken her rule this time was because, well, it was kind of hard for a guy who didn't have her name or number to call her back.

So now what?

The line outside the club had grown another twelve feet since she'd arrived. Sharice did not do lines. Craning her neck forward, she looked to see if John was at the door. Yep. There he was, his bald, peanut-shaped head glistening in the soft light. He'd let her slide to the front of the line. There'd be no waiting tonight.

Sharice sighed. So what if she got in the club? Somewhere in between the time that she'd pulled out of her garage and pulled into this parking spot, Maxwell's had lost its appeal. The effort it would take to make meaningless small talk with a dozen or more men, in hopes of meeting one she wanted to take home for the night seemed like too much effort. Kind of like finding her contact lens in the Pacific Ocean.

She'd been feeling like this a lot lately, which is why she'd been celibate for months. *Six* months, to be exact.

A group of loud-talking sistahs—whose long hair did a better job of covering their asses than their skirts did—sauntered past the car. Did they really think people thought that horsehair was real?

Stop being so bitchy.

She could just go home. Her attitude was not male-magnet material.

But she didn't want to go home. Friday night was a prime party night, for crying out loud. And it was time for her to get her game back on track.

Sharice pressed the pad of her finger against the screen, turning up the radio. The deep voice of Dr. Love filled the car.

". . . Good luck, man . . . You're on, Jessie. What's your sin?"

Jessie giggled.

Sharice rolled her eyes.

"Well, a couple of months ago, I did a striptease for my boyfriend. It was something I'd always wanted to do, but had never done before . . ."

Dr. Love made a sound of approval.

Sharice snorted. "That ain't nothing. I've done a hundred stripteases."

". . . only it wasn't my boyfriend who saw it. It was my neighbor."

"Damn. I haven't done *that,*" said Sharice.

Dr. Love laughed.

Jessie laughed. ". . . needless to say, the boyfriend's out and my neighbor is in."

"He's 'in'? Literally or figuratively?" asked Dr. Love.

Jessie and Dr. Love shared a chuckle.

Sharice joined in.

"Let's just say he's the new man in my life. Our relationship is wonderful. He—"

Sharice snorted. "I was feeling you until you ruined things with a 'relationship.'" She pressed the screen again, cutting Jessie off in mid-sentence; Sharice shook her head. A person had a better chance of winning the lottery than ending up in a relationship that worked. What was up with most women who were desperate for the big R? Sharice had tried that, twice, believing that she'd found *the one* each time. Instead, she'd discovered Malcolm had been living on the down low, sleeping with men behing her back. And Darrell had been sleeping with anything in a skirt, including whichever of her so-called friends he could get into bed—Sharice's bed.

Nope. She was through with that. Fool me once, shame on you; fool me twice, shame on me. Well, she was not going to be anyone's fool anymore. So now she just looked for a brotha for a good time.

But, for some reason, the "good times" were feeling fewer and farther in between. And Sharice's attitude was getting more and more frustrated. Not to mention her libido. She shrugged, throwing off her depressing thoughts.

Well, she might as well go inside the club. As she reached for her keys, her cell phone rang.

She glanced at the display on the cell phone. It was Shawn. Sharice grinned, no longer nervous now that she was back on familiar ground—being pursued.

She pressed a button to connect the call. "I like a guy who goes after what he wants."

"Uh . . ."

Damn, she was good. The throaty voice worked every time.

"You *do* want something, don't you, Shawn?"

"Yeah . . . uh . . ."

She smiled. He was speechless, though the fact that he was surprised her a bit. From what little she'd been able to see of him in his car, the sly quirk of his lip—which passed for a smile—gave the impression that he was the type to have a snappy come-back.

"Well . . . ?" she prompted, converting the throatiness to a purr.

"Yes. Well. I'm not . . ."

He cleared his throat.

Sharice's smile widened.

"I'd like . . . you. Talk . . ."

She couldn't quite make what he was saying, with the reception so bad. She'd only heard a few of the words and it sounded like he was faraway, in a tunnel, with the wind blowing.

"What?"

". . . see you."

You'd like to see me?" she repeated.

"Y . . ."

Was that a yes?

". . . now?" he asked.

"I can't hear you."

"Are you available now?"

She got it that time. He sounded like he was yelling, but his voice didn't register much louder. Where was he calling from?

Sharice paused. A woman should never appear too available, especially at 11:10 P.M. Even author Greg Behrendt would probably agree with that. She let her gaze drift back to Maxwell's, to the line that now looped around the corner. There'd be a good-size crowd inside. Odds were, even she could find someone interesting inside.

But she had someone who might be interesting right here, right now.

Screw Greg Behrendt. She didn't care if Shawn wasn't "into" her because she had no intention of being "into" him. After all, she wasn't looking for a relationship. She didn't have to go by all the rules.

"What do you have in mind?" she asked.